THE PATRON

EMERSON PASS CONTEMPORARIES, BOOK TWO

TESS THOMPSON

PRAISE FOR TESS THOMPSON

The School Mistress of Emerson Pass:
"Sometimes we all need to step away from our lives and sink into a safe, happy place where family and love are the main ingredients for surviving. You'll find that and more in The School Mistress of Emerson Pass. I delighted in every turn of the story and when away from it found myself eager to return to Emerson Pass. I can't wait for the next book." - *Kay Bratt, Bestselling author of Wish Me Home and True to Me.*
"I frequently found myself getting lost in the characters and forgetting that I was reading a book." - *Camille Di Maio, Bestselling author of The Memory of Us.*
"Highly recommended." - *Christine Nolfi, Award winning author of The Sweet Lake Series.*
"I loved this book!" - *Karen McQuestion, Bestselling author of Hello Love and Good Man, Dalton.*

Traded: Brody and Kara:
"I loved the sweetness of Tess Thompson's writing - the camaraderie and long-lasting friendships make you want to move to Cliffside and become one of the gang! Rated Hallmark for romance!" - *Stephanie Little BookPage*

"This story was well written. You felt what the characters were going through. It's one of those "I got to know what happens next" books. So intriguing you won't want to put it down." - *Lena Loves Books*

"This story has so much going on, but it intertwines within itself. You get second chance, lost loves, and new love. I could not put this book down! I am excited to start this series and have love for this little Bayside town that I am now fond off!" - *Crystal's Book World*

"This is a small town romance story at its best and I look forward to the next book in the series." - *Gillek2, Vine Voice*

"This is one of those books that make you love to be a reader and fan of the author." -*Pamela Lunder, Vine Voice*

Blue Midnight:
"This is a beautiful book with an unexpected twist that takes the story from romance to mystery and back again. I've already started the 2nd book in the series!" - *Mama O*

"This beautiful book captured my attention and never let it go. I did not want it to end and so very much look forward to reading the next book." - *Pris Shartle*

"I enjoyed this new book cover to cover. I read it on my long flight home from Ireland and it helped the time fly by, I wish it had been longer so my whole flight could have been lost to this lovely novel about second chances and finding the truth. Written with wisdom and humor this novel shares the raw emotions a new divorce can leave behind." - *J. Sorenson*

"Tess Thompson is definitely one of my auto-buy authors! I love her writing style. Her characters are so real to life that you just can't put the book down once you start! Blue Midnight makes you believe in second chances. It makes you believe that everyone deserves an HEA. I loved the twists and turns in this book, the mystery and suspense, the family dynamics and the restoration of trust and security." - *Angela MacIntyre*

"Tess writes books with real characters in them, characters with flaws and baggage and gives them a second chance. (Real people, some remind me of myself and my girlfriends.) Then she cleverly and thoroughly develops those characters and makes you feel deeply for them. Characters are complex and multi-faceted, and the plot seems to unfold naturally, and never feels contrived." - *K. Lescinsky*

Caramel and Magnolias:
"Nobody writes characters like Tess Thompson. It's like she looks into our lives and creates her characters based on our best friends, our lovers, and our neighbors. Caramel and Magnolias, and the authors debut novel Riversong, have some of the best characters I've ever had a chance to fall in love with. I don't like leaving spoilers in reviews so just trust me, Nicholas Sparks has nothing on Tess Thompson, her writing flows so smoothly you can't help but to want to read on!" - *T. M. Frazier*

"I love Tess Thompson's books because I love good writing. Her prose is clean and tight, which are increasingly rare qualities, and manages to evoke a full range of emotions with both subtlety and power. Her fiction goes well beyond art imitating life. Thompson's characters are alive and fully-realized, the action is believable, and the story unfolds with the right balance of tension and exuberance. CARAMEL AND MAGNOLIAS is a pleasure to read." - *Tsuruoka*

"The author has an incredible way of painting an image with her words. Her storytelling is beautiful, and leaves you wanting more! I love that the story is about friendship (2 best friends) and love. The characters are richly drawn and I found myself rooting for them from the very beginning. I think you will, too!" - *Fogvision*

"I got swept off my feet, my heartstrings were pulled, I held my breath, and tightened my muscles in suspense. Tess paints stunning scenery with her words and draws you in to the lives of her characters."- *T. Bean*

Duet For Three Hands:
"Tears trickled down the side of my face when I reached the end of this road. Not because the story left me feeling sad or disappointed, no. Rather, because I already missed them. My friends. Though it isn't goodbye, but see you later. And so I will sit impatiently waiting, with desperate eagerness to hear where life has taken you, what burdens have you downtrodden, and what triumphs warm your heart. And in the meantime, I will go out and live, keeping your lessons and friendship and love close, the light to guide me through any darkness. And to the author I say thank you. My heart, my soul -all of me - needed these words, these friends, this love. I am forever changed by the beauty of your talent." - *Lisa M.Gott*

"I am a great fan of Tess Thompson's books and this new one definitely shows her branching out with an engaging enjoyable historical drama / love story. She is a true pro in the way she weaves her storyline, develops true to life characters that you love! The background and setting is so picturesque and visible just from her words. Each book shows her expanding, growing and excelling in her art. Yet another one not to miss. Buy it you won't be disappointed. The ONLY disappointment is when it ends!!!" - *Sparky's Last*

"There are some definite villains in this book. Ohhhh, how I loved to hate them. But I have to give Thompson credit because they never came off as caricatures or one dimensional. They all felt authentic to me and (sadly) I could easily picture them. I loved to love some and loved to hate others." - *The Baking Bookworm*

"I stayed up the entire night reading Duet For Three Hands and unbeknownst to myself, I fell asleep in the middle of reading the book. I literally woke up the next morning with Tyler the Kindle beside me (thankfully, still safe and intact) with no ounce of battery left. I shouldn't have worried about deadlines because, guess what? Duet For Three Hands was the epitome of unputdownable." - *The Bookish Owl*

Miller's Secret
"From the very first page, I was captivated by this wonderful tale. The cast of characters amazing - very fleshed out and multi-dimensional. The descriptions were perfect - just enough to make you feel like you were transported back to the 20's and 40's.... This book was the perfect escape, filled with so many twists and turns I was on the edge of my seat for the entire read." - *Hilary Grossman*

"The sad story of a freezing-cold orphan looking out the window at his rich benefactors on Christmas Eve started me off with Horatio-Alger expectations for this book. But I quickly got pulled into a completely different world--the complex five-character braid that the plot weaves. The three men and two women characters are so alive I felt I could walk up and start talking to any one of them, and I'd love to have lunch with Henry. Then the plot quickly turned sinister enough to keep me turning the pages.
Class is set against class, poor and rich struggle for happiness and security, yet it is love all but one of them are hungry for. ......Where does love come from? What do you do about it? The story kept me going, and gave me hope. For a little bonus, there are Thompson's delightful observations, like: "You'd never know we could make something this good out of the milk from an animal who eats hats." A really good read!" - *Kay in Seattle*

"She paints vivid word pictures such that I could smell the ocean and hear the doves. Then there are the stories within a story that twist and turn until they all come together in the end. I really had a hard time putting it down. Five stars aren't enough!"
- *M.R. Williams*

EMERSON PASS

The School Mistress of Emerson Pass
The Sugar Queen of Emerson Pass

RIVER VALLEY

Riversong

Riverbend

Riverstar

Riversnow

Riverstorm

Tommy's Wish

River Valley Bundle, Books 1-4

LEGLEY BAY

Caramel and Magnolias
Tea and Primroses

STANDALONES

The Santa Trial
Duet for Three Hands
Miller's Secret

THE PATRON

EMERSON PASS CONTEMPORARIES, BOOK TWO

TESS THOMPSON

For my very first very best friend, Pamela Odom Burkenpas. Thanks for all the memories and the ones yet to come. Long may we run.

PROLOGUE

I was eight years old the summer I found home. I'd come to Emerson Pass, Colorado, sickly and pale from the Seattle mist and nagging gray to the land of indigo skies, deep rivers, and the sound of tall grasses rustling in morning air that smelled of wild roses and sunshine.

At the beginning of that summer, on a sunny day in June, Nan and I had already eaten our lunch, thickly sliced ham layered between pieces of homemade peasant bread slathered in butter. We'd washed them down with lemonade so cold it had made my throat ache. After we'd had our rest in the shade, Nan suggested we bring home a bouquet of wildflowers to decorate the kitchen table. My grandmother wasn't one for lounging around. If the sun was up, so was she. A rule I'd learned after only a week in Colorado.

Nan and I walked along the bank of the river collecting brightly colored flowers that I had no name for in her worn wicker basket. I didn't have a name for any of the trees or plants I saw. The trees seemed to come in many varieties here. There were some like the ones we had at home with green needles that smelled of the Christmas tree lot around the corner from our apartment during December. Here, my favorites of all the trees had leaves shaped like hearts. Breezes whispered through the leaves and made a sound like tiny hands clapping. They clapped for me.

Narrow as a board and strong as an ox, Nan wore a blue cotton dress that flapped around her long legs. A straw hat covered her silver hair, which she wore in a blunt bob cut just below her ears.

The river flowed gently and was a color of green I'd never seen before. "Why is the river so green?" I asked.

"Because the waters run deep. Like you."

"Deep like me." I didn't know yet what that meant or how true it was. I hadn't yet learned of metaphors or analogies. All I knew was that Nan talked that way sometimes and I loved it. I loved her.

Her arm, tanned to a golden beige from her summer work in her garden and alongside Pop in the horse barn, rippled with muscle as she dipped to clip a daisy for our bouquet. I looked at my own arm. Next to her, I was pale and sallow of skin. All winter and spring, I'd suffered from head colds and a recurring eye infection. I could not escape the chill no matter how much money my mother spent on the electrical bill in an attempt to warm our drafty Seattle apartment. Finally, blaming the cloudy, misty weather for my poor health, she'd packed me up and shipped me off to my Nan and Pop. I was to spend the entire summer on their small horse farm. Soaking up sun and my Nan's hearty cooking, I'd come home transformed, Mom felt sure.

For the first few days I missed my mother. But Nan loved me fiercely and made me feel safe and known in her warm, sun-drenched kitchen. "We'll dry you out and fatten you up before we send you back to your mother," she'd said to me that first morning.

"Nan, what's the reason Mom didn't come here with me?" I asked now as I plucked a purple flower from the ground.

"This place makes her sad."

"Why?"

"She loved a boy very much and when he broke her heart, she had to run away to the city to try to forget all about him."

The idea of my mother loving a boy was impossible to picture. She raised me alone with no mention of why I didn't have a father like most of the others in my second-grade class. "Did she forget all about him?"

"I don't think so." Nan set down the basket and squinted her eyes, looking at something across the river.

I followed her gaze. I couldn't see anything other than the sparkle of the sun on the gentle ripples of the river.

"Did you know him?" I asked.

"Not as well as I thought I did."

Another riddle. Later, I'd understand. At least I figured I would. Mom often said I was too young to ask some of the questions I asked her. Maybe I was also too young to understand everything Nan told me.

I observed her strong, broad hands as she adjusted her hat. My mother's hands were the same, only they were always stained with clay because she made pottery in her wheel. She sold her pieces at summer art fairs, but most of our money came from her job at the department store downtown that smelled of rich ladies.

"Nan, will I ever grow strong like you?"

"Oh, yes. You're a sunflower. Do you know about sunflowers?"

"Not really."

"They start out from a small seed. But once they break through the ground, they tilt their face upward, and the sun makes them taller and taller until they explode with a glorious yellow flower as big as my hat brim. Then, after they're all grown, they make hundreds of seeds. In that way, they make sure the next generation will also be able to grow toward the sun. Always tilt your face toward the light, my love, and you'll be fine all your life."

"Have you been fine all your life?"

"I've had the most glorious life of all. Do you know why?"

"Because of tilting your face up at the sun?"

"That, yes. But also because of your Pop. We've loved each other very well for forty-five years. That's the most important thing, Crystal. The love of your partner. You must choose wisely. When he comes, the idea of love might scare you, but you must do it anyway."

"Was my mom a sunflower?"

"The most beautiful one I ever saw. Like you will be someday."

"Will you still be here then?" I asked. "When I'm beautiful?"

"I hope so. I'm already old. Did you know I was forty when I had your mother? We didn't think the good Lord would bless us with a child. We'd been married twenty years by then. I couldn't believe it when the doctor told me."

"Is that old to have a baby?" I didn't know anything about babies. All I knew was that my mom had only been nineteen when she had me. I'd overheard her tell someone that once.

"It's pretty old but not impossible. I had a friend who had a baby at forty-four. We thought we should have a club for geriatric mothers of babies."

"You won't die soon, will you?" I didn't even want to think about my world without Nan.

"I will eventually but not any time soon, God willing. Watching you grow makes me want to stay here as long as I can. I sure would love to live long enough to see you all the way grown. But whether or not you can see me here on earth, I'm always right there." She tapped my chest. "In your heart. Whenever you need me, just call out and I'll answer."

A shadow passed overhead, covering the sun for a moment. Nan put her dry, warm hand on my arm. "Look up, Crystal. That's a bald eagle."

A bird with wings as wide as I was tall seemed to ride the wind. Mesmerized by her graceful flapping, I watched as she swooped low over the grasses that swayed in the breeze and made the music of the meadow.

"I've never seen one this close," Nan whispered as she took my hand.

The powerful creature dived into the grass and came up with a small field mouse in her beak. We squeezed each other's hands as she soared up and into the blue.

"Isn't she something?" Nan asked.

"Yes," I breathed. The strength and power of the eagle reverberated inside my own body. I grew robust as I stood there in the aftermath. She was there inside me just as the deep river and wild roses were. From then on, they lived inside my body and soul. They were me and I them.

On the way home, the warmth in the car made me drowsy. Nan didn't believe in naps. She said they kept a person from sleeping properly at night. I fluttered my eyelids to stay awake. "Nan, what's it like here at Christmastime?"

"Magical. They put lights up in all the trees and the storefronts. And it's all white with snow. The skiers come, of course, which we like because they bring money to the good folks who live here."

I peered out the window at the northern mountain. The wire and posts of the chairlifts seemed lonely hanging over the snowless brown ski runs. I turned back to look at the quaint, orderly main street of town. Hanging baskets with purple and yellow flowers hung from the brick buildings. People roamed the sidewalks as if they had no place to be other than exactly where they were.

"Did you know that no two snowflakes are alike?"

"How do you know?" They were so small, how could anyone see the differences?

"They put them under microscopes. I think, anyway."

A little girl with a golden braid sat on a bench outside an ice cream shop. Her cone had a scoop of pink ice cream. Next to her, a blond man ate one with chocolate. My favorite. I sighed, wishing I could taste that sweetness on my tongue.

Nan must have noticed my covetous gaze. "Should we stop for a scoop?"

"Really?"

"Sure. We'll bring a bowl back for Pop, though, or he'll be sad. He loves ice cream."

"Who doesn't?" I asked.

Nan parked on the street, and we hustled over to the shop and each ordered a cone. She got a weird kind called rum and raisin, but I went with chocolate. She asked the clerk to set aside a scoop of maple nut for Pop. "It'll melt if we bring it out with us."

I nodded, then licked my cone. My eyes widened at the creamy, rich flavor. "This is the best ice cream ever."

"Everything in Emerson Pass is better," Nan said.

We walked outside. The little girl and her father were still seated on the bench. The man called out to Nan. Everyone knew her here. "Joy, how are you?"

"Jack Vargas. I haven't seen you in months."

"I've been working in Denver during the week. The company has an apartment there."

"Brandi, you're getting so big," Nan said to the girl.

The little girl ducked her head. Shy, like me.

"This here is my granddaughter, Crystal. She's here all summer, Brandi, if you'd like to come over to the farm to play."

Brandi raised her gaze to inspect me. "Where do you live normally?" Her voice was as creamy and sweet as the ice cream. She had round eyes like a doll. Her skin was tanned and her yellow hair had white streaks in it as though she spent a lot of time outside. A pair of jean shorts and a peach-colored tank top were probably a lot more fashionable than the overalls Nan had pulled out of a box of my mother's old things. Brandi was pretty. Too pretty to be my friend.

"Seattle," I answered between nervous licks of my cone.

"That's far away," Brandi said.

"I had to come on the airplane."

"All by yourself?" Brandi asked.

"Yes, but they made me stay with a lady the whole time. She was kind of mean. She gave me a pin, like a pilot has on his uniform."

"Really? I'd like one of those. I've never been on a plane."

My earlier envy of her beauty lessened. I was a city girl who had been on a plane. That gave me a little something anyway, even if I was skinny and pale as a ghost. "You can come over and see it if you want."

Brandi looked up at her dad. "Can I?"

"I'd have to check with your mother, but I don't see why not." Jack Vargas looked a lot like his daughter, tanned and blond. His hair was cut as if he'd be on TV delivering the news. Actually, now that I looked at him more closely, he kind of looked like a Ken doll. Even his tan shorts and blue T-shirt seemed like something I would dress my Ken doll in.

He turned to Nan. "She looks like Jennifer at that age. I think I remember those overalls."

"You know my mom?" I asked, so surprised I almost dropped my cone.

"They were friends when they were little," Nan said. Why did she have the "Don't ask for another glass of water and it's bedtime" voice?

"Sure, right." Jack tossed the rest of his ice cream cone into the trash can next to the bench. "How's your mom? Is she here?"

"No, she just sent me. Nan says this place broke her heart." Is that what she said? I had a feeling I hadn't quoted it quite right.

Jack Vargas looked down at the ground, as if there might be something on his shoe.

"All right, then. We have to go." Nan motioned toward the car with her chin. "I'll get Pop's ice cream."

I gave Brandi a shy smile. "Guess I'll see you around."

"Not if I see you first." Brandi giggled. "My dad always says that."

I walked away, still smiling. Maybe I'd made a new friend?

I'd had no idea then that Brandi would become my very best friend in the world. That first summer turned into many more with my Nan and Pop. They were killed in a car accident the year I turned twenty, just shy of their eightieth birthdays. Everyone in town said they went out together, just as they always had for most of their lives.

Four years after their death, the richest man in Seattle came into the restaurant where I worked and asked me out; I said yes. I'd said yes again when he asked me to marry him. Even when the trolls of the internet tried to take me down, I stayed tall and sure like a sunflower. I knew I had not married him for his money. He'd been my heart. My true companion. My soul mate.

Then he died. Then I lost our baby.

A part of me died with them.

I could no longer breathe in the city of grays and mists. So I went home. Home to Emerson Pass and its indigo sky and snowflakes and Brandi. If someone had told me what awaited me there, I wouldn't have believed them. The secrets of the past rose from the ashes to change my life.

1

CRYSTAL

What is it the Buddhists say? To live is to suffer? I don't know if they're right, but by the time I turned thirty, I knew three truths on which to base my life. To love greatly was a risk that could and often did lead to pain. There wasn't enough money in the world that could cure a broken heart. The only antidote to a soul split wide open was service to others.

On a morning in November, I padded to the window of Brandi's guest room and drew back the curtain. A frost covered the ground. Fallen leaves glistened under the late-autumn sun. I hugged myself, shivering from cold.

The sound of the garage opening was followed by Trapper's truck backing out of the driveway. He and Brandi had a doctor's appointment with their ob-gyn in Louisville. Twenty weeks. They'd learn the gender of their baby. She would be fine, I told myself. The baby too. Soon I would have a little baby who would be like a niece or nephew. Brandi had already asked me to be his or her godmother.

From behind me, the creaking of the bed drew my attention. I turned to see that Garth had wakened. His long legs tangled up in the sheets, he lifted up on one elbow and gave me one of his lazy smiles. His wavy dark hair had flattened on one side during the night. In combination with an imprint of the sheet on his cheek, he looked like a little boy. But this was no child. This was a man. A good man. *Good folks*, Nan would have said.

"Morning," Garth said with that sexy drawl of his. He'd spent time in a lot of places in the country, but his accent came from being raised by a Texan. "City Mouse, you all right?"

He called me City Mouse because he'd watched me try to cut wood into kindling one day. Until the fire came roaring through the southern mountain and took both our homes, he'd been able to see my house and yard from his deck. The flames would have taken me, too, if not for Garth. My devastatingly handsome dark-haired neighbor swooped in like that bald eagle had snatched the mouse and gotten me out of there alive.

Garth Welte. My eagle.

He'd saved me, and I'd given myself to him. My body, anyway. In the dark, I came alive under his touch. I was free of memories of Patrick then. In the mornings, though, I returned to the shadows, ashamed and guilty. This was the last time, I'd assure myself. But then another night would come.

"Are you cold?" Garth asked. "You want me to get you a sweater?"

That was Garth—always asking how I was doing or feeling. The laid-back drawl and low timbre of his voice soothed me like a favorite song.

I sat on the side of the bed, careful not to touch him. If I did, we'd be right back doing what we did together all too well. "I'm fine."

"I know what you're thinking," Garth said. "That last night was our last time. I'm moving out, and we need to get on with our lives. Separate from whatever it is we've been doing."

"We're a broken record." I peeked up at him from under my lashes. "I don't know why we can't seem to stop."

"Could it be because we don't want to?" He sat up, positioning a pillow behind his back.

2

"But you know the longer we do this, the harder it will be to stop." I smoothed my hand over the cotton blanket.

"And neither of us wants to get involved emotionally," Garth said.

"That was a statement, not a question, right?" Had he changed his mind? Was he starting to fall for me? I had no idea what went on in that brain of his. As concerned as he always seemed for my well-being, he kept his own feelings to himself.

"I know what you want me to say." Garth ran a hand through his hair.

"You do?" I asked.

"I do, and I can't say it anymore."

"Garth." What was he doing? The rules had been clear. Sex. Friendship. That's where it stopped. There would be no talk of anything long term. No feelings allowed.

"I know. I know I'm changing the rules. Or I want to."

I sprang up from the bed and wrapped myself around the bedpost. "No, you don't just up and change the rules."

"I'm sorry, but I can't lie to you. I'm not made that way. Every time we end up in bed my feelings deepen for you."

"Deepen?" I disentangled from the post and stepped backward toward the windows. Deepen was a verb, a changing thing. The deep green of the river. Like me. Isn't that what my Nan had said on that day so long ago?

"I didn't want to." His eyes, the color of the apple-cinnamon tea my mother was so fond of, glittered at me from across the bed.

"I'll never love anyone but Patrick. You know that."

"That's what you say," he said softly. "And if that's true, then you're right. We have to stop doing this." He stared at his hands. A muscle flexed in his cheek. He was gritting his teeth. Sometimes in the middle of the night I heard him gnashing them. He needed a mouth guard. But that's the kind of thing a wife suggests, not a woman participating in a casual fling.

"I don't want to hurt you," I said.

"I know that."

"If you've decided you're ready for more, I'm holding you back from meeting the right person." If anyone should have all the family trimmings of life, it was Garth. He was kind and patient and so very good. I'd watched him with the children at the shelter where we'd set up a place where the families who'd lost everything in the fire could stay until their new homes were built. He had a gentleness about him that drew the children to him.

The money for the shelter had come from me, but Garth was the heart of the effort. Especially when it came to the kids.

"I didn't think I wanted something bigger than this," Garth said. "I came here to live without complications. My divorce was enough heartbreak for a lifetime."

I nodded. Garth rarely mentioned his ex-wife. However, it didn't take a genius to understand how hard it had been on him. His parents had divorced after his brother's death, and he'd vowed to himself that he would never be part of a failed marriage.

I should never have let this get started. I hadn't planned on sleeping with him. But after the evacuation we'd ended up at the same campsite. We'd been emotional and in need of comfort and had fallen into bed. Or in this case, a sleeping bag. I'd had too many swigs of whiskey. When he invited me into his tent, my fear and loneliness betrayed my better judgment. To my mortification, the whole thing had been a disaster. Afterward, I'd cried in his arms. I'd have thought that would be the end of it, but when we both ended up homeless, Brandi and Trapper had invited us to stay with them. Our bedrooms were way too close. The very first night, I slipped into his room. From that night on, we'd tried to resist each other, but somehow our chemistry kept bringing us back to the same place.

"Clearly the Welte men aren't lucky in love," Garth said with a wry smile. "But that doesn't stop my dad."

His father had been married four times to progressively younger women.

"I'm very fond of you," I said. "You've been a great friend. I'd hate to lose that." The thought of walking out that door crushed me. Thinking of being here without him left me chilled to the core. Still, I had to let him go.

"You're right," he said, sounding so defeated that I inwardly cringed. I'd done this to him. "We can't go on like this. I'm not the smartest man in the world like Patrick was. But I know people. I know what it feels like when a woman loves me. I can feel it in my hands every time I touch you. So go ahead, Crystal, deny it to yourself. I know better. But until you're ready to let yourself live again, there's no hope for us."

I started shaking. Garth had never spoken to me this way. The raw emotion and anger in his voice scared me. Not as smart as Patrick? Did he think I found him lacking because of who I'd been married to?

"This has nothing to do with you missing anything," I said. "This is about me."

He cursed under his breath. "You've got that right."

"I'm sorry," I said.

"Stop saying that." He plucked his boxer shorts from the end of the bed and threw back the sheet before standing.

I averted my eyes to keep myself from gazing at his spectacular form. He'd been a winning Olympic skier when he was young. Even in his midthirties, skiing and working out had kept his body in great shape.

Skiing.

A ski trip had killed Patrick when the private helicopter they'd rented had crashed. *No survivors.* That's what they'd said to me. Not, *your husband was killed. There were no survivors.*

Even now, three years after his death, anger sparked in my chest. Why had he chosen that trip? I knew the answer. He lived for adrenaline. Garth was the same. He tore down the slopes with that same reckless quality that killed my husband. He'd been all about risk and living large with no thought to how his behavior might have heartbreaking consequences for the woman who loved him. There was no way I would ever go through that again.

"It's not because of anything you're lacking," I said. "You're a skier. A daredevil. Which means I cannot possibly fall in love with you, even if I wanted to."

He turned slowly to look at me. "What do you mean?"

"As you know, Patrick died on a ski trip." I said this flatly and without emotion, even though my stomach churned. "Do I have to spell it out?"

"I'm a skier? And you think that's dangerous?"

I let go of the bedpost and backed up toward the windows. "Yes. I know how fast you ski down the slopes. You set the world record, for heaven's sake."

"A dozen years ago."

"You could die."

"But I'm not going to."

"You don't know that." Supposedly that ski trip was perfectly safe too. Just last year a man died on the Emerson Pass slopes when he lost control and hit a tree. "There was that guy last season," I said out loud.

"He was an amateur on a slope he had no business being on." Garth spoke quietly and calmly, as if I were an animal about to charge at him. "That was completely different from anything I do."

"You share too many qualities with my late husband. And I won't be left alone again."

"I'm not sure what we have in common. He was a brilliant billionaire tech guy. I'm a mediocre attorney and *former* Olympian."

"It's a quality. I can't explain it. A recklessness."

Garth grimaced as he grabbed the T-shirt hanging from one of the bedposts and pulled it over his head. "I'm not reckless. I've spent my whole life trying to find stability. Skiing is not reckless, it's just something I love." He sat on the edge of the ottoman. "My entire life was defined by my little brother's death. I've had this feeling that I had to live for both of us. Every day I ski is with that in mind. I'm still here when he didn't get to be. Racing down a mountain makes me feel alive."

"I know. Which is why I would never ask you to give it up." I crossed my arms over my chest. "Not for me."

He rubbed his chin. "We have a connection, even if you think it's only physical. A closeness that doesn't come along every day."

"We have chemistry in the bedroom," I said, defensive. I didn't enjoy being the bad guy. "But we've both known this wasn't a long-term thing."

"You'll be rid of me." Garth took his jeans from the arm of the chair, but instead of putting them on, folded them over his lap. "My house is done."

I looked away, unable to stand the look of hurt in his eyes and in the tone of his voice. "We're friends. That won't change."

"Sure. That's good." The finality in his tone told me he'd had enough. I'd managed to successfully push him away.

As he tugged his jeans on, I slipped into my robe, suddenly aware of how thin my pajamas were. If I wanted us to stay apart, then I shouldn't be running around half naked.

"I'll see you later?" I asked.

"Probably not. I'll stay at my house tonight."

He sounded so grim I almost reached out to him but knew that wasn't fair. If we were to stay apart, I had to be strong.

When he reached the doorway, he turned back to me. "Did you have the kind of chemistry we have with your husband?"

I blinked, surprised by the question. How could I answer truthfully and not give him hope?

"Tell me," he said.

"He and I loved each other very much." Despite what others claimed, I'd married him because I loved him, not because of his money. The press had gone for my jugular when we'd gotten

7

married. Forty-four to my twenty-four, rendering me a gold digger according to Twitter. "We enjoyed all aspects of a good marriage."

"Was it as good as us? Because I find that hard to believe." His eyes glittered with intensity as he stared me down.

"The things we've experienced together—I've never had that with anyone else, no. Not even Patrick."

He smiled again, this time a little triumphantly. "Yet you claim there's nothing here worth exploring?"

"Sex isn't everything." *I sound ridiculous*, I thought. *Like a child*. No one had ever given me as much physical pleasure as Garth. Still, I couldn't grant him my heart.

"True enough," he said. "But you said yourself we're friends too. What's better than being friends with the person you go to bed with every night?"

The air seemed to leave the room. "I'm not there. I'm sorry."

"Fair enough. At least now we know where we stand."

He didn't give me a chance to say anything else as he opened the door and disappeared into the hallway.

Discombobulated, I sat on the side of the bed. Why did I feel strange and shaky? *I do not care about him,* I told myself. *He's just really good in bed. That's all this is.*

Anyway, this is how it happened. Love had sucked me in once and convinced me that all the broken, missing parts were fixed, and then he died on me.

Had I worried about my husband's ski trip? Not at all. Back then I was still so stupidly sure everything would work out. I'd found the love of my life. For three lovely years we were happy.

After I'd moved to Emerson Pass and bought a home from an elderly gentleman perched on the southern mountain, I'd contemplated opening a restaurant. I could afford it, after all. The amount of money I'd inherited from Patrick was more than a hundred reasonable people could ever spend in a lifetime, unless one was interested in buying small islands and that kind of thing. However, I was conservative by nature. Nan and my mother had taught me that simplicity was best. My needs were simple. I wanted a quiet, unassuming life in the place where I'd been the happiest as a child. Garth had not been in the plan.

I went back to my maiden name. Other than a few friends, no one knew I was the widow of a famous tech billionaire. I'd opened a kitchen shop as a distraction from my grief. Perhaps because I'd been raised by a potter, I particularly loved curating beautiful pieces from small artisans and businesses around the world. In addition, I'd started giving cooking lessons once or twice a month in the kitchen. They'd become popular with the tourists especially. So much so that I'd hired a young chef, Mindy, in need of work to take over some of the classes. She'd been such a delight that I'd ended up hiring her full-time as my manager. Recently, she'd asked if she could buy me out, and we'd worked out a deal between us. As much as I'd thought it was a good idea to have a passion project, it felt right to transition it to someone who needed and wanted the work more than I did. By the end of the month, the paperwork would be completed.

However, as I heard the shower start in Garth's room, I had to admit I was not doing a particularly good job of understanding my feelings. I sat back on the bed, unsure of what to do or think.

I wished I could talk to Nan. I needed her clear-eyed vision to tell me what to do. I touched my fingers to the spot on my chest she'd tapped that day by the river. *Nan, what am I doing?*

2

GARTH

All the way on the drive to my house, I replayed the conversation with Crystal. I could kick myself. Me and my big mouth. I'd revealed too much. So much for playing it cool. But darn it all, I was sick to death of acting as though I didn't care. Pretending that I hadn't fallen in love had started wearing on my soul. Keeping my feelings to myself, which I knew instinctively was the right way to stay in her life, had become impossible. Everything about her made my knees weaken. Her cooking, graceful body, quick mind, and soft heart. Yet my feelings didn't matter. She wasn't ready. She might never be. I truly needed to get myself together and walk away. I hadn't set out to get my heart broken again. Here I was, though, mooning over a woman I couldn't have.

Fine, I'd fallen for her. There was nothing to be done about my feelings or her lack of them. Anyway, she was way out of my league. A billionaire doesn't marry a two-bit lawyer and former ski champion.

Then there was this revelation about skiing. I hadn't known until today that part of her reservation was my favorite hobby. I had no idea how to reassure her that my skills far outweighed

10

the risks. Most ski accidents happened to amateurs, not Olympic athletes.

I blamed my fate on my parents. They'd named me after Garth Brooks, thus guaranteeing a life that played out like a three-chord country song. Divorced by thirty from a woman who took half of my carefully saved nest egg, I'd decided to follow what was left of my heart and move to Emerson Pass, Colorado. I'd sold everything I owned and poured my time, energy, and money into building a new home nestled in the mountains. Somewhat reluctantly, as I'd figured out too late that I didn't really care for lawyering, I'd opened a family law practice. Any spare moment, I spent on the ski slopes. What had once earned me a gold medal at the Olympics was now my beloved hobby. Being an attorney was my job. The slopes were my passion.

Everything was moving along all right until a fire came roaring through the mountain, destroying everything in its path. I'd rescued my beautiful neighbor right before our houses went up in flames. Quite by accident I'd fallen in love with her. Tragically, she was in love with a ghost. If that doesn't sound like a country song, I don't know what does.

The best thing I could do was get out of Trapper's house. If I stayed there, Crystal and I would never stop breaking our promises. My contractor had called yesterday and said my house was ready. As much as I'd felt as though we barely escaped with our lives the day of the fire, I felt the same now. For self-preservation, I needed to move back into my own place.

I passed through town. Red and yellow leaves still clung to the branches of the trees, but soon they'd be gone. We'd have our first snow by the end of the week if it was a typical year. As much as I loved ski season, I loved autumn in Emerson Pass. The skies were often startling blue in contrast to the leaves and the redbrick buildings that lined Barnes Avenue. Today, town was quiet. Tourists didn't come until the slopes opened. This place was frozen in time, especially the downtown area. The original brick buildings from the original settlers remained, albeit with face-lifts and modern windows.

I passed by the market and the bar and grill, two staples for permanent residents. To get to my small office next to the newspaper, I'd have turned right. But I wanted to go out and see the house before I went in to work. I didn't have an appointment until later. Across from the bar and grill, Brandi and Crystal shared a building for their shops, a bakery and a kitchen store. The hanging flowerpots held mums this time of year. Soon, the street would be decorated in lights for the holidays.

Emerson Pass skiing would begin soon. People came from all over for ski vacations during the winter. Town would bustle with visitors. I preferred the quiet months when the population shrank to permanent residents. However, I was happy when tourists came to spend their money. My clients were always residents. In family law, most of the cases I dealt with were custody agreements. Most of the time, a divorcing couple could come to terms, but every so often a nasty one like the one I was working on now came my way. I had a bad feeling it would go to court. The divorcing couple were wealthy, and each wanted full custody of their four children. Neither was willing to back down, which meant the billable hours kept coming.

At the end of town, I took the road that led up to the southern mountain where my house was tucked into the trees. Well, what used to be trees. They'd cleared all the burned ones out and replaced the scorched earth with new dirt and gravel. Already, seedlings had sprouted. Life continues. Even after devastation.

I drove down the long driveway I shared with Crystal. The charred remains of trees stuck up from the black ground like ugly birthday candles. The work to clear the lot hadn't yet reached this part of the property. They'd focused first on the lot where my house had been, clearing dead trees and what remained of the house.

The rebuilding had gone so quickly it was almost hard to

believe. I had a feeling Crystal had something to do with that. She wouldn't confess when I asked how she'd gotten everything rolling so quickly, but I was certain if I followed the money, it would lead right to her. Whenever I brought it up, she always said I'd saved her life, therefore the debt was on her, not me.

From my deck, I'd been able to see Crystal's house and yard. When the fire happened, I'd had more warning than her. I'd torn down her driveway, worried she wouldn't understand how quickly the fire was coming. She was so shaken that she'd only grabbed a few items and jumped into my car. We'd sped out of there as the fierce winds brought down parts of the forest. Both of our houses were destroyed.

She'd insisted that my house be built first. We were sharing a team of builders from Northern California called Wolf Enterprises that included Jamie Wattson's interior designer brother, Trey. Jamie had only just opened her inn when the fire crushed her dream. I'd run into her in town a few days back and she said she thought she'd be able to open by late spring. She'd said it in an optimistic tone that didn't match the defeat in her eyes. Debt had a way of doing that to a person.

My yard was empty. For months, whenever I'd come by, the driveway had been busy with trucks and workers. I parked outside the garage and practically ran to the front door. My stomach fluttered with excitement as I used my key.

I actually exclaimed out loud at the sight of the front room. The floors were made of a dark walnut and paired with light walls. A river stone gas fireplace took up one end of the room with the kitchen on the other. An entire bank of windows ran the length of the room and faced the northern mountain. I'd had the house built using the same rustic, Japanese-influenced farmhouse plan I'd used for the first house. With flow between the different areas of the house, there wasn't a square inch of wasted space. Rustic beams inserted into what was a traditionally Japanese style gave the home the feel of the farmhouses I'd dreamed of as a kid.

I wandered into the master bedroom, also built on the first floor and with windows that looked out to the mountain. I'd splurged this time around and had them add another fireplace, as I'd regretted not doing so the first time. Despite the room being empty of furniture, it had a cozy, restful vibe. Upstairs were two more bedrooms, a Jack and Jill bathroom, and a den that could be used for a television room or an office.

I stood by the windows that looked out to the foothills. This was a house for a family. Why had that never occurred to me before? All these bedrooms? The gorgeous kitchen with an island where people could sit and chat with the cook?

The cook. I groaned softly. God help me, I'd pictured Crystal there.

The fact that I'd become a family law attorney only to get divorced myself was not something I liked to think about. When I'd married, I wanted more than anything to remain so for the rest of my life. I'd wanted children, too, but as we ended up in a miserable marriage, I was glad my wife had refused to have any. We'd married right after college. Looking back, I could see clearly that neither one of us was mature enough to be in a relationship. We'd hung in there, though, until she'd met someone else.

After it was over, a friend asked me how I'd married a woman who didn't want children. Hadn't we discussed it beforehand? We had. She'd told me she was open to the idea, but could we spend a few years enjoying each other first? Her request seemed perfectly reasonable. Sadly, there wasn't much enjoyment of each other in our marriage. Mostly, we fought. We could fight about any subject on the planet. It was like our superpower as a couple. Finally, we'd agreed that we were simply not suited. Then she'd taken half of my savings and assets, and off she went.

I'd come to Emerson Pass to ski and mend my broken heart. The original plan had been to stay for the winter and then return to my practice in the city. But the longer I was here, the more I knew I wanted to stay. By spring, I'd bought the house plan and started construction.

Now here I was again, essentially starting over. The house was finished but empty of furniture and decor. I'd ordered everything to be delivered in the next few days. If I were to stay here tonight, I'd have to borrow a sleeping bag from Trapper.

My stomach growled. I'd left Trapper's without any breakfast. Usually, Crystal whipped up a batch of muffins or eggs for me. I'd grown too accustomed to Crystal's cooking over the last few months. Often, I'd kept her company while she prepared dinner. Brandi and Trapper always took an evening walk together before dinner. When they returned, they'd shower, and then the four of us would sit out on their deck and enjoy a leisurely dinner as the sun set. I worried that we were disrupting their honeymoon period, especially since the baby would come in early April, but they assured us it was fine.

The four of us had such a fun time together. Brandi and Trapper felt like family to me now. Being there had reminded me of what it had been like to be a family. Before my little brother died and my mom left, we'd been happy.

I pushed all of these thoughts out of my mind. I'd see if some of my buddies wanted to meet at the bar and grill in town for supper. Since I'd been living with Trapper, I'd become close with his two best friends from high school. He'd grown up with Huck and Breck, and through him I'd gotten to know them both well. Breck anyway. Huck, who ran the newspaper in town, was harder to know. Whatever had happened to him while covering the Middle East as a war correspondent haunted him. Trapper said he'd always been intense and prone to broodiness, but since he'd come home Huck's dark side had seemed to nudge out any former lightness. Still, he was fun to hang out with over beers. Breck, the town vet, was the opposite. Sweet and unassuming, he was quick with a smile and a joke. He was the kind of man another man could rely on if he ever got into a scrape.

Yes, dinner in town was what I needed. *Put Crystal out of your mind*, I told myself. *You have a good life here and your house is finally ready. Time to start again.*

———————

Huck and Breck were already seated when I arrived at the bar and grill. Since it was sparsely crowded tonight, they'd lucked into the best booth near the woodburning fireplace. The lights were dim, but the fire warmed up both the temperature and the atmosphere.

Huck nodded as I approached. "What's up, Welte?"

"Not much."

"Congrats on getting your house finished," Breck said.

"Thanks." I clapped him on the shoulder before scooting into the booth next to him. "I figured that was as good a reason as any to get together for dinner."

"You bet," Breck said. "Not that we need one."

"True, but it gives Breck's mom a break," Huck said. "She feels the need to make dinner for us every night when she should be taking it easy."

"She loves it," Breck said. "She's always had a soft spot for you. No one knows why, since you're such a grouch."

"I'm not a grouch," Huck said.

"Not to her, anyway," Breck said.

Huck, after the fire, instead of moving in with his parents at their estate on the original Barnes family property, had opted to stay with Breck and his mother instead. Breck, I knew from previous discussions, had moved in with his mom because he was worried about her living alone. His dad had died when he was fifteen, and since then he'd looked after his mom, even taking over her veterinary practice so she could retire.

As far as Huck went, I was curious if there was bad blood between him and his parents. If so, he never mentioned it to me. I figured Breck knew the story, but men don't ask these things.

We were distracted when the server came to take our orders.

I did a double take when I saw that it was Stormi, our local photographer, wearing a green apron and carrying an order pad. Why was she working here? She had her own studio and also did weddings or special occasions. In addition, she worked part-time at the newspaper as a photographer. Were things so tight she had to take on yet another job?

"Hey, when did you start working here?" Breck asked.

"Since yesterday," Stormi said, a trace of New York accent apparent in the chewing of her vowels. "I used to work at restaurants back home just to make the rent." She was slight, with several tattoos etched into her fair skin. Her shiny brown hair stopped at the nape of her neck with bangs that framed green eyes the color of a vintage soda bottle.

"Isn't this jerk paying you enough?" Breck asked with a nod toward Huck.

"The same crappy wages as always." Stormi had the cutest spattering of freckles and one of those adorable noses, belying her overall edgy persona.

"Nice," Huck said.

"It's the wedding business that's tanked," Stormi said. "With the fire, I lost a lot of bookings. No one wants to come here and have a scarred mountain in the background."

"That's ridiculous," Huck said, sounding very much the grouch that his friend had said he was. "Only the southern mountain was hit. The lodge and northern mountain are scenic for even the snootiest city folk."

"People might be afraid to come here," Breck said.

"Also stupid," Huck said.

"Regardless of your opinion that most of mankind is stupid, Huck, until we get back to normal, I'm making some extra cash working here." She pointed at me. "Garth, don't you dare give me that look of pity. I'm tough. And fine."

"I wouldn't think of it," I said. "We all know you're tough. But still, if you need anything, let us know, okay?"

"Like you have anything you could do for her," Huck said.

I chuckled. "Yeah, I'm not exactly rich."

"Moral support's nice too," Stormi said.

"How's Tiffany doing?" Breck asked.

Stormi raised an eyebrow. "Why do you ask?"

"No reason, just that her income's reliant upon the wedding trade too." Breck plucked at the wrist of his flannel shirt. "I haven't seen her around much. We usually see each other at the dog park."

"Isn't it obvious?" Huck asked. "He has a huge crush on her."

Breck shot him a dark look. "Dude, not cool."

This was news to me and apparently to Stormi.

"Really?" Stormi asked. "Tiffany doesn't know that."

"I'd like to keep it that way," Breck said. "Despite Oscar the Grouch's invasion of my privacy."

"I won't say a word," Stormi said. "You're wise to keep it to yourself."

"Why?" Breck asked.

Stormi's eyes widened. "Don't you know? She lost her fiancé. He died. Very tragic. She's not ready to meet anyone else."

"That seems to be going around," I muttered under my breath.

"Do you think there's zero chance she'd go out with me?" Breck asked. "Because we both really like dogs."

"I'd say you'd have to be her friend first. She's innocent." Stormi narrowed her eyes. "Not the type who's going to jump into bed with you just because you happen to be hot."

"There's more to me than just my pretty face," Breck said, grinning. "But thanks for the compliment."

"Is there?" Huck asked. "I don't see it."

"You have more in common than just the love of dogs," Stormi said. "She's like you—nice all the time and always concerned for others."

"Which you find difficult to understand," Huck said.

Stormi's eyes flashed. For a second, I thought she might

unleash her thunder on him. Instead, she gave him a withering glance that would have made most men dive under the table. "Finally, Huck, something we have in common. We're both best friends with nice people."

With these two, I was never sure if they hated each other or were insanely attracted.

Stormi glanced back at the bar where her boss was pouring drinks. "Listen, I better get to work here before I get fired. You guys want a pitcher? There's a special tonight." She gestured toward a whiteboard with a list of food and drink specials scrawled in purple. "Rocky Mountain Breweries has a seasonal ale they're pushing if you want to try it for cheap."

We all agreed and then ordered a plate of garlic french fries to start. No one could get enough of Puck's wedge fries.

"What's up with you?" Huck asked me after Stormi left.

"Who, me?" I asked.

"Yeah, why the sudden dinner invite?" Breck asked. "We know you prefer to dine with your girlfriend."

"She's not my girlfriend," I said.

"Whoa, that sounds like the words of a bitter man," Huck said.

"Did something happen?" Breck asked.

"She basically kicked me to the old curb," I said.

"I thought you two were just having fun?" Breck asked.

"That was the idea," I said.

"Did you scare her off?" Huck asked.

"Basically." I sighed, miserable.

"What did you do?" Huck asked.

Breck shot Huck a look. "Don't make him feel bad by saying something rude."

"I wasn't going to," Huck said, sounding hurt. "Why do you always assume the worst of me?"

"Tell us what happened," Breck said, ignoring Huck.

"I kind of told her how I felt this morning, and then she

dumped me." I traced the grain of the table with my thumb. "I'm an idiot."

"You're not an idiot," Breck said. "You care about her. There's nothing wrong with that."

"If it's reciprocated," Huck said. "Which apparently it isn't. You should move on. Half the women in town want to sleep with the former Olympian turned slick lawyer."

"I'm hardly slick," I said. "And I don't want anyone else. I want Crystal."

"That's a problem," Breck said. "That I understand."

We were interrupted when Stormi appeared with our pitcher of beer and three glasses. "Your fries will be out in a minute. Do you boys want the burger special? It's under six bucks tonight."

"Nah, I'll take the chopped salad," I said. "Extra chicken."

"Tacos for me," Breck said.

"I'll take the special," Huck said. "As the only one here who needs to practice frugality."

Stormi looked as if she wanted to give a sassy retort but refrained. "Got it. Thanks, guys." She turned on her heel and walked away. I couldn't help but notice that Huck's eyes followed her. For a man who claimed to dislike her, he seemed pretty interested.

3

CRYSTAL

Brandi texted me midmorning to let me know they were keeping her for additional tests. They wouldn't be back until dinnertime. Worried about Brandi and the baby in combination with my disturbing conversation with Garth, I fretted all afternoon. In an attempt to occupy myself, I'd spent hours putting together dinners I could freeze for the first weeks after the baby was born.

I knew something was wrong the moment Brandi and Trapper walked into the kitchen. I'd prepared an early dinner for them, knowing they'd be hungry after their doctor's appointment.

"What's happened?" I asked, looking from one to the other. Brandi had her long blond hair pulled back into a ponytail. Her pretty face was blotchy and her eyes red. Had she lost the baby? I gripped the edge of the kitchen island to steady myself.

Trapper put one arm around his wife's shoulder. "The good news is, we know that the baby's a girl."

"And she's doing fine," Brandi said.

Then why was my best friend's voice shaking?

"Okay," I said. My heartbeat raced as I waited for her to finish.

"I have to go on bed rest for the remainder of the pregnancy," Brandi said. "Otherwise, I could go into labor too early."

I sighed with relief. "Well, we can do that," I said. "I'll help with whatever you need."

"She's supposed to go straight upstairs," Trapper said. His deep brown eyes were troubled. The baby they'd lost couldn't be far from their minds.

"Okay, well, let's get her up there," I said. "Don't worry, honey, I'll take care of you."

Brandi's eyes filled. "What about the bakery?"

"Between your dad and me, we'll make sure everything runs smoothly without you," I said. "Your manager is doing well. Think of it this way—you were going to take maternity leave. It's just starting a little early."

"Are you sure?" Brandi asked. "What about your kitchen shop? And all the work you're doing at the shelter?"

"Positive." Having more to do would be good for me. Helping my best friend would be good for her. Trapper had his hands full with the building of his new ice rink. We'd lost the old one in the fire, and he was rebuilding a state-of-the-art facility for training athletes as well as an outside rink for recreation. "Anyway, Mindy runs the kitchen store. I just pop in once in a while."

"You're the best," Trapper said to me. "What would we do without you?"

"I'm the one who's been living here for months," I said.

"And cooking most of our meals," Brandi said.

"Take her upstairs, Trap." I was already thinking through all the meals I would make and freeze for them. "I made a beef stew and biscuits. I'll put two plates together for you."

"Where's Garth?" Trapper asked.

"Still at work, I think." I answered as if it were of no concern. "His house is finished. He might be getting things organized over there. I'm not sure he's even coming back here tonight."

Brandi picked up on my evasiveness immediately. "Did

something happen between you?"

"He wanted to take it to the next level, and I'm just not there." I let this tumble from my mouth, eager to have it said and done with.

Trapper and Brandi exchanged a glance. I knew what they thought. They thought we made a great pair. Brandi had encouraged me over the last few months to entertain the idea of something more serious. I was always quick to dismiss their romantic notions.

"Are you sure that's what you want?" Brandi asked.

I flushed. "I'm not sure, but it's better for Garth this way. This whole thing was getting much too complicated."

"Fine, but this discussion will be continued later," Brandi said.

Trapper helped her from the stool and took her hand. "Come on. Let's get you settled."

"I'm going to get so fat," Brandi mumbled.

"More of you to love," Trapper said.

"You say that now," Brandi said.

Brandi and I were chatting in her bedroom when her dad appeared in the doorway with an old-fashioned recipe box in his hands.

"I found this while cleaning out another corner of the attic." The box was made of silver tin and had a hinged top. "It's full of Lizzie's recipes."

"Is this the first time you've seen it?" Brandi asked as she snatched the box from Jack and lifted the lid.

I moved from where I'd been sitting in the window seat to perch on the side of the bed. Brandi set the box between us. Inside the box were graying notecards, each with a recipe on them scrawled in small, neat script. They were in remarkably good shape considering they were a hundred years old.

"You two have fun," Jack said. "I'm off to Christmas shop."

"Remember I've been very good this year," Brandi said.

"I'll have to ask Santa about that," Jack said before disappearing into the hallway.

Brandi rustled through the recipes and pulled a card out of the box. "It's for shepherd's pie." She handed it to me.

The recipe included detailed instructions for a classic shepherd's pie made from lamb and topped with mashed potatoes. Brandi pulled one out for a biscuit recipe made with lard. At the bottom of the card, Lizzie had written: *American biscuits taught to me by Merry. Serve with breakfast or supper on cold days. Good with or without jam, but be sure to use a nice cube of butter between the top and bottom pieces.* "These cards are heart diseases waiting to happen," I said, joking.

"Yes, but I bet they were delicious." Brandi put the biscuit card back and pulled out one for an apple pie. "They all worked so hard back then that they burned off all the calories."

We spent the next hour looking through the entire box. There were recipes for a rosemary-and-red-wine beef stew that made my mouth water and another with tips for the perfect pie crust.

Don't mess with it too long or you'll make the crust tough.

On each of the cards were additional words of advice beyond just the recipe itself, as if they were written to someone specific. Perhaps to her daughter? What a legacy to leave behind. Would I have any such thing to leave behind when I left the earth? Would I have anyone to leave it to? An emptiness came over me. Years of solitude stretched out before me. Brandi and Trapper would have their children, but what would I have? I thought about Garth and his confession this morning. Was I making a mistake sending him away? Could I ever love him? He would be a great man to make a family with. Yet I couldn't see a future. Not with him or anyone. I'd had my chance with my one true love, and now I would have to spend my life alone.

"Have you noticed they seem like notes to someone?" I asked.

"I think so too. To Florence, I'd guess. She was Lizzie and Jasper's only child."

"You could do this for your daughter," I said. "Write down all your tricks and tips for your recipes at the bakery."

"Who knows how her generation will keep their recipes."

"On tablets or computers, most likely."

"Or something we can't even imagine yet." Brandi looked over at me. "Do you think I'll be a good mother? Given my own?"

"Wait a minute, are you actually worried about that?"

"Yes, it keeps me awake at night," Brandi said. "Worried that somehow my mom passed down her coldness to me and that it only comes out through motherhood."

"No way. You're made for this, just like Jack."

"I hope you're right."

"I am," I said. "You have Trapper, too. He's going to be fantastic, like his dad."

"True. I'm not alone."

"I wonder if Florence ended up with these cards or if they sat in the attic all these years?" I asked as I glanced down at one for a perfect white cake.

"I'd like to think Florence used them. It must have been something, cooking back then for such a large family that wasn't even your own." Brandi's eyes misted. She fanned her face. "That could make me cry just thinking about it."

"Why?" I asked, amused by her pregnancy hormones.

"I wonder how it was for her, really? Like under all that English stoicism?"

"Your family isn't getting any smaller." I touched her round belly before pulling out a card. This one sounded like the perfect dish for a cold winter's night accompanied by one of those American biscuits. I laughed as I handed Brandi the card. "Look at the directions on this one. She describes how to twist the chicken's poor neck and then pluck it before carefully cutting it up."

Brandi shuddered. "I don't think I could kill a chicken with my bare hands. Plucking all those feathers must have taken forever." She turned the card over, then laughed. "She says in here to do it before you have your breakfast. What does that mean?"

"Less likely to lose your breakfast that way?" I suggested. "She worked so hard all her life. I wonder if she ever felt too tired to go on? Or if she was ever resentful of Quinn?"

"She didn't seem to be from what we've read in the letters she sent home to England," Brandi said.

"We're not as tough as Lizzie."

"Different times call for different types of strength." Brandi placed her hand over her belly and turned over to lay on her back. "Sometimes I don't know if I'm strong enough to get through the next twenty weeks. I'm scared, but I don't want to be because I need to be calm for my baby girl."

"You're strong enough. Everything's going to be fine."

"If I lose another one, I don't know if I can make it through. Even with Trapper here this time."

"We're going to keep you nice and safe here in this bed and in twenty more weeks, a healthy baby will be in your arms."

She closed her eyes and drew in a deep breath. "From your mouth to God's ears."

"Do you remember the first time we met?" I asked, hoping to distract her.

"I can't remember a time when you weren't in my life. It seems like you were always my best friend."

"Nan had taken me into town for groceries and then surprised me by saying we could have ice cream. You and Jack were outside the shop with cones of your own. You had strawberry."

"The best flavor of all."

"You know that's not true," I said, laughing at our long-standing joke.

"I remember being at your Nan's and making cookies. It was

her recipe I used for my first ones. I started obsessively tweaking ingredients until I figured out the best combination. The secret's using chocolate chunks, not chips, by the way."

She rolled over to look at me, resting one arm on her stomach. "Thanks for being such a good friend."

"Stop it, you're going to make me cry. Anyway, it's me who should be thanking you. Without you—well, I don't know what I'd have done."

"We've had some tough times," Brandi said. "But our friendship has always been there to catch us when we fell."

"Absolutely."

She was quiet for a moment as she traced the flower pattern etched into the cotton quilt. "Can I ask you something?"

"Anything."

"This thing with Garth, do you really think it's over? Because you seem happy with him."

"He makes me laugh and he's a great friend and we have amazing chemistry, but I don't love him. I wish I could. But I'm either not ready or he's not the right one. I don't know if I'll ever feel like I did about Patrick for anyone else. I simply can't imagine the rest of my life with him. That's why I had to end things before he got any deeper."

"It was the right thing to do. I'm sad, though. I want you to have someone to grow old with. To have a family with. Garth's such a fine person."

"I thought I'd have that with Patrick." I smiled, remembering our courtship. He'd swept me off my feet, dazzling me with his intellect and passion for his work and life. I'd fallen fast and hard. "Nan used to tell me that my one true love was out there and when I found him, I'd know it. I did, too. Patrick was my once-in-a-lifetime man." I flopped over on my back and looked at the ceiling. "As great as Garth is, he's not that. I had him and then he died. End of story."

"I don't want that to be the end," Brandi said.

I didn't either, but that didn't make it any less true.

4

GARTH

A little after seven, I said good night to Huck and Breck and headed to my car. Once inside, I realized the windshield had frozen over, so I turned on the defrost and waited. I'd parked in a space that faced the brick building. Huck's truck's headlights flashed in my rearview mirror before he headed out to the street. His defrost must work better than mine. My windshield had only melted the ice at the bottom.

I looked around me. The parking lot was empty except for me and one other car, which I assumed belonged to one of the staff. A forecast earlier had said an unexpected storm would roll in sometime tonight. People wanted to beat the snow home. Downtown had emptied fast and now had an eerie feeling of desertion, as if I were the only man left.

I wasn't sure what to do. I'd vacillated all evening between going home to my new, empty house or back to Trapper's. The furniture I'd ordered was supposed to arrive early next week. Sleeping on the floor next to the fireplace didn't appeal to me. On the other hand, I didn't want to see Crystal. I had to break ties. Staying at my own house was the only option that made sense.

Crystal had not been far from my mind all night, even during the fun time with the boys. Her revelation about skiing had taken me by total surprise. I felt like an idiot. Why hadn't I thought of it before? That she had reservations about a man who sped down slopes as easily as walking made perfect sense. To her, I was reckless. A risk-taker, as her late husband had been. One big red flag if there ever was one.

Could I give it up for her? I supposed I could. But did that compromise who I was? Could I come to her half of the man that I had been? Even with all that said, she might not ever be ready. I needed to face that fact.

As much as I'd fallen for Crystal, I couldn't give up who I was for her. Not skiing. Other things, yes. A sport that had defined so much of who I am was nonnegotiable. All the choices and sacrifices my dad had made for me. I mean, a person could give up waffles if their wife hated them.

Not that she'd asked me to give it up. In fact, she'd been clear that even without my risky sport she had no interest in pursuing the kind of relationship I wanted. How ironic. Wasn't it supposed to be the man who avoided commitment?

Now my fingers twitched. I wanted to call or text and see how she was doing. No, I needed to stay away. She wanted space. I needed space. This was all for the best.

I texted Trapper that I was going to my house. I had a sleeping bag in the trunk of my car. Roughing it for a few nights wouldn't kill me.

He returned the message right away. *You sure? It's cold.*

I've got a sleeping bag. I'll be fine. Crystal and I need some space from each other.

A memory of the first night Crystal and I had stayed together raced through my mind. We'd been in sleeping bags in a tent, having narrowly escaped with our lives.

I got another text from Trapper. *I get it. I'm sorry. I know you care about her a lot. Don't give up, though. She might just need some more time.*

Another text came through before I could answer.

29

Brandi has to be on bed rest. The doc's worried about premature labor.

I cursed under my breath. If they lost the baby, I didn't know if Brandi could take it. They already had one baby in the town's cemetery. I wrote back. *I'm sorry. Is there anything I can do?*

Just get back to your house asap. This weather has me nervous.

Will do. Give Brandi my love, okay? And let Crystal know I'm not coming back tonight. I don't want her to worry.

I flipped the windshield wipers on, hoping to speed up the process. They caught a chunk of the ice and flung it upward.

The windshield had nearly defrosted when Stormi came out the back door of the bar and grill. I rolled down my window and called out to her. "Hey, do you need a ride?"

She sprinted over and leaned down to talk to me. "Nah, I can walk. My apartment's above the newspaper office."

"You sure?" I'd forgotten she rented from Huck. The poor girl was too beholden to him, especially since he didn't like her. "Did your boss send you home?"

"Yeah. The place emptied out once the storm warning came through." She zipped up her Nordic-style jacket and pulled the faux fur–lined hood over her head. "It's icy. Be careful driving back to Trapper's."

"I'm used to driving in this, though. I'll be fine."

"Cool." She rubbed her hands together. "I'm off then. Have a good night."

Did she always walk home alone in the dark? I didn't like that idea. Emerson Pass was a safe place, but even in small towns bad things happened. "Wait, please let me drive you. I don't want you walking in the dark by yourself."

I thought she'd decline again, but instead she shrugged. "Sure, why not?"

I turned on the seat warmer on the passenger side as she jogged around the back of the car and then got in beside me.

"You always walk home alone?" I asked before putting the car in Reverse and backing out of the parking space.

"This is my first night at the bar. But yeah, I'd planned on it. My car's in the shop. Again."

"Sorry to hear that."

"One more reason why I needed an extra job." She sighed. "I can't ever get ahead."

"This summer will pick up."

"I hope so. Or I may have to get out of Dodge."

"Really?"

"Yeah, I love it here, but it's been rough since the fires," Stormi said. "I make nickels at the paper. And what's there to take pictures of lately?"

"The winter festival's coming up in a few weeks, right?" Emerson Pass had a holiday festival the Saturday after Thanksgiving. The tradition went back a hundred years. A celebration of the end of World War I and the Spanish flu had stuck in our little town.

"Yeah, man, I love that cheesy festival."

I chuckled as I pulled out onto the street and turned left. "Me too."

"Trapper's dad playing Santa gets me every time."

"Same here. Crystal's organizing a huge toy and food drive this year." Always back to Crystal, I thought, disgusted with myself.

"I may be one of the ones who needs canned food," Stormi said. "I'm not sure how I'm going to make my rent this month."

"That's rough. Sadly, I don't think you're the only one." Since the fires, the usual tourists we expected in the summer and fall had not come. "Once the snow starts, the slopes will open and people will be back."

"I hope so."

She sounded so defeated I immediately felt the urge to fix it all for her. "You let me know if you need a loan, okay?"

"That's sweet but no. Not how I roll." She crossed her ankles. Her jeans were tucked into combat boots. Even her clothes gave the message that she was armed and ready for battle. No one could hurt her.

However, I didn't buy it for a second. Nothing could disguise the young, vulnerable woman under all that bluster. "You have any siblings?"

"No, thank God."

"Why do you say that?"

"My mother couldn't afford me, let alone any more of us. She did her best to make sure I felt like crap about myself. I'd have hated watching her do that to someone I loved. How about you?"

I wanted to ask more about her mother, but I didn't know her well enough. "I had a brother. He died when I was ten. Cancer."

"Sorry. That's tough."

"Thanks." I glanced over at her as I approached the newspaper office. Situated off the main street of town, the office was in one of the original brick buildings. Up in the window of Stormi's apartment, a shaggy dog's face appeared. "Who's that cutie?"

"Sassy. She's my shelter dog. Breck found her wandering down the road. Said if I took her in, I'd have free vet visits for life. Don't ask me what kind of dog she is because no one knows, not even Breck."

"She's adorable."

"She's the best thing in my whole life."

"Maybe I should get a dog," I said under my breath.

"Everyone should get a dog. Especially if they're lonely. Like us."

"I'll think about it."

"Good. Okay, thanks for the ride. It was better than walking home in the cold." She opened the door and slipped out, then squinted up at the sky. "The snow's about to start. Get home quick."

I promised her I would but waited until she was safely inside before pulling away.

My heart leaped when I heard the sound of the heartbeat that I'd plugged in for Crystal coming from my phone.

Checking on you. Come home. The roads will be bad.

She wanted me to come home. I sat at the red light in the middle of town, thinking. What should I say to her? Should I give in and tell her I was on my way and would stay another night? But if I went to her, we were doing the same thing we always did. Again, we were like a bad country song. Or were we more like a children's puppet show? Was I the soft, fuzzy puppet made from a sock and she the puppeteer? I was helpless to control my own actions.

I was used to helplessness, though. That I had no control over the outcome of things had become apparent to me at an early age. No one remained under the false assumption that we have control of our lives when they watched their little brother fade away into nothingness.

No, I would not respond to her text. I had to make this a clean break. I would go to my new house tonight and that would be that. I'd be done with this inevitable broken heart that waited for me if I continued as we were. She didn't want me in her life in the way I wanted. The sooner I was out, the better.

As I headed out of town, the promised snow began to fall. The flakes were large and mean, more ice than snow. They hit my windshield faster than the wipers could swipe them away. Without warning, it was as if I were driving into a thick blanket.

I white-knuckled the steering wheel and crawled along, hoping to stay on the road that led up the southern mountain to my house.

I'd been ten years old when my brother died. Before his death, our family had been as ordinary as any on the block of our suburb. But after months of chemo and hospital visits and finally the home hospice where the sound of the oxygen tank filled the house, we lost Christopher and our family was forever changed. When I returned to school, it was as if a cloud of cold fog followed me around. Kids averted their eyes when I walked down the hallway. Even my best buddy, Jason, seemed to think of me differently. Tragedy, death, and decay clung to me. I was now the boy whose brother had died of cancer instead of just regular old me.

Looking back, I could see that children don't know how to process the idea that someone they knew was no longer alive. How was it possible? Where did we go when we died? At least, that's how it was for me. I couldn't understand how my brother could be there one minute and gone the next.

My mother was a blank page. I'd come home from school to find her staring out the window, still wearing her pajamas. Dad handled it a different way. He went to work, and then he went to the bar. He wouldn't come home until after I had gone to bed and left before I got up.

One day, I came home from school and there was a note on my bed telling me that my mother was leaving.

I'd sat staring at that note until Dad came home. My mother had called him at work and left a voice mail.

"It's just you and me now, kid," Dad had said.

"Will you take care of me?"

"Absolutely. I'm sorry you're stuck with me, though."

For the next year or so, we made our way together as best we could. He came home right after work. We ate from cans and the frozen section. My mother had moved across town to an apartment. Strangely enough, she got a job as a secretary in small law practice similar to the one I ran now. She came by to see me on Friday afternoons before Dad got home from work. We didn't have much to say to each other. Mostly, I sat at the table doing homework while she made some kind of casserole. She was always gone long before Dad's car parked in the driveway.

When I started sixth grade, I joined the ski club. Everything changed for the better after that. My coach saw talent and spent extra time with me. When I wasn't skiing, I was thinking about skiing. Speeding down those slopes felt like the only thing in my world that made any sense. There, with the wind in my face, I was free.

Dad found a purpose through my sport. By the time I started high school, my coaches were pushing me hard. I skied every day during the season. Off-season, I worked on strength and agility. The parameters of my life were those of an athlete. Nutrition, workout plans, and evenings watching footage of downhill speed skiers became my world.

Dad ate it up. He'd always been good himself but had never considered it a sport. Now, though, he saw my potential. Being a man who loved adventure and competition, he poured his energy into me. He became my manager and biggest supporter. Along with my coaches, he pushed me hard to get ready for the 2010 Olympics. That was our mantra, day and night. Qualify for winter 2010.

When my marriage started to fail, all the fighting and bickering over nothing, I thought about my mother a lot then, wondering if I was like her. Was there some quality inside me that made it possible or even inevitable that I'd walk away from a marriage?

Now, as I crept along, I started to pray. I was in a full sweat and wondering if I should pull off the road and walk the rest of the way. If I did so, would I be able to see any better or would I freeze to death?

I rounded a sharp corner, perhaps a little too fast. The car started to slide. I tried to correct, but the road was too icy. I was airborne, and then the car rolled. The seat belt held fast, crushing into my chest and stomach. I'm not sure how many times I rolled until I hit the tree. A noise of metal against a tree was the last thing before blackness overcame me.

———————

I woke at the table in the kitchen of our old house. Christopher sat across from me, reading the back of the bran flakes box. His blond hair shone in the sun that streamed through the window. The wallpaper with the apples in vivid greens and reds decorated the walls. Mom's apron hung over the back of one of the chairs.

"Garth, look at this!" Christopher pointed at the picture on the front of the box. It was of me, racing down a hill. The gold medal hung around my neck.

"You did it! You really did it." Christopher's eyes sparkled green and pure. He wasn't sick. His cheeks were rosy and his body robust. "I knew you could do it." His expression turned from joy to sorrow "I'm sorry for what I did."

"Forget about that. I don't care about the mitt. I'd let you borrow it every day if I could."

"It was wrong to take it without asking." He smiled. "Did you know when I first got sick I thought God was punishing me for losing it?"

"I overreacted. It was stupid," I said. He'd taken my baseball mitt and lost it. I'd made a huge deal about it and made him cry. "I'm sorry. I was a stupid kid."

"But it's not the mitt I'm sorry for. The other thing. The big thing."

"What did you do?"

"I was sick. For so long. All Mom could do was think about me. You got lost."

"It wasn't your fault. You didn't ask to get sick. Mom was just being a mother. She only wanted to make you well again."

"It wasn't right that she left you." Christopher's eyes filled with tears. "I tried to get her to stay. But I couldn't reach her. She was too sad. I was her baby, so that made it worse. Plus, you were always so strong. So much like dad. A survivor. She knew you didn't need her like I had."

"Mom would've rather had it be me."

"No, it's not like that," Christopher said.

"It felt that way to me."

"Let go of that one. Forgive her. It's only hurting you now—

holding on to all that anger." His freckle-covered nose wrinkled. "I'd have loved to be there when they put that medal around your neck. But I was up here all along. Looking down on you, cheering you. Jesus too. He loves the Olympics."

I laughed. "I always wondered about that. Like does God have a favorite football team?"

"He has a favorite quarterback. I mean, Brady switched teams and still won the Super Bowl."

I laughed again—the belly laugh I used to share with my brother. Then it occurred to me. Was I dead?

"Is this it? How it all goes down? I die in a car accident?"

"No, you've still got a lot left to do. It's not true, you know."

"What's that?" I asked

"That only the good die young." He smiled his brilliant smile. "You're one of the good ones, brother. Don't forget that. There's more for you to do. Your purpose is quite clear."

"But what is it?"

"Family."

"As in, have one?"

"Not make one, but build one."

"What's the difference?"

"You'll see. Keep your eyes open. There's another thing— Mom and Dad. They're supposed to come back together."

"I don't know if you can see this from up here, but that ship has sailed. He's on his fourth wife."

"Doesn't matter. Bring them to Emerson Pass for the holidays."

"Dude, that's a bad idea. You haven't been here."

"Trust me."

And then he was gone, leaving only blackness.

5

CRYSTAL

As I cleaned Brandi's kitchen, I waited for a return text from Garth, but it never came. The snow was falling as hard as I'd ever seen it. Wind had picked up, too, howling through the trees. We were in a full-blown blizzard. *Please, God, don't let him be out in this.*

I jumped when my phone rang. I scuttled over, hoping it was Garth. To my surprise, it was my mother.

"Hi, Mom," I said. "What's up?"

"Hi, honey." Mom hesitated. "I was wondering—could I come visit for a few weeks? I'd stay at the lodge."

"You're always welcome. But why? I thought you had your new art show opening in a few weeks."

"That kind of fell through." Her voice shook, followed by a sniff.

"What happened?" She was supposed to have a show at her boyfriend Romeo's gallery during the month of November. As well as she did now, she still felt insecure about her work. This show had been a boost to her confidence.

"I pulled the contract. There's no way I'm letting that snake display my work."

I went hot. "What did he do?" Like my late husband, Romeo

had made a fortune in high tech. He'd sunk a lot of money into the Seattle art scene and owned a huge gallery in the coveted downtown area. In just five years it had become *the* gallery for emerging and established artists. I found him pretentious and obnoxious. Unlike my mother, who oozed with talent, both as a critic and a creator, Romeo wouldn't recognize quality unless someone with an eye told him so. During their two-year relationship, I'd kept all that to myself. I wanted nothing more than for my mother to be happy. If he was the one she wanted, so be it.

"Do you remember the assistant? Moira?" Mom asked. "The one with all the tattoos?"

"Sure." Moira had been at my mother's last holiday party. A skinny thing that reminded me of a wisp of smoke. Not just because she smoked copious cigarettes on my mother's balcony but because, despite being in her twenties, she was gray and small and elusive. "Don't tell me—he's been sleeping with her."

"That's right."

My heart sank. Poor Mom. She was kind and beautiful and way too trusting. When I was young, she'd been focused on me and her art. Despite having to work menial jobs to keep us fed and working on her pottery in the wee hours, I'd never gone without. When I was in high school, a gallery owner in San Francisco offered her a show. Her work took off, and she was able to focus only on her creative endeavors. Soon thereafter, she bought a loft downtown where she lived and worked.

After I left home, she became increasingly aware that she wanted and needed a companion. Romeo had been the third man it hadn't worked out with. Like the others, the relationship had lasted a few years before blowing up, followed by a long period of time where she remained happily single, concentrating on her work. None of them were good enough for her, yet she gave away her power to keep them happy. I'd hated the way she'd diminish herself to feed their fragile egos. Knowing this about herself, after the second failed relationship, she'd promised to remain single. Then stupid Romeo had come along and changed her mind.

I wanted so badly for her to find someone to settle down with. She'd had me when she was nineteen and had sacrificed so much to raise me alone, including finding a nice man when she was young.

"Mom, I'm surprised you want to come here, but I'd love it." The memory of that day so long ago when I'd asked Nan about why Mom never visited Emerson Pass came to me. A boy had broken her heart. I'd asked her again later, when I was teenager, "Shouldn't Mom be over whoever it was who broke her heart?"

Nan had looked out the window in her kitchen with a faraway look in her eyes. "My Jennifer was always a hard one to pin down exactly." It was true. My mother was like the wind, free and powerful yet hard to see. Despite how fun and beautiful she was, there was something below the surface that hinted at something deeply heartbreaking.

I'd asked my grandmother then for the first and only time if she knew anything about my father.

She'd shaken her head. "Whoever he was, it happened after she'd already left us for Seattle. She refused to say anything about him."

The only time I'd ever had the courage to ask my mother about my unknown father, she'd told me he was someone just passing through Seattle. She didn't even know his name. "A drunken evening with a stranger. Don't ever do that, do you hear me?" Then, uncharacteristically, she'd shut down any more questions. She'd always encouraged me to be curious about all things, to explore and question. But not this. The identity of my father was not something she wanted to discuss. So we didn't.

The hole left by his absence was just that. This dark, cold, unknown space of emptiness. From time to time, I thought about doing one of those DNA tests, but something always stopped me. If I'd found him, this nameless man, I would disrupt everyone's life. His, my mother's, and my own. What good would it do for any of us? For this reason, I left it alone.

"Mom, I could use your help. Brandi's on bed rest. I've got my hands full with the shelter and all the rest. I'd love it if you could help me look after her."

"Oh no. Is she all right?" My mother was very fond of Brandi. Over the years, Brandi had come to visit us many times.

"Yes, she's fine for now. The baby's fine, too. But she has to stay on bed rest or she might go into premature labor."

"She must be worried sick."

"She is," I said.

"Plus, her parents' divorce must be hard on her."

"Not really. Brandi's been happier since her mother moved away." Her mother, Malinda, had already found a boyfriend. I felt bad for Jack, but I thought both he and Brandi were better off without her toxicity.

"Why's that?" Mom asked.

"You know how Malinda was."

"Only from what you've told me."

"Trust me, she's better off. Especially now. She doesn't need any stress."

"Agree." A slight pause before she asked, "How's Jack doing?"

"He's good too. Excited about the baby."

"I bet he is. He's always been a family guy," Mom said. "I mean, from what Brandi's said anyway."

"Absolutely. There's no better father than Jack Vargas. Although I think Trapper's going to give him a run for his money." I told Mom how Trapper had been online researching the safest baby equipment and making spreadsheets to decide which to buy.

"Trapper's a sweet boy," Mom said. "I'm looking forward to seeing him."

"When can you come?"

"I'll try to get a flight out for Denver tomorrow. If that's all right?"

"Whenever you want to come is fine with me. I'll send a car for you. The weather's bad and I don't want to drive all that way."

"Are you sure? A driver seems extravagant."

"Mom."

"Yes, right. Money's no object."

"Not if it means you'll come visit," I said. "I have a guy here with a big four-wheel drive type of vehicle. He'll get you here safely."

"That would be lovely. I'm anxious to get out of here and to see you. My heart's pretty bruised, honey."

Part of me had thought she'd use the weather as an excuse and say she'd come later with no specific date. Eventually, she'd decide against the trip and cancel on me. However, there was a certainty in her voice that made me think otherwise. "Mom, I have to ask. Why now? You've never wanted to come here."

"People change."

"They do?"

"Well, sure. Anyway, you and Brandi need my help. It's good to have a purpose. It'll help keep my mind off Romeo."

"I'm sorry, Mom. I know you really cared about him."

"It's not the first time I've had my heart broken, unfortunately. But as they say, what doesn't kill you makes you stronger?"

I chuckled. "Mom, that's not supposed to sound like a question."

"I wish it wasn't."

We chatted for a few more minutes about flight schedules and arrival times. I almost suggested we have dinner with Garth until I remembered that was no longer an option. I hadn't mentioned him much to my mother. She knew he was my neighbor and that we were both staying at Trapper's. Other than that, I kept my complex feelings about him to myself. I didn't want to get her excited. In addition, talking about him with her would have made the relationship feel more real. The more real it was, the harder it would be to walk away from him.

I felt a pang in my chest at the thought of Garth. Since I'd been busy all day helping Brandi and Trapper, I'd been able to put him somewhat out of my mind. Now, however, darkness had fallen and the thought of him not coming home tonight hurt more than I liked to admit.

After Patrick's death, if not for my mother and Brandi, I'm not sure how I would have gotten through. People always say that. After a tragedy, one inevitably thinks about the loved ones who were there by your side. Both my mother and Brandi had been there for all the good and bad moments of my life. My graduation from culinary school. My short stint on the runway. The glorious days of my first chef job. My wedding day. The best day of my life. They both had been there beaming at me as I walked down the aisle.

Don't think about it now, I told myself. *I can't shed another tear. Not today.*

And then another thought came. One that I hadn't expected. Would the tears be for Patrick? I wasn't certain. Was I mourning the loss of Garth? Had I sent him away when I really wanted him to stay? Had I sabotaged something beautiful? Made up a reason to send him away? He was a skier. But he was a real one. Not a rich high-tech mogul who bought an expensive ski vacation with his other geeky friends.

Garth was an Olympic gold medalist. He knew the slopes the way I knew my way around a kitchen knife. I hadn't cut myself in years. A ski accident was unlikely. So what was this really about? Was it truly that I was just too afraid to risk losing someone again? It made no sense, if you really thought about it. Lightning doesn't strike the same tree twice, does it? And yet the thought of giving my heart fully to someone again seemed impossible. But Garth? Was he the same type of man as Patrick had been? Yes, they were both adventurous. Did the similarity end there? Garth was a family man. The type of man you called when you needed someone. Was I making a mistake?

As much as I hated to admit it to myself, the physical aspects of my time with Garth had been breathtaking. He took my breath away. He increased my breath. He gave me breath. Was it enough to risk the possibility that he might at some point leave me? Even if we had forty years together, at the end he would die, and I would be left alone to grieve the man I loved all over again. Would it be easier because we'd had more time together than Patrick and me? That I could not answer.

"Mom, I should go. Call me in the morning and let me know what time your flight is."

"I'll look forward to it, baby."

We hung up, and I finished what was left of the dishes, then went to the patio doors to peer out into the storm.

I shivered again. A nagging dread trickled its way down my spine. A sense of foreboding filled me. Something was wrong. I could feel it.

I paced around my bedroom. Garth was out there in this weather. Trapper had confirmed that Garth was on his way to his own house. Given my calculations, he should have been there an hour ago.

"Dammit," I whispered to myself as I reached for my phone and typed in a text.

Please, text me back. I just want to know if you're all right.

Nothing. It said delivered but not read. I wanted to scream. He wasn't coming back. I hugged myself as a chill entered my bones. He was in trouble. I knew it.

Many nights around this time Garth and I would meet in one of our rooms to watch television or a movie together. We'd fallen into the habit of domesticity and friendship, not to mention our fun between the sheets. Tonight, however, I was alone for the first time in many months. I didn't know how I had let myself get into this position, or when exactly I'd let my guard down. Now I was in too deep.

Why hadn't he replied to my text earlier? I'd seen that he read it. Usually, he responded right away. But what did I expect? I'd sent him away. Yet some part of me had hoped that he would come home anyway. I knew his house was empty of furniture. He wouldn't even have a place to sleep. Knowing him, he would want to give me space, and probably sleep on the floor so as not to cause me any discomfort.

I am a weak person, I thought to myself as I typed in another text.

I'm starting to panic. Please tell me you're all right.

Nothing.

I went to the window and peered into the night. At least six inches had accumulated in the last thirty minutes. Trapper had already called Breck and Huck. They'd confirmed that he was on his way home before the weather turned for the worst. What had taken him so long to get here? Had he stupidly stopped somewhere and then set out too late?

I plopped down on my bed and covered my face with a pillow.

I spoke to him silently. *Please be safe and mad at me. Please let that be the reason you haven't written back.*

Feeling unsettled and sure I'd be awake all night, I climbed into bed. I tossed and turned and checked my phone dozens of times. At some point, exhausted, I fell asleep. When I woke next, the light through the window told me that morning had come, bringing with it clear skies. I grabbed my phone. Still no messages. I got out of bed and went to the window. Trapper had already cleared a spot in the driveway. He was going out? At least six feet of snow covered the yard. Would the snowplows have come through already? I glanced at the clock. It was almost nine. How had I slept so late when Garth could be hurt? Shivering from worry and cold, I put on my flannel bathrobe and was about to go downstairs. A tap on the door beat me to it.

"Crystal, are you awake?" Trapper asked from the other side of the door.

I hurried over and yanked open the door. The moment I saw his expression, I knew I was right. Garth was hurt. My heart beat faster as he stepped into the room.

"Is it Garth?"

"Yes, he slid off the road last night on his way back to the house."

My chest tightened. I could hardly breathe. "Is he alive?"

"He's alive. As far as they could tell, he ran off the road because of the storm. They airlifted him to Louisville."

I stumbled backward. The bed caught my fall. *No*, I screamed silently. I'd known something was wrong. "Louisville?" The hospital in Emerson Pass was small but usually adequate. "If he's in Louisville, that means it's bad, right?"

"His leg needed surgery to repair the broken bones. He broke a few ribs as well. When they found him he was unconscious. Between the weather and the tree he crashed into, it took some doing to get him out of there. They're still doing tests on his brain. He hit his head hard on the windshield."

The room spun as I wrapped my arms around my middle. I was afraid I might be sick. "He's going to be all right, isn't he? What else did they say?"

"They wouldn't tell me much over the phone, other than the surgery on his leg. I'll know more once I get there."

"How did you find out about the accident?"

"I called our local hospital, then the ones in Louisville until I found him." Trapper's eyes were bloodshot. He'd been up half the night too.

Why hadn't I thought of calling the hospitals? I couldn't even do that right. Garth deserved so much better than me. "Why didn't I think of that?" I asked out loud.

"Brandi was the one who suggested I try to find him. I

couldn't get any information until early this morning or I would have woken you."

A car accident? A stupid car accident? What was it about machinery that didn't hold up its end of the bargain?

"The roads have been cleared. I'm going to go the hospital. Can you stay with Brandi?"

"I should go to him," I said.

"No, let me go. I don't want you driving. You're too upset, and the roads are going to be slick."

For some reason that made no sense whatsoever, I was hurt. Of course Trapper was on his contact list. Trapper was his best friend. I was only someone he'd been sleeping with. God, I hated this. I hated everything about it. Not only that he was hurt, but that I was right. People I cared about died. This is what happened when you loved people. They left you.

"Plus, I need you to stay with Brandi."

"Yes, yes. It's just that I'm scared."

"Me too. But he's tough."

"What did they say? The doctors. How bad is it?"

"They didn't say much. Only that I should get there as fast as I could."

"Oh my God, Trapper. This cannot be happening again."

He came to sit next to me on the bed and took one of my hands. I looked into his warm brown eyes desperate for reassurance.

"I can understand why you're afraid. I am too. But you have to pray, okay? Have faith that God's going to be there by his side."

"Why does it feel like if I'm here and he's there that—" I stopped myself. What was I trying to say anyway? That my ability to be here or there made any difference in the outcome? It didn't matter that I'd been waiting in a hotel room in Alaska. Patrick didn't return to me.

"I totally understand." Trapper's kind eyes glassed over with unshed tears. "You feel like you need to be there because if you're not something bad will happen. But I'll take good care of him, I promise. I'm going to bring him back to you. This is not how the story ends."

I couldn't stop the tears from coming. "This is my fault. I sent him away. He should've been home for dinner instead of out there in the snow and dark and icy roads."

"No, this was not your fault," Trapper said. "This was an accident. That's all."

"An accident, right. A stupid accident."

"This is going to be all right, do you hear me?"

I trembled. "Please, just tell him—tell him that I'm thinking about him. I mean, if he wakes up."

"He'll wake up. And he'll be glad to know you're thinking of him." Trapper gave me one last pat and got up from the bed. "I have to go. I want to be there when he opens his eyes. Do you mind checking on Brandi?"

"I will. And please, text me when you know more."

"You'll be the first."

I watched him walk to the bedroom door. He turned back to give me a reassuring smile. Trapper Barnes was the type of man who always expected the best of everything to happen. I hoped he was right this time.

6

GARTH

I woke in the hospital to see Trapper's worried face peering at me from where he sat in the bedside chair. They must've had me on some heavy drugs, because I was feeling no pain. What had happened exactly? I could remember rolling and nothing after that. Except the dream. The dream of Christopher.

"Hey, buddy." Trapper rose to his feet and came over to stand next to the bed.

"Hey. What in the heck happened?"

"You banged yourself up pretty good," Trapper said. "Broke your leg and cracked a few ribs."

"I hit a patch of ice." I tried to sit up, but pain in my ribs stopped me. "But I don't remember anything after that."

"You were knocked unconscious. Took some doing to get you out of the car. Do you remember being in the ambulance? They said you woke up at some point in a lot of pain."

"No. I don't remember any of that."

"Your leg was broken in a few places. Required surgery."

Stunned, I stared up at him. What did this mean? "How bad is it?" Would I be able to ski again?

"You'll be good as new before you know it," Trapper said.

"What about skiing?" I asked.

"Doc says you'll be fine as long as you do the physical therapy once you're healed," Trapper said. "You'll have to sit this season out. But who knows? Maybe we'll have a snowy spring."

I sighed, relieved. "How did you know I was here?"

"It took some doing ." Trapper drew closer. "I couldn't get here until this morning because of the roads."

"Does Crystal know?"

"Yes. She was as scared as I was."

"I'm sorry, man. I've never seen it come down like that. Like it was fine one moment and the next I couldn't see a foot in front of me."

"Crystal had a feeling you were in trouble. I thought maybe you'd just let your phone die and didn't have a charger. But she was right."

I winced, thinking about Crystal's reaction. If she'd worried about skiing, what would a bad car accident do to her? "I'm sorry I worried you guys. How's Brandi? The baby?"

"They're fine. Bed rest isn't her favorite, but she'll do anything to keep the baby cooking in there for as long as possible." Trapper glanced at the doorway, almost as if he expected his wife to be there. "She's tough, you know?"

"I do, yeah."

"As far as Crystal goes, she was sick with worry. I don't know what that says, other than she cares for you a lot more than she thinks she does."

"What good does that do me, though?"

"Be patient. I see a happy ending in your future," Trapper said. "Women are like wine. You can't open them until they're ready."

"You're way too optimistic about everything. Still, I'm hanging on to everything you just said."

"Given her reaction when she heard you've been hurt, she's not ready to say goodbye forever. She's just really afraid. This is going trigger a lot of stuff for her. Don't give up on her. She's been through a lot." The corners of his eyes crinkled. "All of which means you need to bounce back quickly. You need to prove to her that a little car accident can't keep a good man down for long."

A happy buzz replaced some of the pain in my body. Was it true? Did she care about me enough to override her fears? To Trapper's point, only time would tell. Since the fire, my instinct had been to take care of her. I'd kept her safe that day, and ever since I'd wanted to continue to do so. Now we would be on different footing. I was in a cast with two broken ribs and a busted-up leg. There had never been a time when I was that vulnerable in my life. I didn't like it.

A doctor wearing scrubs hustled into the room. He was a small man with stooped shoulders and a round belly. His manner was just efficient and brusque enough to give me confidence that I was in good hands.

"Garth, I'm Dr. Baker. I'm the surgeon who worked on your leg. I'm the best there is, so you're going to heal up just fine. How are you feeling?" He came over to the bed as he pulled a small flashlight from his white jacket pocket.

"I'm a little fuzzy on the details of how I got here," I said. "But my friend filled me in on most of it."

He shone the light into my eyes. "Yes, you would be. You managed to give yourself a concussion. Given your former profession, I'm surprised this is your first one."

"I was lucky that way," I said. "And now, not much happens in my law office."

Dr. Baker didn't smile at my joke as he moved to the end of the bed to read from my chart.

"Will I live?" I asked, joking again.

"You're going to be fine, but it's no laughing matter when the Jaws of Life have to pull you out of a car," Dr. Baker said.

I exchanged a glance with Trapper. "My friend didn't tell me that part."

Dr. Baker placed the clipboard back on its hook and fixed his gaze on me. "Once your leg heals, you'll need some physical therapy. Ribs will heal over time, but you're going to have to baby them. I'd like to keep you another day for observation and to let you start to heal in a safe environment. A concussion is serious business. Not to mention the fact that you won't be getting around too easily for a while."

"I guess it's a good thing I'm retired from skiing. But you think I'll be able to ski again?"

His white eyebrows rose and then knit together as if my question displeased him. "You won't be able to participate this season."

I sighed. "Bummer."

"If you behave and give yourself a chance to heal properly plus do your physical therapy once the cast is off, you should be good for next season."

"I'll do whatever it takes," I said.

"It'll take some getting used to, but after a few days you should be able to get around using your crutches." Dr. Baker stuck the clipboard back on the end of the bed. "However, err on the side of caution. We don't want you to reinjure yourself before everything heals."

"I'll make sure," Trapper said.

The doctor went over a few more details before he left. I wasn't sad to see him go. "Well, shoot, this is not how I wanted to spend my winter, but I'm glad to be alive."

"You scared the hell out of me."

"If I'd been conscious, I'd have scared myself."

"You'll need to come back to live with us until you're better," Trapper said.

"I'm going to call my dad and ask him to come stay with me. Given Brandi's situation and this thing with Crystal, I'd prefer to go to my house. Anyway, my furniture arrives next week. Dad can help me with all of that."

"Until your dad is able to get here, you can stay with us. The couch in the office pulls out. You can sleep in there so you don't have to deal with the stairs." Trapper went to the window and looked out into the bright day. "I should probably head for home. The roads are slick. After the snow, the temperatures dropped and everything's frozen. I want to get home before dark."

"You're a good friend," I said. "I owe you big-time for everything."

"That's not how it works. We don't keep score."

"If we did, you'd be way ahead."

We both chuckled. I winced from the pain in my ribs.

His expression darkened. "Are you in pain?"

"A little," I said.

"The nurse will be in soon. Ask her for more pain meds when she gets here." Trapper yawned.

"Dude, I'm sorry. This is such a hassle."

"Don't be. I'd expect the same treatment if I needed you."

"Please, go home," I said. "I'm not going anywhere until tomorrow, and there's nothing you can do for me. Go take care of your wife."

"I *should* get back to Brandi. When they spring you, I'll come get you. Until your dad can get here, you should stay with us."

A horrible thought struck me. "How am I going to bathe?"

"Sponge bath. Which I can tell you right now is not going to be done by me."

"I best leave that duty out when I call my dad."

"Your phone is here on the table. After I leave, you should get in touch with Crystal. I gave both the girls an update when I got here, but she'd like to hear from you."

"I'll text her," I said. "If you really think I should."

"I do." Trapper handed my phone over to me. "I charged it for you. Call me if you need anything. Other than that, I'll see you in the morning, okay?"

"You got it," I said.

He placed a hand on my shoulder. "Glad you're all right. I was doing some pretty heavy praying on the way here."

"I guess it wasn't my time," I said, thinking of my dream.

"I guess not. See you later."

He grabbed his jacket from the chair and headed toward the door. I waited until his footsteps had faded before picking up my phone.

After Trapper left, I lay there staring at my phone. Trying to get the courage to call her. Our conversation from yesterday morning seemed so long ago. A strange urgency filled me. A sudden need to talk to her, to tell her about my dream. Had I been in some sort of half a life state? Have I been about to cross over to the other side? Or was it simply a dream because of a head injury?

I punched in Crystal's number. It rang three times before she picked up.

"Garth?"

"Hey, yeah, it's me."

"Are you all right?"

"I won't be skiing for a while. But other than that, I'm fine." *Skiing? Way to go,* I thought. *Bring it up immediately.*

"I've worn a path between the bed and dresser here in my room," she said. "Worrying."

"I'm sorry to have scared you."

"I know," she said.

"I'm going to ask my dad to come stay with me."

"Stay here at Brandi's. I'll look after you."

"I'm going to need a lot of help. I'm not sure it's a good idea that it comes from you."

Silence greeted me from the other end of the phone for a few seconds before she spoke. "That's fair. Regardless, I want you to come home. I want you here. I want to be the one who takes care of you."

"I can't be around you."

"Why?" she asked, softly.

A tear leaked from one eye and traveled down my scruffy cheek. The meds must be making me soft. "I can't be casual with you any longer. I know we signed up for some fun and nothing more. This is much more than that to me. I want all of you. Not just the part that happens at night. As wonderful as that is. I can't be around you and not want what you can't give me. It's better for us to be apart."

"I understand."

"This thing between us has started to hurt too much," I said, as if I needed to further explain myself. "I don't want to get hurt again."

"I don't want to hurt you."

It's too late, I thought.

She was quiet for a moment. My heartbeat thumped between my ears.

"Take care of yourself, okay?" Crystal said.

"I'll do my best."

I hung up the phone and lay there, tears leaking from my eyes and dripping into my ears. What had I done to myself? I'd fallen in love with a woman incapable of returning my feelings. Now, along with my broken leg and ribs, I had a heart to heal too.

I called my dad next. "Dad, it's me."

"Garth. How are you, kid?"

"Not so great." I explained to him about the accident. "I'm going to need some help at the house."

"You want me to come?"

"Could you?" He might not be able to, I realized as I waited for his answer. He had a life of his own.

"You betcha. I'll get a flight as soon as possible. Good Lord, what a fright you must have had."

"I didn't really know what had happened until I woke in the hospital." I paused for a second. "It was weird, Dad. I had a dream about Christopher when I was knocked out."

"Yeah?" I sensed the hesitancy in his voice. My dad didn't like to talk about him.

"It seemed superreal."

"What did he say?" Dad asked. "Did he give you some instructions?"

"Not really. He said he was sorry for all the fuss and that Mom didn't pay attention to me while he was sick. Or something like that."

"He was always sweet that way." My father's voice had grown softer. "I can remember him apologizing about getting cancer."

"Yeah, he was like that in my dream."

"Listen, son, I should go. I'll need to book the flight and car and everything."

"Sure."

"I'll let you know when to expect me. I'm sure glad you're all right."

"Thanks, Dad."

"You call your mother?" Dad asked. "To tell her about your accident?"

"Not yet. Should I?" She and I rarely talked.

"She'd like to know about a thing like this."

"All right, then. I will."

"Love you, kid."

"Same. I'll see you soon." I hung up and put the phone next to my good leg. Tears leaked from my eyes once again. It had to be the meds making me loopy and sad. Not that the woman I loved didn't want me or that my dad couldn't talk about my brother. Or that I had no earthly idea what to say to my own mother.

Call her. You promised Dad, I told myself. I punched in her number and waited for her voice mail. Usually it went straight there. In truth, I would rather leave a message.

She surprised me by answering. "Hi, Garth."

"Hey, Mom. Nothing alarming or anything but I've had a little accident. I'm in the hospital."

"Goodness, Garth. How bad is it?"

"I broke my leg and a few ribs. I'll be fine. Dad thought I should call and let you know. He's coming out to help me. I don't need you to do anything. I'm not calling to ask for anything." Why had I even brought that up? She hadn't exactly offered.

"I know you're not. It was very thoughtful of your father to think of me." Her voice was soft and low in my ear. The soothing tones of my mother that I'd so often craved after she'd left us.

"How are you?" I asked.

"Same. Nothing new." I could see her in her tidy apartment, smoothing a blanket over her slim legs. It was a Saturday. She would be home from work today and reading on the couch or watching television. She liked old movies.

"Good. That's good."

"Would you like me to come out?"

"Um, no, that's not necessary. You don't have much time off. I wouldn't want you to eat up your vacation time by coming to see me."

"All right. Well, you take care. Please call and let me know how you're doing. Give your father my best."

"Sounds good," I said, more jolly than I felt. "Thanks, Mom."

"Bye now."

We hung up. I wanted to fling my phone against the wall. Instead, as I'd done since we lost Christopher, I closed my eyes and tried to think of something else. Anything but the rejection from my mother. *Tulips*, I thought. *I'll plant tulips in my yard.* In the spring, they bloom and bring cheery color to the world. Yes, tulips.

7

CRYSTAL

I stood near the windows of my kitchen shop waiting for my mom to arrive. The driver had called to say they were safely on their way and should arrive around six. As promised, I saw his large, black SUV pull up to the curb a few minutes after the hour. I ran out to greet them as Mom exited the car. She looked gorgeous and glamorous in a camel-colored coat and tall black boots over leggings. Her light blond hair hung in loose waves around her shoulders in a style much too young for a woman my mother's age, yet she pulled it off beautifully. When I was growing up, I'd thought my bohemian-style mom was the most beguiling woman in the world. I still thought so. She was also the most fun.

I ran out of the front door toward the SUV. "Mom!" I shouted. Her face lit up at the sight of me. She gingerly made her way toward me over the icy sidewalks. Seconds later I had her wrapped in my arms. She was slim but dense from her daily yoga practice.

"Darling, you look divine," Mom said as she drew away to get a better look at me. Her strong hands squeezed my upper arms before she turned back to thank Mikey. A large, bulky man with a deeply pocked face, he also worked as a bouncer in a night club in Louisville. I had a suspicion he was a former mobster in Witness Protection but I never asked too many questions.

I slipped Mikey a tip before he hauled Mom's huge suitcase from the back. "Would you mind putting it in my car?" I asked, pointing to where I'd parked in front of the bakery.

"Sure thing, Miss."

A few minutes later, we headed to my car, waving to Mikey as he drove away.

"Goodness, what do you have in that suitcase?" I asked Mom. "You packed like you're never leaving."

She laughed as she slipped into the passenger seat. "I brought a lot of shoes."

"I hope some of them are appropriate for the snow." The roads had been plowed earlier and were clear and dry. I wished they'd been last night when Garth was out.

We chatted about her flight and a few other mundane topics as we drove toward the lodge. The flight to Denver had made her nauseous, and she gratefully accepted the bottle of water I had in the car. "I left Moobie with the neighbors. Their little girl loves him."

Moobie was my mother's lazy, fat cat.

"I'm sorry about Romeo," I said.

"It's a double punch because of the gallery space. I was excited." She tugged at the collar of her coat. "But it's not to be. The universe has other plans for me."

"Are you all right, though?"

"I'm feeling better just being here."

We exchanged a smile as I pulled into the long driveway that led to the lodge. Decorative lanterns lit the driveway. Strands of sparkling lights twinkled from the front awnings. Soon, the large fir tree would be decorated for the holiday season as it was every year.

I left my car in the capable hands of a valet and wheeled my mother's suitcase into the lodge. Warm air blasted our faces as we walked into the lobby. Built in the 1940s, the lodge had a glamorous yet rustic feel to it. A large stone fireplace was a showpiece. Plush chairs and dark wood tables were set before a stone fireplace and facing the large picture windows that looked out to the mountain. Several families with copious ski gear were checking in at the front desk.

"Should we have dinner here at the lodge?" I asked as we walked toward the front desk.

"Do you have to get up early for the bakery?" Mom asked.

"No, Brandi's morning baker has it covered." As it turned out, the bakery wouldn't need as much time and energy as I'd first thought. Brandi's assistant manager was very capable. When I'd met with her earlier, she'd assured me that she would be able to take over some of Brandi's responsibilities. I didn't want to tell my mom too many details because I'd made such a big deal about her being here to help. Mostly, I just wanted her here with me because I missed her. "Plus, Jack's keeping an eye on things."

"Jack won't let anything go amiss, I'm sure."

"Why do you say that?" I asked.

"Well, I mean, from what you've told me, he's the responsible type."

"That's true. He's the best," I said. "Brandi's lucky to have him."

A flicker of pain showed in her eyes. I shouldn't have mentioned the father subject. She never said so, but I had the feeling she felt guilty over my fatherless childhood.

While she checked in, I wandered over to the windows to look at the view. The lights for night skiing lit up the mountain. Only a few skiers were out tonight. Next weekend we'd be flooded with ski vacationers, but for now it was quiet and peaceful.

"It's lovely this time of year," Mom said as she came to stand beside me.

"How long has it been since you were here?"

"My parents' funeral. So what's that? Two decades?"

"Give or take." Neither of us said any more about their funeral. We'd made a pact long ago to talk about how splendidly they'd lived not how they'd died.

"Do you want to take your bag up to the room," I asked, "while I get us a table for dinner?"

She agreed. "I'll freshen up a bit first."

"Take your time. I'll order us wine." I found us a cozy table in the bar near a roaring fire. Piano music played softly in the background. When a server came by, I ordered us each a glass of chardonnay. By the time our drinks arrived, my mother had appeared. She'd changed into a pair of loose jeans, a black sweater, and flats. A turquoise necklace that had probably been made by one of her talented friends in Seattle hung around her neck.

Mom tilted her head, obviously observing me closely. "There's something different about you."

"There is?" I touched my fingertips to my hair.

"Not your hair. Your aura."

I rolled my eyes. "Honestly, Mom, you're such a hippie sometimes."

She narrowed her eyes, still watching me. "Have you been having a lot of sex?"

I almost spit out my sip of wine. "Mom!"

"You have. I can see it in your face. Who?"

I sighed. There was no way I was getting out of this conversation without spilling it all. "You remember my neighbor, Garth?"

"The hot cowboy? Of course I remember him. He saved your life, after all."

"How do you know he's hot?"

"I looked him up." She gave me a smug smile. "Even I know how to google someone. What a career he had, too. Very impressive."

"He's been staying at Brandi's," I said. "In the other guest room."

"Yes, you mentioned that."

"And one thing led to another."

"Oh really?" Mom asked, even more animated than she'd been even the moment before.

I shook my head. "Don't look like that. It was just a casual thing. We've ended it."

"That's a shame,"

"He was starting to get too serious," I said.

"And you didn't like that."

"I don't have any interest in getting involved like that ever again." I paused to take in a breath. "He was in a car accident yesterday."

"Oh no, that's awful. Is he all right?"

"He has a broken leg and two cracked ribs. I had this bad feeling that he was in danger after I hung up the phone with you last night. The storm roared in out of nowhere. He got stuck in it and slid off the road. Smashed into a tree. They had to airlift him out of here."

"I'm so glad he wasn't hurt worse," Mom said.

"Me too. The whole thing scared me to death." I glanced up at the server as she set a basket of bread on the table. She introduced herself as Bree and asked if we were ready to order.

I'd glanced quickly at the menu before Mom came down and knew exactly what I wanted. "Mom, are you ready?"

"You order for me, honey," Mom said to me.

"We'll both have a cup of the butternut squash soup to start," I said. "Then we'll share the beet and goat cheese salad. For our main course, we'd like the salmon."

Bree had the rugged appearance of a person who loved the outdoors. She nodded in obvious approval at my order. "Will you share the entrée?"

"No, we'll each have one." The lodge wasn't known for large portions.

"My daughter's a trained chef," Mom said.

Bree smiled politely. "I hope you'll enjoy your meal."

"I'm sure we will. Thank you."

Mom waited for Bree to walk away before leaning closer over the table. "Are you sure want it to be over? You and Garth."

"It was just supposed to be a fun thing. Something casual. There's something about the man I can't resist."

"I knew it," Mom said. "Sex."

"We enjoy each other that way." I flushed. "More than we should."

"What's wrong with having a bit of fun?" Mom asked. "You've always been too serious."

"The whole thing was getting too complicated."

My mom lifted perfectly plucked eyebrows. "What does our hot cowboy want?"

"He wants to take everything to the next level. He's that type. The marrying kind."

"Then why did you get involved in the first place?"

I looked away from her intense scrutiny, stung by her question. "He didn't at first present that way. He's divorced and said he didn't want anything serious either. We agreed to have fun."

"You have feelings for him. I can see it."

"Maybe."

"You don't want to because you think you should remain loyal to a dead man the rest of your life?"

When she said it like that, I sounded crazy. "I don't know. I guess so." I moved my finger up and down the stem of my wineglass, avoiding her gaze.

"What is it really?" Mom asked. "There's something you're not telling me."

"He's a skier," I blurted out.

"What's that got to do with anything?"

"Patrick died on a ski vacation." I knew the minute it was out of my mouth that my mother would pounce.

"Let me get this straight. Because your husband died on your ski trip, you can't get involved with a skier?" She folded her hands on the table. Her fingernails were always cut short for her work. Often they were stained from clay, but tonight they'd been buffed into a nice shine.

"That about sums it up."

"This is not at all the same." She touched her fingertips to one of the stones in her necklace. "Patrick died in a helicopter, not skiing."

"To me, it feels similar. Too familiar."

"Isn't Garth retired from professional skiing?" She asked this in such a reasonable tone that I knew she was trying not to let her impatience with me come to the surface.

"He is. But he still skis. A lot." What was it about being with my mother that reduced me to a petulant child?

"Again, not the same. Patrick hired a helicopter to take him and his rich friends on a very dangerous ski trip in the back-woods. All very dangerous in good conditions. They knew the risks going out in weather like that."

Was she resentful of Patrick's choice to go out that day? She'd never even hinted at this before. What she said was true. The helicopter company had told me the pilot decided on his own to take Patrick and his friends out even though a storm was expected that afternoon. I had a feeling Patrick had paid him off to take them out anyway. They skied all day and were caught in the storm on the way home. This was something Patrick would do, weighing the odds that they could beat the bad weather and get back to the lodge before conditions grew worse. "You know how he was, Mom." Going with the risky choice had made him feel excited and alive.

"I don't know why he had to take that kind of risk. Not when he had you and..." She trailed off, not wanting to bring up my miscarriage.

"I'm angry sometimes too."

"I loved Patrick, but I don't know why a man with a wife behaved the way he did."

"You've never said that before."

"I don't like to upset you. My anger is my own to deal with."

I took a moment before admitting to my mother something I'd only recently come to terms with myself. "I think if he'd loved me more, he would have chosen to come back to the lodge instead of going out that day in very questionable weather." I sighed. Speaking the truth was like coming up for air after swimming underwater.

"He didn't think about it that way," Mom said. "To him, it was all a game. One he was accustomed to winning."

"I suppose that's true." An image of him from that morning flashed before my eyes. I'd been watching him from the upstairs window at the lodge as they were loading into the van that would take them to the helicopter. Perhaps sensing me, he'd looked up and waved. I'd placed my hand over my heart, a gesture to express my love. He'd given me a grin and a thumbs-up.

"Honey, he loved you." Mom reached across the table to cup my cheek in her cool hands. "Of that, I have no doubt."

Her touch brought the sting of unshed tears. "Isn't it strange that the quality you're attracted to in a person can be the very one that kills the relationship?"

Mom's gaze flickered to the wall behind me. "Yes, it's that exactly." I detected a deep sadness. One she usually kept hidden from me. Was there someone in particular she was thinking about? Romeo or one of the others? "Was there ever anyone like that for you?" I wanted to ask about my father and if it were him, even though I knew better. She'd told me whenever I asked that he'd been a one-night stand. A man she didn't know well enough to even remember his name.

Mom took a sip from her wineglass but didn't answer my question. "You remember Patrick for who he truly was and the choices he made before giving up on Garth."

Bree was behind the counter making a racket with a cocktail shaker filled with ice. The pendant lights over the bar were made of blue glass and shaped like teardrops. "I don't know if I can let myself care about someone again. Not the way I did with

Patrick. I don't know if I'd live through losing someone a second time."

"You might not lose him."

"People go away," I said. "In one way or the other."

"Sadly, we know that to be true."

"I wish it wasn't," I said. "Or I wish I were braver. One or the other."

"Jack Vargas and I dated in high school," Mom said.

"What? Were you serious?"

"I thought so. But you know how that goes. A teenage girl doesn't always have the best judgment."

"How come you never told me?"

She studied her wineglass. "I don't know. You and Brandi are so close, I didn't want either of you to feel strange." Mom looked up at me. "He never mentioned it, then?"

"No, not to me or Brandi."

"I was nothing to him, I suppose."

"Did you break up when you left for art school in Seattle?"

"No, he went to work at a summer camp to make money for college and met Malinda and next thing I knew they were getting married. And that was curtains for me." She said it lightly, but the hurt in her eyes was unmistakable.

"They married because she was pregnant," I said.

"I know. There was never a finer person than Jack Vargas. He couldn't have made any other choice but to marry the girl he got pregnant. I was already supposed to go the art institute, but I'd hoped there was a future with Jack. I didn't know quite how it would work, but we'd talked about him coming to Seattle with me. But then he wrote to me at the end of the summer that he'd gotten one of the other camp counselors pregnant and they were getting married." Her voice caught as she clutched the stone in her necklace. "He broke my heart."

I stared at her in amazement. All of a sudden, certain things made sense. "Is that why you never wanted to visit?"

She nodded. "I didn't want to see them together. And then, ironically, you and Brandi ended up best friends."

"I wonder why he never said anything to Brandi?"

"Probably for the same reason I didn't. He didn't want it to be awkward between you two. Or it meant nothing to him. Like a blip in his life."

"Mom, you don't have feelings for him still, do you?" I stared at her, completely thrown by this new information.

She waved her hands in a dismissive gesture. "Don't be silly. We were high school sweethearts, that's all. What you said made me think of Jack. The thing I loved about him was the thing that drove us apart."

"What was that thing?" I asked.

She hesitated, obviously thinking through how to explain it to me. "He had old-fashioned ideals—hard work, integrity, loyalty, kindness. He was like my dad in those ways. All those things made it impossible for him not to marry Malinda. Even if he had loved me like I thought he did, he would have done the right thing."

We were interrupted by Bree bringing out our cups of soup. After she left, we ate in silence for a few minutes.

"They were never happy," I said. "Jack's a new person since the divorce. Malinda was kind of horrible."

Mom didn't say anything as she reached for a piece of bread.

"Jack's in and out of Brandi's house every day. Will you be all right if you run into him?" I watched her carefully.

I could swear her hands trembled when she placed her spoon next to the bowl. "It's been ages and ages. I'll be fine."

Interesting thing to say, I thought. Was she trying to convince herself?

"Do you think he'll find me old?" She touched her fingertips to her cheekbones.

"First of all, you're beautiful. Second, he's aged too."

"Is he still handsome? He had the most wonderful hair."

"It's silvery now, but thick. Very attractive. He's in good

shape, too." I sometimes saw him running along the road that led to Trapper's.

I tried to imagine them together. My artistic, eccentric, and sophisticated mother with straightforward, earnest Jack Vargas? An odd pair for sure. Even if they suited each other in high school, thirty years had brought many changes to both of them. Mr. Vargas was Emerson Pass. Tough and ruggedly handsome, made from the finest materials, like the mountains and sky. My mother was more like a fine city sculpture.

"Mom, you'll find him different than you remember from high school. You're not the same person."

"Of course you're right. It's just nostalgia for an innocent time in my life. Those were happy days."

"I always thought you hated it here."

"It wasn't Emerson Pass that I hated."

I reached out to touch her hand. "Mom, that must have hurt so much. To find out he'd been with someone else when you thought he was your future."

"Being betrayed by Jack Vargas was the last thing my young heart thought would happen. Afterward, I was never the same. Like you, I stayed away from men for years and years. All the time you were little."

"I thought you weren't interested because of me."

"No, it just took twenty years for my heart to heal."

"Mom, I had no idea. I'm sorry."

"It's all right now. As they say, a lot of water under the bridge."

And now here she was, returning home after all these years. When I'd spent summers here, my grandmother had often told me how anxious Mom had been to move away to a city. "She had big dreams, honey," my grandmother had said. "Dreams too big for this town or our little farm."

Now she ran in circles with rich, artistic people. In fact, I'd gotten the job at the restaurant where I'd met Patrick because I'd been granted an interview as a favor to my mom. Her friends were sophisticated and rich, as Patrick's friends had been. Would she find Jack Vargas too provincial after all this time?

I imagined her now, eighteen and on her own in Seattle. She'd probably gone out for the evening as a way to mend her broken heart and met some random man and ended up pregnant with me.

"Did you ever regret having me?"

"No, honey. You were an accident but not a mistake." She reached and pressed her hand against my wrist. "You've been the very best thing in my life. God had a plan for me, and it was you."

"And your work too."

"Yes, my work has been a blessing too. It's never how you think."

"What's that?"

"Your life. It never ends up like you think it will."

That was the truth.

8

CRYSTAL

By the time I got home after visiting with my mother, my mind was reeling. I wanted one thing and that was to talk to Brandi. Trapper was in his office speaking on the phone and waved to me as I headed toward the stairs. The door to Brandi's bedroom was open a few inches, so I peeked in to see if she was awake.

She was sitting up in bed with the television on when I tapped on the door. "Hey there. I just wanted to let you know I'm back."

"Come in. Tell me everything." She clicked the television off and looked at me expectantly. "I've been bored stiff. How's your mom?"

I sat beside her on the bed. With her hair pulled back in a braid and a face free of makeup, she looked almost like the girl I'd first met. Her pregnant tummy made an adorable bump under the blankets.

"Well, it was an interesting night," I said.

"What did she do now?" Brandi asked, eyes gleaming. "Wait, don't tell me. She met some foreign diplomat on the plane who's invited her to Paris for the month of February."

I laughed. "Not that. But she had a bombshell just the same."

"What is it? I can tell it's something good." Over the years, we'd delighted in my mother's antics, mostly because she was so different from us. As much as Brandi and I loved the simple life here in Emerson Pass, we enjoyed hearing my mother's stories about the interesting people she met.

"Okay, brace yourself. This is a doozy."

Brandi smoothed her hands over her bump. "Even better."

"Your father and my mother dated in high school."

Her eyes widened. "What? No way. How didn't we know this?"

"She said she never mentioned it because she didn't want us to feel weird, especially when he was married to your mom."

"I can't believe it." She shook her head. "But they're so different. How were they ever a couple?"

"She was totally in love with him. In fact, it took her twenty years to get over him."

"You're kidding."

"I'm completely serious. I don't know how he felt about her, but she was head over heels for him. She admitted that's why she didn't like to visit here when I was a kid. She was afraid to run into them. He broke her heart when he got your mother pregnant."

"Holy crap."

"I know. She thought he might move to Seattle with her to go to college, and then he wrote to her about your mom and the baby. Can you imagine how blindsided she must have felt?"

"I can't believe my dad did that."

"He was a kid," I said. "With a lot of hormones."

"Still. He cheated. That's like the opposite of the type of person he is. He was loyal to my mom all those years when she was terrible to him."

"Honestly, I think that's why she's never found the right guy," I said. "She compares them all to the memory of your dad."

"How sad." Brandi brought her thick yellow braid over her

shoulder. "That's like me and Trapper. I never stopped loving him the entire ten years he was away."

"I don't think this was like you and Trapper. This seemed more one-sided. I don't think he loved her the way she loved him."

Brandi shook her head, obviously disagreeing with me. "No, I don't think Dad ever loved my mother. He did the dutiful thing. Maybe he loved your mom but had to marry the girl he got pregnant. Think about this—I loved the boy I loved in high school for ten years and Trapper loved me back. Maybe it runs in the family. Can you imagine if they got back together like Trapper and I did?"

"Don't get too excited. Over thirty years has gone by. They have nothing in common now."

"But how fun would it be if they fell in love all over again? We'd be sisters. Jennifer could be my stepmom. We'd have the perfect family."

I patted her knee. "You're such a romantic."

"Come on, it would be amazing." She smiled, all dreamy and sparkly. "My dad deserves someone special after being married to the Mom-ster all those years."

"That we can agree on." I got up from the bed to pull down the shades.

"Garth's getting released in the morning," she said. "Trapper's going to get him and bring him back here. His dad's coming out in a few days."

"It'll be good to have him back with us." I traced the flower pattern sewn into the comforter with my finger. "The house feels empty without him."

"Interesting." She smiled innocently, but I knew better.

"I'm off to bed now. Don't dream up any schemes to get our parents together. This is not *The Parent Trap*."

"Wouldn't it be great if it was?" Brandi asked.

We said our goodnights, and I wandered down the hall to my room. I stopped at Garth's door, wishing two things. One, that he was in there, and two, that I could go in and have him wrap me in his arms.

––––––––––

The next afternoon, when I heard Trapper's truck pull into the driveway, I flew to the door and yanked it open, watching as Trapper helped Garth out of the truck. Garth's left leg was in a cast that went over his knee. They'd given him crutches, which he now stuck under his arms. He winced as he made his way up the stone path toward the front porch. His ribs hurt, I assumed. At least there had been no serious injury to his head. He'd texted me earlier that the test results indicated no permanent damage.

"Howdy," Garth said to me as I ran out to greet them.

I searched his face, reassured by the calm in his brown eyes. "Welcome home," I said softly.

"I'm glad to be here. The hospital food can't touch yours." He hadn't shaved. The stubble gave him a harder look than normal.

"Tell me you have dinner," Trapper said. "It's all we talked about during the drive here,"

"I just took a pan of lasagna out of the oven," I said.

"Great, I could eat a pan by myself," Trapper said. "But first I need to see my wife. Has she been good and stayed in bed?"

"Very good. She's anxious to see you, though."

They followed me into the kitchen; Garth's crutches made a bumping sound against the floor. The air smelled of Italian spices and tomatoes from my homemade sauce.

"If you two will excuse me, I'm going to see my wife. Start without me." Trapper gave us a quick smile before exiting the kitchen, leaving me alone with Garth. It had never been awkward between us but now, overcome with emotion at the sight of him, I didn't know what to say.

He made his way over to the kitchen sink. "I'm starving, but I'm also dying for some water."

"Here, let me do it for you." I scurried over to the cabinet and grabbed a glass, then filled it with water from the filter on the refrigerator. "Would you like to sit?"

"Nah, I'll be upright for a few minutes. Feels good after all that time in bed." He took the glass from my outstretched hand and downed the entire thing. "Much obliged." He set the empty glass on the counter.

"Are you in pain?" I asked.

"A little." He grimaced. "My ribs more than my leg."

"I'll fix you a plate."

"You're a sight for sore eyes." He smiled as he seemed to take me in as someone would a long-lost loved one.

"As are you. When I think how close you might have come to..." I stopped myself, unwilling to say what had haunted my thoughts since we got the call.

"Don't go there. I'm fine." He hobbled over to the kitchen table but didn't pull out a chair. "I hate to ask but could you help me into a chair?"

I rushed over to him and lent him my arm as he lowered into the chair.

"Darned if that doesn't hurt like a you-know-what." He grimaced and let out a small groan.

"Did they give you any pain medication?"

"He gave me something, but it makes me sleepy. So I best eat first or my head will end up in the lasagna."

Suddenly, I felt a need for a glass of wine. "I don't suppose the doctor will let you have wine?" I asked.

"I won't tell if you don't."

I cut him a healthy square of lasagna and brought it over to him. Then I opened a bottle of Chianti and poured us each a small glass. As I took it over to him, I fought the urge to touch him. I allowed myself one brush of my fingers over his stubbly cheek. "You scared me."

"I know." He caught my hand and brought it to his mouth. "But do I look any worse for wear?"

"If I were to say anything at all, I'd say you look as good as ever."

"I missed you."

"I missed you too," I said quietly. "More than I should have."

"Should or wanted?"

"That's the same thing."

"Not exactly."

I escaped and went back to the counter to cut a piece of lasagna for myself. When I returned to the table, he hadn't touched his food yet. Instead, he stared down at the plate. "Are you in pain?"

"No, I'm fine."

"Then eat. I spent all afternoon on that thing. Even the sauce is homemade."

He dug into his lasagna. After the first bite, he groaned. "Good Lord, girl. You're gonna make me fat."

"That's what Brandi said," I said.

"How's she holding up?"

"She's been fantastic. Especially when you consider what happened with her first baby."

"I can tell Trapper's scared. I've never really seen him that way. I can't lie. It kind of freaks me out."

"I'm the same way. But he's strong too. They'll get through this and as long as Brandi's careful, the baby's going to be fine."

We ate in silence for a few moments. When he'd finished, he pushed his plate away. "That was ridiculously good.

"I was surprised to hear your mother's in town," he said. "Is everything all right with her?"

"She's had a bad breakup and called out of the blue and said she needed a change of scenery. I was shocked she wanted to come here. Usually she'd ask me to meet her somewhere."

"She knew you wouldn't want to leave Brandi."

I ate a bite of lasagna before answering. "She told me something last night that explains why she never wanted to visit here. She and Brandi's dad were high school sweethearts. He broke her heart when he came home married to the girl he'd gotten pregnant at his summer job. She flat out told me she couldn't cope with seeing him with her or their baby. I had no idea about her and Jack, let alone that it kept her away from here."

"Does she know he's divorced now?" Garth asked.

"She does."

"Do you think there's any chance the two of them could reconnect?"

"You and Brandi—romantics. I don't think there's any chance of that." I explained to him about what had happened.

"Jack would have some explaining to do to get out of that one," Garth said.

"I think so."

Garth had this way of listening with complete attention. I never felt the need to rush through details. My husband had been the opposite, so often on one device or another while talking with me. His mind had gone faster than most. He'd been able to track our conversation as he answered emails or played with code. I'd always forgiven him for his multitasking. Only occasionally it had left me with the feeling that I hadn't quite eaten enough to be full. Garth left me satiated, like the perfect slice of lasagna.

I inwardly cringed. Why was I comparing them? I'd loved Patrick. No one could or should replace him.

"What is it?" Garth asked. "I lost you. Where did you go?"

I smiled. "I was just thinking about what a good listener you are."

"I'd listen to you read the dictionary just to hear your voice."

I flushed, pleased and embarrassed by the compliment.

"Something strange happened to me," Garth said. "When I was knocked out, I had a dream about my brother. Only it was more than that. It was like I was in the space between life and death."

The space between life and death. The hair on my arms stood up as I took in a deep breath. "What happened in the dream?"

"We were in my parents' old kitchen. Christopher was the

age he'd been when he got sick, only he wasn't sick. He was perfectly healthy, just sitting at the table eating cereal. It felt so real but also different. A glimpse into the afterlife. The place where we go when we die."

"Did you want to stay there?" I asked, anger rising.

"I didn't, no. He told me it wasn't my time. That I had work still to do. He also told me I should get my parents back together. That they belong together."

"You're kidding."

"That's what he said. What do I do with that? Especially considering my father is now married to his fourth wife."

"It could've just been a dream, brought on by a head injury."

"I called my mother yesterday. She acted like she wanted to come out here, which is super weird."

"How long has it been since you talked to her?"

"I can't remember." He looked at the clock that hung on the wall over the sink. "We never have much to say. There's so much space and time between us. So much distrust on my part."

"Which is understandable." What was wrong with her? How could she have left her precious son? Yes, she lost a child. But she had another one. A child who obviously had needed her. *Still* needed her. The sins of our parents followed us around. One of the many things we had in common. My unknown father. Garth's absent mom. "Everyone leaves, it seems."

He gazed at me, a mixture of sadness and confusion in his eyes. "What do you mean?"

I drained my glass. "When I heard about your accident and how close you were to death, everything I feared came rushing back to me. I can't trust someone not to die on me. And then you almost did."

"I didn't, though."

"You just said that you might've been in the place between life and death." I stopped, afraid I might cry. The anger in my voice surprised even me.

"I know you're angry at me. But you don't get to be. Because I didn't die. I'm right here. I don't plan on dying anytime soon."

"I'm sorry."

"Don't be. Life's messy. People are messy. When two people are together, there's a bigger mess."

"When you say it that way, messy doesn't sound so bad."

"I'm scared of losing you too," Garth said. "Don't think for a second you're alone in that. I've never met anyone I've felt more suited to be with. I don't think I ever will. I don't want to, for that matter."

"Is it my cooking?" I asked, joking to avoid going as deep as he'd just gone.

"That has a lot to do with it." He smiled and reached for his glass. Before he could pick it up, I covered my hand with his. "I stood outside your door last night for like five minutes. I'm pathetic."

"We've had some good times in that room." His voice turned husky. "Sadly, we're not going to revisit those times anytime soon. Not with this." He gestured toward his cast.

I giggled, imagining how we could work around a cast. "We might be able to move past the broken leg, but your cracked ribs could be a problem."

"We'd have to be very creative."

We were interrupted when Trapper came into the kitchen. I abruptly stood and knocked my hip on the corner of the table. "Trapper, let me make you a plate."

"Sorry to interrupt," Trapper said.

"Not at all. Is Brandi hungry too?" My cheeks flamed. Why had he walked in just at that moment? I couldn't wait to be back in my own home. As much as I'd enjoyed being with people, I craved my own space.

"She said she'd like a small piece," Trapper said. "Emphasis on small. She said you're overfeeding her."

I busied myself putting their plates together as Trapper poured himself a glass of wine. He then sat at the table with Garth. "How you holding up?"

"Fine," Garth said. "I'll take some pain meds before bed."

"Brandi told me about your mom and her dad." Trapper said. "My wife has the wedding planned already."

Garth and I both laughed. "I told her not to get carried away," I said.

"Jack's such a good man," Trapper said. "I'd love to see him happy. Brandi would too."

"He broke my mother's heart," I said. "I don't see a happy reunion."

"I wonder, though," Trapper said. "He might have carried a torch for her like I did for Brandi all those years we were apart."

"Stranger things have happened," Garth said.

"You guys didn't see her face when she told me about what had happened. That's the kind of heartbreak that stays with you forever."

The next morning, I was up early making bacon when I heard a knock on the back door. I opened it to see Jack Vargas standing on the back porch carrying a bag from Brandi's bakery.

"Hey there," I said. "Come on in. I just made coffee."

"I brought scones." He stepped inside and shrugged out of his jacket. "It's cold this morning. I feel another snowfall coming."

"That's what the forecast says," I said.

"Everything's going fine down at the shop. I thought I'd come by and let Brandi know."

"She's still asleep as far as I know."

He sat at the island. "Do you think Brandi will mind that Susan's doing so well? My daughter's poured her heart and soul into that place."

"Yes, but she's about to give her heart and soul to the baby. The bakery will seem less important."

"True enough. Brandi changed my life. She was all I cared about. That's for sure."

"Did you ever regret having Brandi so young?"

"Absolutely not. Even though Malinda and I couldn't make it work, we gave Brandi a stable home, and that's all that really mattered in the end."

"I would have liked to have a father." Why had I said that? I hadn't meant to reveal something so personal.

"Did you ever meet him?" Jack asked. "Forgive me. It's none of my business, but I've always wondered."

"No, my mother didn't know him. One of those 'passing through' kind of things. He never knew about me." Embarrassed and slightly defensive, I flushed with heat. It felt like a betrayal to my mother to tell him that. I'd already filled in the missing pieces. A young girl, brokenhearted after her high school sweetheart got someone else pregnant, sought comfort from a stranger, which resulted in me. Could it be that Jack Vargas was my father? I quickly dismissed the idea. For one thing, Brandi was old than me. The timing wouldn't add up.

"I'm sorry. That must have been hard."

"It was fine. My mom was enough. She's got the energy of two people."

"I remember. She was a force."

Then why did you do what you did? I thought. Horrible Malinda instead of my phenomenal mother? What was he thinking? "She's here in town for a visit. Did Brandi mention it to you?"

One eyebrow shot up as he turned toward me. "No. She never comes here."

Interesting. He knew that? Did he know it was because of him?

"She called out of the blue and asked if she could come out." I thought about whether or not to tell him the story of her breakup with Romeo but decided against it. I didn't want him to know she'd been dumped for someone else. Again.

"Did she ever tell you we dated in high school?" The corners of Jack's eyes crinkled as he smiled.

"Just last night, actually." My voice hardened. "She said you broke her heart."

Bless him, he had the decency to look embarrassed. "I know I did. We had big plans. I ruined them."

Shocked by his confession, I blurted out, "Then why did you do what you did?"

Jack dipped his chin before looking back up at me. "Not my finest hour. It was a mistake, after too many beers at a bonfire. Just that one night. That one mistake cost me the only woman I've ever loved."

Only woman he ever loved? Was he serious? Could it be possible that he'd loved her as much as she loved him? "She didn't visit here because of you and Malinda."

His eyes reddened. "I'm sorry to hear that."

"She didn't want to run into you."

He flinched as if I'd smacked him. "I can understand why. I hurt her—turned her love into hate."

Not hate, I thought. Just a hurt so big that it kept her away from the place where she'd grown up.

"She loved it here," Jack said.

"I always thought the opposite," I said.

"I wondered why she never visited." He touched the spot on his hand where his wedding band must have been not so very long ago. "I always figured I'd feel it in my bones if she came home. Maybe I was right. I had a dream about her last night."

Did that mean something? Had God had a hand in this? A small ray of hope lit my heart. "She's had a recent breakup. That's why she wanted to come see me."

He scratched the back of his neck. "I'm sorry to hear that."

Was he?

"I got Brandi out of my mistake, so I can't wish it all away, but the last thing I ever wanted to do was hurt your mother. It's one of my biggest regrets. I have a lot of them, unfortunately. My carelessness caused so much pain. To all of us, really."

TESS THOMPSON

I softened, touched by his obvious remorse. "You were young. No one makes the best decisions at eighteen."

"You're kind. I don't deserve it, but thank you."

"Everyone deserves forgiveness, especially from themselves." Like me? I'd killed the baby growing inside me with my selfishness. The miscarriage had been my fault. I hadn't been able to forgive myself yet for begging God to kill me, too, after I lost Patrick. I hadn't yet known I was pregnant. My grief killed my own baby. I knew it as well as I'd ever known anything.

Jack leaned his backside against the island and folded his arms over his chest. "Do you think your mother would have a drink with me? I'd love a chance to tell her in person how sorry I am for what I did."

I chose my words carefully. The last thing I wanted was to betray my mother's trust. However, this man before me was so clearly decent. I'd known him as a loving father to Brandi. Now, more than ever, I understood he'd sacrificed his own happiness for his daughter's sake. There was a stability about him, too, like a hundred-year-old oak. My willowy mother, more like a tender aspen, needed an oak. What would have happened if they'd been able to stay together? The answer was too strange to truly contemplate because neither Brandi nor I would be here.

"I'm not sure if she'd want to have a drink or not, but it wouldn't hurt to ask."

"It *could* hurt," Jack said wryly. "If she says no."

"An apology would help her, I think. You can do that over the phone if she refuses to see you."

"That's all I want." He gripped one hand around his opposite wrist. "After I wrote to her and told her what I did, I never heard from her again. I've thought about that a lot over the years. The silence and what it said. I believe it would've helped her to be able to lash out at me. Instead, she ran away to suffer alone. I'd like to give her the opportunity to unleash some of that anger."

"Would you like her number?"

He didn't answer, other than to hand me his phone.

82

9

GARTH

I woke in Trapper's office confused about where I was for a moment. A second later, it all came rushing back to me. I groaned softly, wondering what to do first. As if in answer, my leg and ribs throbbed. Pain medicine would be first. The sofa bed creaked as I reached for the prescription Tylenol bottle. I popped one in my mouth, followed by a drink from the glass Crystal had left by the bed. For a few minutes, I lay there, trying to muster up the energy to get out of bed. Finally, I gingerly reached for my crutches and managed to hoist myself onto my one good leg.

Between the pain and the poor mattress, I'd had a terrible night. My eyes felt scratchy, and my head ached. After hobbling over to the bathroom, I leaned heavily against the sink and inspected myself in the mirror. I looked as bad as I felt. Bloodshot eyes, greasy hair, and the three-day stubble made me look like I'd been on a bender. I wanted a shower in the worst way. However, the doctor had been very clear that I was not to get my cast wet. The hospital had sent me home with a cast cover for the shower. Still, I didn't see how I was supposed to stand in the shower with crutches for support. If only it were summer, I could have had Trapper simply hose me down in the backyard.

I looked longingly at the shower. I'd have to settle for a sponge bath and a shave.

Crystal had brought my toiletries down from the guest bathroom upstairs. Using my crutches for support, I lathered my face and shaved as best I could. I cut myself twice and cursed both times. My foul mood grew worse by the minute. I used a washcloth to wipe myself down, but I was pretty sure I stunk. Not to mention my hair, which was matted down on one side of my head like a kindergartner before his mother got to him with the brush. I combed it and slicked it back from my forehead, then brushed my teeth. By the time this was all done, I wished I could go back to bed.

Using my crutches, I clomped into the kitchen. The smell of coffee and bacon improved my mood considerably. As did the sight of Crystal standing by the island with Jack Vargas.

"Good morning," Crystal said, a little too chirpy. I'd interrupted a conversation between them that had seemed serious. What was that about?

"Morning," I said. "Jack, good to see you."

"You too. Sorry to hear about your accident." He gave me a sympathetic smile. "I'm glad it wasn't worse."

"Me too." Right now, I couldn't imagine feeling worse.

Crystal drew nearer, inspecting me with the eyes of a caretaker. "Did you sleep?"

"Not much. I feel awful."

"Did you take anything for the pain?" Crystal asked.

I nodded, then moved over to stand next to the island. "It hasn't kicked in yet."

"It said online that you're supposed to get ahead of the pain," Crystal said. "I'll help you with that today."

I mumbled a thanks and then scooted onto one of the kitchen table chairs.

"Can I get you coffee?" Crystal asked. "I've got bacon and can fry you up a few eggs. Jack brought scones from the bakery."

"Sounds like heaven," I said. "I'm in a foul mood."

"No one can blame you for that," Jack said. "I broke my leg one time and it was a real pain to shower. My wife had to help. Neither of us enjoyed that."

"How did she help?" I asked, curious. "Because I could use a shower in the worst way."

"I sat in the tub on a stool with my broken leg covered in the plastic thing," Jack said. "Did they give you one of those?"

"Yeah."

"Then my wife scrubbed me up," Jack said. "Harder than she had to."

Crystal handed me a cup of coffee with a spoonful of cream, just the way I liked it. I took a grateful sip.

"Jack, do you want some eggs?" Crystal asked.

"I couldn't impose that way," Jack said.

"Nonsense. I'm making some for Garth anyway." She pointed at the table. "Sit. I'll get you coffee. Cream. One teaspoon of sugar, right?"

"You have a good memory," Jack said.

"I never forget what people eat or drink but, in this case,, that's exactly how I have my coffee," Crystal said. "Making it easy to recall."

"I'd love another cup." Jack came to sit with me at the table. "I had one at the bakery this morning while I was waiting for them to package up the scones."

Trapper came into the kitchen. His hair was damp, and I caught a hint of his shaving cream. Who would have thought I'd feel jealous over a good shower?

"Hey Jack, what're you doing here so early?" Trapper asked.

"I came by to check on you guys. Is Brandi awake?"

"Yes, and freshly showered, which improved her mood considerably."

"Must be nice," I said under my breath.

Crystal brought a mug of coffee over to Jack. "Trapper, what do you want for breakfast?"

Trapper opened the bakery bag. "I can't stay. I'm meeting

someone from the city for the rink inspection. I'll just take a scone with me. Oh, good, there's a lemon one. I love those." He pulled his phone out of his jeans pocket. "Jack, I'll text Brandi that you're coming up in a few."

The ice rink had been lost in the fire. Trapper had decided to resurrect it. His dream, as a former professional hockey player, was to create a training program for kids to come from all over the world. Now that it was almost completed, he would be able to get started on building his program. He'd also had an outdoor rink built for recreational purposes. Inspired by the stories of the first residents of Emerson Pass and their infamous skating parties, anyone would be able to skate for free.

Scone in hand, Trapper headed out the back door.

"Jack, how do you like your eggs?" Crystal asked.

"Any way you like to cook them," Jack said.

After Jack left, Crystal fixed her attention on me. "Are you feeling any better?"

"Your breakfast helped."

She took my empty plate to the sink and rinsed it before returning to the table. "Jack asked for my mother's number. He wants to take her for a drink. To apologize for what happened."

"Do you think she'll agree to it?"

"I'm not sure. I just don't want her hurt. This could open a lot of old wounds. On the other hand, an apology might provide healing."

"I hope she'll be all right, either way."

"Do you want me to help you take a shower?"

I blinked. "That's a switch of subject."

"I know you want one. I'm the perfect person to do it since I've seen...all of you."

"I do feel really gross." I'd have to keep control of myself or the bath would be even more embarrassing.

She brushed the palms of her hands over the front of the apron she always wore when in the kitchen. "Let's do it."

"Now?"

"No time like the present. Don't tell me you're suddenly shy after all the nights we've spent together." Crystal grinned.

"You're enjoying this a little too much."

Her face turned a little more sympathetic. "Don't worry. I'll let you scrub your boy parts."

"You're not funny."

She laughed. "Come on, let's get it over with."

Crystal prepared things in the bathroom while I changed from my sweats and T-shirt into my birthday suit, covered by a terry cloth robe. Our plan was for me to sit in the bottom of the tub and use the handheld shower to rinse me off.

"I'm ready for you," Crystal called to me from the bathroom.

I trudged toward her with my stupid crutches under my arms. When I arrived, she had the cast's sleeve in her hands.

"Sit on the toilet there and I'll cover it up."

I did as instructed, feeling worse about myself by the minute. She gingerly placed it over my foot. "Here, I can pull it up," I said, only too aware of my unwashed junk.

Once I had the plastic case over the cast, the suction cup sealed around my skin.

"Turn around," I said.

"It's not like I haven't seen it all before."

"Not all shriveled up like this."

She laughed and turned around. "I won't hold it against you."

I shrugged out of the bathrobe, worried I smelled. "All right, I guess I'm ready." I stood, using the crutches.

"Here, set one aside," she said. "Give your weight to me on the other side and we'll get you in there."

"Fine." I leaned on her as I stepped into the tub with my unbroken leg followed by the one in the cast. She then hung on to me as I lowered onto the bottom of the tub.

"Damn, that hurts." I winced from the dart of pain coming from my ribs.

"I'm sorry," she said.

By the time I was seated, she was panting from the strain.

"Are you all right?" I asked.

"Sure. You're heavier than you look, though."

"Great, thanks."

Crystal took the crutch from me and put it beside its mate. I sat there naked in the tub, feeling like a little boy.

She frowned as she picked up the handheld showerhead and turned the spigot to let the water flow through. Water spurted out, hitting her in the face. She let out a scream of surprise.

"I think I can do this myself," I said. "Now that I'm in here."

"No, I'm fine." She turned the water on me.

"There's nothing wrong with my hands." I covered my face as the spray assaulted my hair.

"Good." She turned the spigot off and poured a bit of shampoo into my hand. It smelled like flowers.

"This is girl shampoo."

"Scrub it up or I will."

It felt great to lather up my hair. When I was done, I closed my eyes and let her rinse my head. Even though I was perfectly capable of doing it myself, I wasn't going to turn her away. Not when she was kneeling on the floor of the bathroom, all her attention on me.

She poured some kind of liquid soap that smelled of citrus into the sponge and then used it to wash my back and arms and chest. As she scrubbed, I watched her. Pink-cheeked and breathing heavily from the effort, it didn't take much of an imagination to think of our other antics.

"What?" Crystal pushed a stray hair behind her ear.

"You're pretty."

She rinsed the sponge and me, then added more soap. "Here, you can do your boy parts."

"Thank God." I took the sponge from her outstretched hand. "Turn around. I can't have you watching me."

She laughed again but obliged by getting to her feet and turning toward the door.

By the time I was done, I felt like a new person.

"Can you help me out of here?" I asked.

"We got you in here, right?"

"I'm afraid you're going to hurt yourself," I said.

She handed me one of the crutches before kneeling to wedge her shoulder under my armpit. Between the two of us, we managed to get me to my feet. It wasn't pretty, but success came just the same. Then she helped me into my robe and assisted me out of the tub.

"This sucks," I said, shivering.

"You're a grumpy patient."

"I don't like being so reliant on someone else."

"Someone or me?" Crystal asked.

"Anyone. But especially you."

"Why?"

"Because I'm supposed to take care of you," I said. "Not the other way around."

"How old-fashioned of you."

"You say that like it's a bad thing."

"You're sweet but stubborn, and frankly, not a very good patient." She cupped my face in her hands. "I'm just glad you're here, grumpy or not. Now, let's figure out how to get that furniture delivered to your house earlier than promised. We need to get you home."

I could hear my phone buzzing in the bedroom. "Will you run and get that?" I asked. "It might be my dad."

She hustled over to the bed where I'd left the phone. "It *is* your dad. His flight's been delayed until late tonight. He won't be here until midnight."

"Great. More good news."

"Don't worry, I'll help you. Let me call the furniture company and see if I can get them to come out today."

I was too tired to protest and simply nodded.

CRYSTAL

After a little haggling that included an absurd delivery cost, I had the furniture store agree to send a truck to Garth's with his bedroom and only guest room furniture, a sectional couch for the living room, and a dining room table and chairs.

That afternoon, I drove Garth up to his house to make sure we were there when the furniture arrived. I hadn't been there since they'd finished and had never been in his house before the fire. They'd done a beautiful job. Tall ceilings with exposed beams made it a perfect mountain retreat. A river rock fireplace was the center of the living room, which looked out to the valley below.

"What do you think?" Garth asked, leaning on his crutches.

"It's beautiful." The floors were made from wide-planked walnut and gleamed even on this dark day. A bank of windows ran the entire front of the house. "Is it the same as before the fire?"

"Pretty much. I made a few tweaks."

The sound of a truck coming down the gravel road drew me away from the windows. "That's them. Right on time."

"How much did you have to pay for this?"

I chuckled. "You don't want to know."

"I never thought I'd be so happy at this point in my life that the master bedroom is on the main floor," he said as I went to answer the door.

For the next hour, the delivery men brought in the furniture and put it where Garth instructed. Most of it needed to be put together, so the afternoon was busy and loud. The delivery company showed up with mattresses for the master and guest room right around the time the workers were done. They'd just left when the doorbell rang again with our order from Amazon. I'd purchased sheets, blankets, towels, and a coffeepot. I figured we could get takeout for dinner until I could get his kitchen stocked with items from my shop.

I waved to the UPS driver before bending down to get the package. By the time I had the sheets in the washer, Garth had collapsed onto the long portion of his sectional couch. He'd gone for a sage-green cotton, mostly because it had been in stock. I liked it, finding the color warm and peaceful. He had his head propped on a pillow. Right now, his complexion was a similar shade of green. All this had worn him out.

I gave him another pain pill and covered him with one of the blankets. "Rest for a bit."

He didn't answer, other than to close his eyes.

I turned on the gas fireplace. Outside, the light had dimmed. Soon it would be dark. I turned on the overhead lights in the living room but used the dimmer to keep it from being too bright. Lights strung on the rafters of the patio came on as I stood looking out at the view. The house felt cozy and safe.

For the next hour, I read on my phone while Garth napped.

"Hey. How long was I asleep?" Garth asked.

I turned to look at him. "Not long."

"Come sit closer to me. I want to see you better." He patted the spot next to his good leg.

My stomach fluttered at the low tone of his voice. I hesitated. Was it a good idea? In the past, I couldn't keep my hands off him whenever I was near him. In the end, desire overruled caution. I slipped out of my boots and sat next to him, careful not to jostle him. I could see the effects of the pain pill in the lazy droop of his eyes.

He lifted his arm. "Right here, baby."

Fine. Just give in to it, I told myself. *You know you want to.* I lay down, snuggling into the crook of his shoulder.

"Does it hurt if I touch you?" I asked.

"Nope. Quite the opposite."

Snow began to fall, dancing prettily in the lights. Every nerve in my body burned as fiercely as those lights. "What do you want for dinner? We can have something delivered."

"Pizza?" His voice was lazy and smooth as silk.

"Thai or barbecue?" Those were his favorites. He enjoyed anything sweet, like his heart.

"I'm feeling barbecue tonight," he said. "With extra chicken. Is that all right with you?"

"Whatever you want is what I want."

"If only that were true," he said, under his breath.

I let that one go. Any response would lead to the kind of discussion I didn't want to have tonight. I called down to the pizza place in town. They took the order and said they'd deliver them in less than an hour. Less than an hour, as if that were fast. This was the kind of town that figured an hour's delivery time was speedy. In the city, that number would be cut in half.

I went to the kitchen and filled up the water bottle I'd brought with us. Garth probably needed liquid.

I returned to him and had him take a sip from the bottle before settling down next to him. The snow continued to fall. We needed music to make the scene even more perfect. For the next few minutes, we discussed what he wanted for the kitchen. "I'll get all this from my shop tomorrow."

"Let me pay, at least," he said.

"We'll see." I changed the subject. Talking about money made me uncomfortable. "Do you want to know what I was thinking about?"

"I always want to know what you're thinking about."

"Do you remember how we had to buy a new car for me after the fire?"

"Sure do. We're going to have to buy one for me now. My insurance called earlier. They called it a total so I can get a replacement once I can drive again. Who knows how long that'll be."

"Six weeks if you let your leg heal properly."

"Yes, ma'am."

"Do you know what you want?" I asked.

"Did we already decide on pizza?"

"No, I meant what kind of car do you want."

"Oh, right. Something practical?"

"Maybe something better in the snow," I said, teasing.

"Do you know I love you, City Mouse?"

I stiffened. He'd said the words I'd dreaded coming from his mouth. Was it the pain medicine loosening his tongue?

He continued. "I know you don't love me back, which breaks my heart. However, I'm an optimist. I keep thinking if I stick around, you'll eventually see how I could make you happy."

Happy? What was that exactly? Was I capable of it? I'd been a joyful person before I lost Patrick and the baby.

"Talk to me," he said.

"I don't know what to say."

"I'm sorry. These drugs are making me loopy. Did I just tell you I loved you?" He chuckled, then drew in a deep breath. "It hurts to laugh."

I know, I thought. *It hurts me to laugh, too.* That was the problem with being a widow. I wasn't supposed to be merry. I'd promised to love Patrick forever. Until death do us part. Death had come. Why, then, did I feel disloyal for being here with Garth?

"I love to make you laugh," Garth said. "It gives me the flutters in my stomach. Do you ever have flutters?"

"Yes, I do."

"For me?"

"For you." Tears gathered at the corners of my eyes. This sweet man just kept getting better and better.

Garth let out a small snore. I shifted to look at him. Asleep again. I'd let him sleep until the food came. I snuggled closer, wishing I could rest my head on his chest, but I didn't dare for fear of hurting him.

I stared at the falling snow, wishing I could sleep. Instead, I replayed his words over and over in my mind. What was I going to do about Garth Welte? Love him back? Could I? Would I?

———

The pizza came an hour and five minutes later. Garth woke when the doorbell rang. I leaped up to fetch it from the delivery boy. He was a high school kid I recognized as a frequent visitor to Brandi's bakery.

"Hi, Ms. Whalen. We threw in a salad since it was you."

"That's nice of you. Are the roads all right?"

"Yeah, they're fine. Snowplow came through a bit ago."

I'd already tipped him from the phone so I thanked him and told him to be careful driving back to town. Shivering, I closed the door and went into the kitchen. I'd thought to grab some paper plates and napkins from Brandi's before we headed up here, and pulled them out now. They'd done a fine job on the kitchen. I loved the way the room flowed from kitchen to dining room to living room. As a cook, I enjoyed kitchens that were connected to the rest of the space. When I prepared meals, I didn't have to miss out on any action.

When I prepared meals? What was I thinking? When I prepared them here? For Garth and me?

Garth stirred from the couch, sitting up to look over at me. "Is that pizza I smell?"

"Barbecue. Extra chicken. And a salad."

With the aid of his crutches, he struggled to his feet. "Should we eat at the new dining table?"

"Sure thing." The table he'd picked out was rectangular and could seat eight. He'd chosen two white wingback chairs for either end and a soft teal for the side chairs that paired nicely with the rock of the fireplace and gray granite countertops.

I brought two plates and the pizza box to the table as he eased himself into one of the wingback chairs. He was adapting well to his crutches. It wasn't hard to imagine the kind of athlete he'd been. The kind to win a gold and a bronze medal. His medals. Where were they? Had he lost them in the fire?

"Were your medals in the house when the fire came through?" I asked.

He reached into the pizza box for a slice. "No, they were at my dad's house."

"Why?"

"I don't know. I figured he'd earned them as much as or more than I had. He sacrificed a lot for me to train. Plus, he likes to show them to his various women." He took a bite of his slice.

"I think that's sweet. Don't you want to display them, though?"

"I'm proud of them, yes. But all that was a long time ago now. I don't think of myself in terms of my skiing career."

"How do you think of yourself?" From what I could tell, he didn't have huge ambition. He'd told me he only worked the minimum of what he needed to, saving himself for the slopes, hiking, and fishing.

"I think of what kind of son I am. What kind of friend. I'd have liked to be a big brother for longer than I was."

"You're still a big brother, whether he's still here on earth or not."

"True enough." He winced and drew in a deep breath.

"Do you need more pain meds?"

"Just some Tylenol this time. Those other ones are too strong. I barely remember this afternoon."

I wondered if he remembered confessing his love to me. There was no way I was asking him. Instead, I got up to grab the pain tablets from my purse.

"I'm sorry about what I said earlier." He took the pills from where I'd set them by his plate and tossed them into his mouth, followed by a sip of water. "I don't know what got into me. Other than strong drugs. They loosen tongues as well as take away pain."

"Don't worry about it."

"It's true, just the same."

"Garth."

"I know. I have a big mouth."

"Incapable of keeping things to yourself." I placed my hand over his wrist and looked into his eyes. At first glance they seemed the color of strong black tea. Sitting only inches away and with the glow from the pendulum lights that hung over the table, I could see specks of dark green.

We were saved from further discussion by the sound of a car pulling into the driveway. "Is that your dad here already?"

"Maybe he managed to get an earlier flight." He rubbed under one eye. "Do you mind answering the door?"

I got up from the table to look out to the driveway. Two headlights blinded me momentarily. When they shut off, a man stepped out of a SUV. Sensing motion, the light over the front door switched on, illuminating his face. He was a man in his sixties with thick silver hair and a face that reminded me of Garth. "It's your dad." He squinted into the night as snow fell steadily from the sky. "I think it's your dad."

Garth clumped across the floor to stand beside me. "That's him all right."

Touched by the excitement in his voice, I opened the door and we both stepped onto the porch.

"Hello there. Don't come out here. I got my suitcase and that's it," Mr. Welte called out as he tugged a bag from the back of the SUV. His Texas accent was thicker than I'd imagined. Garth had never mentioned his dad had a drawl. Now I knew where the hint of one in Garth had come from.

"Welcome," Garth said.

"Wouldn't you know—I got picked on one of them waiting list things and got an earlier flight." Mr. Welte stepped onto the porch. Snowflakes had landed in his hair and eyelashes. "Son, good to see you." He put both his hands on the sides of Garth's face. "How you doing, kid?"

"I'm fine," Garth said. "But I'm glad you're here."

"Glad to be of service." He turned toward me. "And who's this pretty little darlin'?"

"This is Crystal," Garth said.

"Crystal, nice to meet you." Mr. Welte held out his hand for me to shake but surprised me by pulling me into a hug at the last second. I could feel the power of his muscles as he almost picked me up off the ground.

After we parted, he gave me a flirtatious grin. "Good Lord, boy, you didn't tell me she looked like a movie star."

"Dad, don't embarrass her," Garth said.

"Embarrass her? Are you embarrassed?" Mr. Welte asked me.

"A little. But I appreciate the compliment just the same."

"See there, son? She appreciates the compliment."

"Come inside," I said. "It's freezing. We have pizza."

"Excellent." Mr. Welte stomped his cowboy boots before entering the house. I made a note to add a mat to our list.

Mr. Welte was about the same size as his son, but his outgoing personality made him seem bigger. Garth's gentle voice and mannerisms were in stark contrast to his father's boisterous laugh and voice. He filled up a space, even one as large as the nearly empty room.

"Boy howdy, this place is fancy." He gestured toward the bank of windows. "You did good."

"You're in luck, Dad. Your bed got delivered today, but things aren't exactly put together."

"Well, don't you worry about a thing," Mr. Welte said. "I'm here to help now. We'll get you all fixed up. I can do the heavy lifting while you recuperate."

I had to admit, an able-bodied man would be helpful. "Are you hungry?"

"Shoot, I could always eat." He shrugged out of his wool peacoat. "Where should I hang this up?"

I took it from him. "We don't have any hangers yet, so I'll have to hang it over the couch."

"Done deal." Mr. Welte grinned at me. "I'm not a fussy man, so you just tell me what's what and I'll do your bidding, you hear?"

"Yes sir," I said.

"None of that now," Mr. Welte said. "I'm Brian to my friends. And anyone who feeds me within the first ten minutes is a friend."

"I like a man who knows how to eat," I said.

"Shoot, girl, it's my superpower," Brian said.

We walked back over to the table to eat. Between bites of pizza, Brian told us about the flight from Vegas—bumpy—and the drive from the Denver airport—snowy. "So thick I darn sure couldn't see farther than the car ahead of me. I was white-knuckling that steering wheel like my grandmother. She was scared of a lot of things, including driving." He pretended to drive, shaking his entire upper torso in a way that made me laugh.

"Dad, where's your wedding ring?" Garth asked.

"Well now, there's a little story around that. My new bride took it upon herself to sleep with her trainer. She done Joləned me."

"Jolene?" I asked.

"Dolly Parton song," Garth said to me. "You'll get used to it after a while."

"It doesn't fit exactly right," Brian said. "Because Jolene is a woman and the one who's cheating with Dolly's man. This was the other way around."

I didn't follow completely, but I nodded politely anyway.

"Marilyn cheated on you?" Garth asked. "I'm surprised."

"Why's that?" Brian asked.

"I didn't think she'd do anything to jeopardize her meal ticket." Garth's gaze flickered to me. "Marilyn wasn't exactly the type who liked to work."

"Now, son, don't be petty." Brian grinned. "Anyhow, it's a good thing I had that prenup, huh?"

"I guess so." Garth sighed. "Seriously, Dad, you've got to stop marrying them."

"Couldn't agree more. From now on, this ol' boy is closed for the wedding business." He tugged on the collar of his flannel shirt. "I've learned my lesson for good."

"Four wives later," Garth said.

Surprised by his tone, I turned to Garth. I hadn't seen him this way before. He almost seemed dour, and I'd never heard him sarcastic before, either.

He met my gaze and must have sensed my disapproval, because he apologized to his father. "I'm in pain. It's making me grouchy."

"Not a problem. I deserve your disapproval." Brian turned to me. "I've really had the lousiest luck with women. Since his mother, my 'picker's' been off."

"Picker?" I asked.

"How he picks women," Garth said.

"Oh, a picker. That's funny," I said.

"She left us, so Mom wasn't too good, either," Garth said.

I cringed at the hurt in his voice.

"She had a breakdown," Brian said. "Who could blame her?"

"Me, I guess." Garth pushed his paper plate aside. "Crystal,

I'm changing my mind about the stronger pill. I think I'd like one, or I'm not going to sleep tonight. Dad, it's good to see you, but I'm tuckered and should go to bed."

"Sure thing." Brian's dark eyes looked troubled as he glanced over at me. "Should I be worried about this?"

"I'm fine, Dad. It's just going to take some time to heal." Garth looked toward the windows. At least five inches of additional snow had accumulated in the last hour. "Crystal, you're staying here tonight. You're not driving in this."

I didn't argue, even though this meant a night where temptation would lead me right into his room. Was there a country song for that?

"I don't reckon I'd enjoy getting back in the car," Brian said. "The roads were rough getting up here."

"You should stay," Garth said to me.

"I thought that was a foregone conclusion," Brian said.

I flushed. I'd wondered if he knew about Garth and me. That answered that question.

"I need to make up the bed in the guest room for you, Brian," I said. "We ordered everything today and it needed washing."

"Let me help you," Brian said.

"No, stay and relax. I'll just be a moment."

I went to the laundry room and grabbed the sheets and towels from the dryer. By the time I returned, both men were up and standing at the bottom of the stairs.

"The guest room and bathroom is the first one at the top of the stairs," Garth was saying. "There's nothing but a bed and empty dresser, but it'll do for now."

"You bet it will," Brian said as he held out his arms. "Here. Give me those sheets and towels. I'll put the bed together myself."

I relented. Garth's skin seemed pale and the slope of his shoulders told me how tired he was. I needed to get him settled. "It's nice to meet you, Brian. I'll see you in the morning."

He gave me a warm smile before patting Garth on the shoulder. "You both get some shut-eye. You'll feel better in the morning."

"Thanks for coming, Dad."

"You know it." Brian headed up the stairs.

"Come on, let's get you into bed," I said to Garth.

He nodded and followed me into the bedroom.

11

GARTH

I climbed into bed, exhausted. Crystal was in the bathroom doing her nightly routine. The sounds of her moving around, opening cupboards, brushing her teeth, and flushing the toilet comforted me. Over the months we'd started a habit of getting ready for bed in our own bathrooms. When we were done, one of us would text the other. *Your place or mine?* We'd switched back and forth in an unspoken agreement. One night I'd initiate the text. The next night, she would.

How had we thought our relationship wasn't going to become complicated?

Crystal came out of the bathroom rubbing lotion into her hands and arms. Another routine she did every night. Her skin would smell very slightly of cocoa butter. She had the lotion shipped in from some boutique shop in California. "A lavish expense," she'd told me once, seemingly embarrassed by the extravagance. I figured she didn't have many. The time and money she gave to others far outweighed any small gift she gave herself.

She drew back the covers on her side of the bed and climbed in. "I see we're keeping to our sides of the bed?"

"Yeah, I guess so." I'd always slept on the right side of the bed. The first night at Trapper's house, she'd taken the left. Was that her usual side? It hadn't occurred to me until now to wonder. "Did you always sleep on the left?"

She stacked her two pillows, then settled on her side. "No. I always had right side when I was married."

"Did it seem strange to you?" I turned my head to look at her. Usually when we talked, I faced her, but tonight it was impossible because of my cast being on my left leg.

"No stranger than being with you. Not strange in a bad way," she added, quickly. Had she seen the flicker of pain her words had caused me? "I mean, simply because you were the first person after Patrick." She smiled as she reached over to push a lock of hair from face. "I'm still embarrassed about our first night."

She'd cried in my arms afterward. I'd filled with sympathy and empathy sorry for her, knowing what it was like to venture out into the dating world after my divorce.

"You were very gracious," she said. "Still, I didn't think you'd ever want to do it again after that."

"I understood more than you realized."

"I've never asked you. Did you date much after your divorce?"

"Nothing more than a few casual flings." Which is what I'd thought Crystal would be. Had I only known how deep my feelings would become, I might have had the sense to stay far away from her.

"Do you ever talk to your ex-wife?"

"God, no. We could barely speak civilly when we were married."

"I can't picture you having a lot of conflict with someone."

"She brought out the worst in me," I said. "She was the type of person who was incapable of seeing any perspective but her own. Which makes it hard to have a loving relationship."

"What made you fall for her in the first place?"

"I was young. I hadn't dated much because I was always

busy training. When we met in college, I didn't know constant drama wasn't normal. Why do you ask?"

"I don't know. I was thinking we really haven't talked about our pasts. I guess we were too busy with the other thing between us."

"And now that I'm injured, we're forced to talk." I chuckled. "God has a sense of humor."

"How do you feel about your dad's divorce?"

"That would take all night to explain." The complex feelings I had about my father and his women were hard to understand, let alone explain it to someone else.

"Try."

I looked back up at the ceiling. "I guess I'm torn between wishing he could find the right person and frustration by the ones he chooses. For one thing, none of them have been age-appropriate. It's suspect, given his wealth."

"Do you think they marry him for his money? But what about the prenups?"

"I don't think they go into the marriage thinking it will end in divorce." I hadn't in my own marriage, even though it was quite clear now how unsuited we were. "My dad never does. He has such faith in the goodness of people. All three of them after my mother were awful." The first had been someone he met at the bar after one of my ski competitions. She was so obviously looking for rich men, but he couldn't see it.

"What happened with wives two and three?" Crystal asked.

"Wife two divorced him and took half his money. She was in it for the cash all along. Honestly, I think she was a grifter. She targeted him. I'm sure she picked up on how lonely he was. At that point, he was accompanying me on all my ski competitions. This was before the Olympics. He learned his lesson after that. Wife three and four both had prenups."

"And number three?"

I groaned. "That was a mess. She was still in love with her ex-husband and married my dad to get back at the guy. She started messing around with the ex and got pregnant. Paternity test and everything. Thank God the kid wasn't my dad's, or he'd have had to pay for a child being raised by someone else. He's a wealthy man. I don't know if I mentioned that before."

"How wealthy?"

"Not like you." I reached under my head to adjust my pillow. "But he's in the top one percent. Investments in everything. He can make money out of nothing. Nothing sketchy. Just smart investments. He's on the board of multiple companies. They pay him for consulting, basically."

"I feel bad for him," Crystal said. "He wants to be married."

"You should've seen him after my mother left. It was ugly. If it hadn't been for my sport, I'm not sure what would've happened to him. After my brother died, my mom hardly came out of her room. He was out at bars every night. Then, one day, she left. Dad had to step up and take care of me. Which he did. I guess we can thank my mother for that at least."

"It must have hurt a lot to have her go."

"I was completely blindsided." I told her how I'd come home and found the note on my bed. "I can recite exactly what it said. 'Dearest Garth, I have to go. Just for a little while. Until I can get my head straight. I love you no matter what. Love, Mom.'"

Crystal placed a hand on my arm. "I'm sorry."

"She never came back. Not really, anyway. Then Dad and I started traveling a lot for my competitions. The visits were fewer and fewer. It's like she wasn't interested in me any longer."

"I wish things had been different for you."

I lifted a shoulder in a half shrug. "It was all a long time ago. My dad made up for it. We're super close." I paused for a second to combat the ache in my throat. "I often wonder what our family would've been like if Christopher had lived. Like would my parents have stayed together? Or was their marriage always doomed?"

"Statistically, it's hard for people to stay together after they lose a child. Do you ever remember them fighting? Brandi says her parents used to fight in their bedroom as if that would keep her from knowing."

"If they did, I can't remember it. She was always quiet and shy. More sensible and timid than my dad, who was a dreamer and obviously the life-of-the-party type. With him, though, she came alive. He could make her laugh and laugh. At least, before we lost my brother. The transformation was like a light suddenly being shut off. Poof, darkness."

"I can remember having daydreams about my dad suddenly appearing. We'd have this wonderful reunion, and my parents would fall in love. Then I'd have a dad who lived with us like the other kids."

"Have you ever thought about doing one of those DNA tests?" I asked.

"Why?"

"To find out who your father is."

She flinched as if I'd flicked her nose. "I didn't want to make a big fuss about it all."

"Why not?"

"Wouldn't it cause us both more harm than good? This man never even knew I existed. Then one day, he wakes up to find he'd fathered a daughter thirty years ago? He probably has a family and a wife. My presence would mess up his life. There's the money, too."

"What do you mean?"

"It would be impossible to know if he wanted a relationship with me or just wanted access to my wealth."

I hadn't thought about that angle before. "Like lottery winners? Long-lost relatives come out of the woodwork."

"Right. We should get some sleep. This was a long day." She sat up and drew closer to kiss my cheek. "I hope you get some rest and wake up feeling much better."

My arm instinctively wrapped around her waist. "Thanks for everything." Her scent made me light-headed.

"You were a trouper," she said, sounding slightly breathless.

"We have furniture and beds, thanks to you."

She traced my jawline with her thumb. "This is dangerous."

"Being in my bed?"

"Your house. Your bed. As if I were a regular fixture in your life."

"It's too late for caution," I said. "For me, anyway. The drugs may have loosened my lips, but what I said earlier is true. I've fallen in love with you. I want you here. I don't want you to ever leave. But my dad's here now to look after me. You're free to go if you want to."

She briefly closed her eyes as a wave of pain crossed her face before opening them to look directly into mine. "I need a little time to sort myself out, but I don't want to leave. I'm not sure I can at this point."

"What does that mean?" My heart skipped a beat. Could I dare hope? Was she falling for me?

"It means that my feelings for you run deeper than I've let on. Your accident proved that to be true. The thought of losing you triggered everything all over again. I'm scared. That's it, plain and simple. Scared to lose you and scared to claim you."

"But you feel it too? This connection between us?"

"I've felt it from the first night I ever spent with you. I need a little time."

"I've got nothing but time, City Mouse."

"Thank you." She tossed one of her pillows to the other end of the bed, then switched off the lamp on the bedside table. I felt her lie down next to me. Through the darkness, she found my hand and slipped her fingers around mine. "Good night."

"Night." I closed my eyes, wishing my cast was off and my ribs weren't busted and I could pull her to me and remind her of what she'd be missing if she walked out of my life. Instead, I settled for the fact that she was here with me. If the snow kept falling, maybe I could keep her here longer. Eventually, perhaps she'd decide to stay forever.

My wish didn't come true. The snowfall ceased while we slept. We woke to a bright, sunny day. However, Crystal didn't say anything about going back to Brandi's except to check in on her. She convinced Dad to go with her to town for groceries. I had piles of work to take care of, so I parked myself on the couch with my laptop.

I'd just gotten off the phone with a client when I heard a car in the drive. With the aid of my crutches, I hobbled over to the front door to see who it could be, expecting the delivery truck with more of the items we'd ordered. A black sedan with tinted windows came to a stop in front of my garage. I could hardly believe my eyes when my mother got out of the car. She clutched a blue purse against her side as she looked around my front yard. I could almost see the tension in her shoulders. What was she doing here? Had she driven from Montana? The sedan didn't appear to be a rental car. Stunned, it took me a moment before I opened to the door to greet her.

She held up a hand and headed toward me. "Don't come any farther. The gravel will be terrible with those crutches."

I obeyed, waiting for her to climb the stairs to the covered porch. Slim and straight-backed, she was dressed in an elegant black coat and riding-style boots. Her dark hair was cut into a short bob that framed her heart-shaped face.

"Mom, what are you doing here?"

"You sounded weak on the phone. Frankly, you scared me. I decided to come visit, even if you didn't want me."

"Why would you think I don't want you?"

"You said not to come." She clutched her purse to her chest. If it were possible, she'd become thinner than the last time I saw her. A good hug might break her in half.

"You didn't want to come," I said.

"Obviously, that's not true," Mom said softly. "I didn't want to hear you say no, so I didn't ask."

"Dad's here. Not at the moment, but he'll be back."

My mother smiled stiffly. "I'm staying at the lodge. We can avoid each other."

Her appearance had shaken me to the core. I thought about my dream. Christopher had said they should be together again. Had my accident done just that? Brought them under the same roof?

She touched my arm. Even through my sweater her hand felt ice cold. "You look well. I don't know what I expected. The word *concussion* had me worried."

"I'm fine. Better today than yesterday." I nodded toward the door. "Let's go inside. It's cold."

I let her go in first and followed with my clumsy gait. She smelled of her perfume, just as she had when I was young. She shrugged off her coat, revealing a light gray sweater over black leggings. Despite the essence of sadness that seemed to float about her head, she'd aged well. Mom gasped when she saw the front room and view. "Garth, it's spectacular."

An image of her small, dingy apartment in downtown Bozeman flashed before my eyes. Thinking of her there all alone depressed me. "Thanks, Mom. It's not decorated much, obviously. It wasn't before the fire, either. I'd only just moved in when it was destroyed."

"What a thing to have happened." Mom set her purse on the dining room table.

"Would you like coffee or tea? Did you drive all the way from Bozeman?"

Her black boots clicked on the hardwood floor as she crossed over to the bank of windows that looked out over the valley. She spoke with her back to me. "No, I left yesterday and stayed overnight at the halfway point. A little motel in the middle of nowhere. Don't ask me where."

"I'm not crazy about the idea of you traveling all alone," I said as I came to stand beside her. In the light from the window, I could see the fine lines in her small face.

110

"Don't be silly. I do everything alone."

Your choice, I thought.

"When will your father be back?" Mom fidgeted with the cross that hung around her neck. "I don't want to be in the way."

"Within an hour, I'd guess. He and Crystal went to town for groceries and to raid her kitchen store for supplies."

She gave me a quizzical look. "Who's Crystal?"

"A friend. She lost her house too."

"Right, I remember the name now."

I nodded and gestured toward the road. "We share the long driveway. They haven't started on hers yet."

She turned slowly from the window to look at me. "Have you and Crystal grown close? Are you dating?"

"She's a friend." I hadn't meant to sound evasive, but it certainly came out that way. How could I explain what Crystal meant to me? My dad seemed to have picked up on the complexity of our relationship and hadn't said a word. However, that was Dad. Obviously, he knew all about complicated relationships with women. My mother, however, was another story. As far as I knew, she hadn't dated since she left my dad twenty years ago. I had no idea what her personal life was like. Strangely enough, she worked as an assistant in a family law practice.

The few times I'd visited her in Bozeman, I'd been struck by the simplicity of her life. She lived in a small apartment and walked to her boss's law office. She always had a stack of books on the bedside table. From what I could tell, they were her only companions. I'd never heard her mention friends and certainly no one special. She was an enigma to me, as she'd always been. This unexpected arrival was among a long line of unexplainable behavior. It was as if she lived in a different realm from the rest of us, floating around like a ghost. I could never quite pin her down.

"What kind of friend?" My mother peered at me with her light blue eyes. Those eyes paired with her dark hair had made her striking in her youth. My father still talked about the beauty of those eyes. One time, after a few drinks, he'd claimed they still haunted his dreams.

"It's complicated," I said.

"Fair enough." That was one thing I could say for my mother. She never pried.

"Mom, I can't believe you're here. What made you decide?"

For a moment, I didn't think she was going to answer. Finally, she said in a voice so quiet I instinctively leaned closer. "I had a dream about your brother."

I recoiled, shocked to hear those words come out of her mouth. Has she had the same dream as I? "What about?"

"It was the night you had your accident, although I didn't know that at the time. He told me you'd almost died. He said I should come to see you. He also said something about your father and me—that we should reconcile or something like that. It was a little fuzzy. Which, now that I know your father's here—it makes more sense. Or less. I'm not sure."

The shock of what she'd just said made it impossible to speak for a moment. "I had a dream too. The night of my accident, I hit my head and blacked out. During that time, he came to me. Or I went to him. I'm not sure which. It was as if I were in the place between earth and heaven. He told me to go back and that I wasn't done with life yet. He also said that I was to bring you and dad back together."

Her eyes widened. She brushed underneath her lashes with her index fingers. Then she drew in a shaky breath. "How extraordinary. But anyway, your father's married. It's not like we could reconcile. Not that we would. I don't know if he'll want to be in the same room with me."

"He's a kind guy. I'm sure he'll be glad to see you."

"Did he bring the wife?" Mom turned back toward the window. Her gaze flickered from left to right.

"No, they split. He's getting a divorce."

"Number four?" The corners of her mouth lifted in a weak smile. "Or were we on five?"

"Four. Marilyn. That's her name."

"Were you surprised?" Mom asked.

"In one way, no. She's a child, and I knew she didn't love him. But in another way, yes. He never talks about the bad stuff. And then suddenly, it's all over, and he's off to the next one. Younger than the last."

Mom laughed, the sound like a thin sliver of smoke. "He could always charm the pants off whomever he chose."

"Yeah," I said, uncomfortable.

The sound of Crystal's car drew my attention. "That's Dad and Crystal."

Mom's thin eyebrows lifted and she spoke so softly I almost couldn't hear her. "Maybe I shouldn't have come. Brian might not like to see me." She sprang to her feel, reminding me of a jack-in-the-box I'd had as a child. Only my mother didn't have a scary, maniacal grin.

My dad and Crystal came in, each carrying shopping bags. "Whose car is in the drive—" At the sight of my mother, Dad stopped and stared.

Crystal and I exchanged a glance. From her shocked expression, it was obvious she knew who had shown up at my house.

"Sam?" My father had always called her Sam, not Samantha.

"Hi, Brian." Mom's voice shook. She came around the couch.

"What are you doing here?" Dad asked, not unkindly but clearly surprised.

"I came on a whim. To check on Garth. I'm staying at the lodge." Her voice was as brittle as a fine piece of glass. I imagined her crashing to the floor and splintering into a thousand pieces.

"Oh, well, okay. Nice to see you." Dad had recovered slightly or at least had quickly hidden the discombobulated effect my mother's presence had on him. "Did you drive?"

"Yes, yes. From Bozeman." Mom turned to Crystal. "I'm Samantha, Garth's mom."

"Nice to meet you. I'm Crystal," she said as she scurried over to the table to set down her bags, then returned to shake Mom's hand.

"You as well," Mom said.

Then, as she almost always did, given any situation, Crystal asked, "Are you hungry? Would you like to stay and eat with us? I'm making Julia Child's chicken in white wine."

"That's my favorite," Mom said. "How strange."

Crystal and Brian smiled at each other. "Brian happened to mention it when I suggested something French. He said you used to order it at a restaurant in your old neighborhood."

"You remembered that?" Mom asked softly.

"Sure. I can't eat anything French without remembering that little bistro," Dad said. "We had some good times there, didn't we?"

Mom nodded as she and Dad locked eyes. "We did."

"You look good, Sam," Dad said.

"You too." Mom smiled as she tilted her head, observing him. "Your hair is just how I figured it would be when you were older."

"I'm old as dirt but still kicking around," Dad said as he grasped his grocery bags harder, making an orange fall out onto the floor, where it rolled under the couch.

Mom bent to pick it up, then stuck it back in his bag. "This reminds me of the meatball song."

"On top of spaghetti, all covered with cheese," Dad sang out, loud and off-key.

We all laughed. Why we all found my dad's terrible singing funny, I couldn't say. But it got us to the next minute. One new minute, which would lead to another. One in which healing could begin.

12

CRYSTAL

S till reeling from Samantha's sudden appearance, I went into the bedroom before starting dinner to call my mother. I'd called earlier to see if she wanted to join me for lunch. In another surprise of the day, she'd said she was meeting Jack instead. She'd agreed to come to dinner at Garth's. Brian had offered to go down to the lodge to get her while I fixed dinner. I thought she'd enjoy a dinner with lively Brian. That was before I knew that Samantha would also be here. I was starting to miss the simpler time at Trapper and Brandi's. Our parents were causing quite the complications in our lives.

Mom answered right away. "Hi, honey."

"How did it go today at lunch?"

"Fine."

I couldn't detect any further information from the tone of her voice. "What does fine mean?"

She sighed. "It was an emotional lunch. I don't want to talk about it."

"Do you still want to come here for dinner? Brian will come pick you up."

Before I could tell her that Sam was also here, she interrupted. "I'm tired. If you don't mind, I think I'll just stay in tonight."

"Oh, sure. Whatever you want." I was surprised. Usually she loved anything social. I told her about Garth's mom. Again, her lackluster response befuddled me. The dramatic turn of events would normally have intrigued her. She would have wanted to know every detail. "Get some rest, Mom. I'll call you in the morning."

"Have a fun night, honey."

I hung up and went back to the kitchen to begin preparing dinner. All three members of the Welte family were sitting in the kitchen. Brian was in the process of putting away groceries and telling Sam about my shop and all the fun items we'd found. Sam was opening a bottle of wine. Garth was sitting at the island looking like a happy child with his parents on an ordinary night.

Seeing the joy on his face was enough to break my heart. Having grown up without a dad, I was familiar with the unrealistic yearnings of a child who wished his or her parents were together. However, I'd never actually known what it was like, whereas Garth had. I felt quite sure that he'd already gone down the path of a happy reunion in his mind, especially given his dream. Who could blame him? Human nature dictated these types of wishes. He wanted his parents to be together. Even after all this time, the desires of the boy he'd once been were strong.

As much as I doubted anything would come of it, I had to admit the scene in the kitchen was a happy one. Sadly, this was the type of evening that could suck him into a false reality. I worried he'd be hurt when his parents left separately and everything went back to normal.

"Hey, Mouse." Brian had started calling me Mouse after hearing Garth call me City Mouse. He was the type of man who got away with using a familiar nickname for someone he'd just met. This might have been part of the problem with all his wives. "Is your mom ready for me to come pick her up?"

"No, she's tired," I said. "She's staying in tonight. I hope she's not getting sick. It's not like her to miss a party."

"I hope she's all right," Sam said. "Airplanes are full of germs. She might have caught something."

"I'm sure she is," I said. "She's going through a rough breakup."

"Sounds all too familiar," Brian said. "I'm sorry she won't be here to commiserate with me."

I went to the refrigerator and pulled out onions and carrots.

Brian held up his paw-like hands. "Put me to work."

I asked him to cut up onions and carrots as I twisted the top from the olive oil and poured it into the new cast-iron Dutch oven I'd brought from my shop.

"Will do," Brian said.

Now that I'd seen Garth's mother, I could see that although he'd gotten his dad's height and strength, his bone structure favored his mother. She had the look of a dancer, graceful and slender, whereas Brian was more of a burly bear. In combination, they'd made a man perfect for darting down a slope on two skinny sticks.

I peeled several cloves of garlic and diced them before tossing them into my pan with the olive oil.

"How much do I owe you?" Garth asked. "You came home with a lot of stuff. Some of which I don't recognize."

I laughed. "You'll find a use for all of it, I promise." I'd picked out a set of white bistro-style dishes, silverware, bowls, pots and pans, and a good set of knives. Brian had already paid for them at the shop.

"I'd like to buy them for him." Sam sat a glass of wine near Garth.

"Mom, no."

"I already got them, Sam," Brian said. "You don't need to spend your hard-earned money."

Sam looked crestfallen. "I'd have liked to."

I hated seeing Sam disappointed. "There are other things he might need, Sam. I have a few ideas. We can talk later."

Sam smiled. "I'd like that, thank you."

Garth seemed about to say something, but I stopped him with a pointed look. I suspected guilt about the past must weigh heavily on Sam's mind. She seemed to be making a concerted effort to look relaxed, but I had the feeling that inside she was a bundle of nerves.

I browned the chicken in olive oil and garlic. The smell of the sizzling oil and garlic filled the room. When the chicken pieces were crispy, I set them aside to add later. "You have those onions and carrots ready for me?" I asked Brian.

He wiped under his eyes. "These onions got to me, but yeah, they're ready."

"You're tough, Dad," Garth said.

"Thanks, Brian." He'd the vegetables coarsely and unevenly, but they'd do.

"What? Did I do a bad job?" Brian asked. "I'm more of a takeout kind of a guy."

"They're perfect," I said.

"You're a liar." Brian grinned as he brought the entire cutting board over to me.

"Never," I said, returning his grin before dumping it all into the pan.

I stirred the onions and carrots into the oil and then returned the pieces of chicken to the pan. A half a bottle of cheap white wine went in next. I waited for it to boil before turning the burner to simmer.

"How about we pour some of the wine Sam opened?" Brian suggested. We'd gotten several good bottles at the store earlier.

"Do it," Garth said. "I didn't take any pain meds today."

"You're feeling better then?" Sam asked him. The tenderness in her voice made my eyes sting. I blinked to keep from tearing up.

"Much better," Garth said.

I couldn't decide if he was telling the truth about the pain. Regardless, I was glad he hadn't taken any more of those pills. I'd started thinking of them as the Truth Pills. I didn't need any more truths out of him tonight.

"What do I do now, Mouse?" Brian asked.

"I need some potatoes peeled." I held up the peeler. "Unless anyone has anything against mashed potatoes?"

"God no," Garth said.

"Consider it done." Brian rinsed the cutting board and went straight to work.

"I could make a salad?" Sam asked meekly. "If you wanted? I'm out of practice in the kitchen but I could probably rustle up a salad."

"You're a great cook," Brian said.

"Not anymore," Sam said. "I don't cook like I did when the boys were little...because, well, you know." She trailed off and smoothed her hand over the granite.

"It's not as much fun to cook for one," I said. An urge to make her feel better had come over me. "After my husband died, I stopped bothering."

"Yes, what's the point of all the fuss just for myself?" Sam asked.

"No one can cook like Crystal," Garth said. "But Mom, you used to make a mean chocolate chip cookie."

"You remember that?" Sam asked.

"Sure I do." Garth patted his stomach. "This boy never forgets a cookie."

Sam gave him a slight smile before heading to the refrigerator to grab the items for the salad. Busy with her hands, Garth's mother seemed to relax a little. Brian seemed in good spirits, making jokes and keeping the conversation going. As the evening wore on, I couldn't help but feel a little optimistic myself. Could it be possible that two people torn apart by grief could come back together over twenty years later? Miracles happened every day. Could this be one?

"Garth tells me you did modeling back in the day." Brian placed a bowl of peeled potatoes in the sink.

I flushed as I set a pan of water on the cooktop for the potatoes. Whenever anybody asked me about it, I always felt like an imposter. I didn't see myself as a runway model with my narrow face and gangly limbs. However, the gigs had paid for culinary school. For which I would always be grateful. As Brandi had once said, it beat stripping any day. Not that either of us knew anything about that line of work.

"It was only for a few years." I rinsed the potatoes and went to work cutting them into even pieces.

"She doesn't like to talk about it," Garth said.

"Why is that?" Brian asked. "God gave you a gift, just like he did Garth. Why not use it?"

"I prefer to be behind the scenes," I said. "Like in the kitchen. But it paid for culinary school, so that made everything worth it."

"She was the head chef at one of the most famous restaurants in Seattle," Garth said.

"Not really famous," I said. "More like popular."

"However you want to describe it," Garth said. "You were a star."

"Not really." I brushed aside his compliment. The head chef who had hired me had been fired for sexual harassment and they'd needed someone to take his place. What was supposed to be temporary had turned into a full-time offer. I'd been over the moon. "I happened to be in the right place at the right time."

"The head chef couldn't keep his hands off the staff," Garth said. "So they moved Crystal from one of the line cooks to the boss chef."

"It was my husband Patrick who was famous." The night Patrick had come in for dinner with business associates, the whole place had buzzed. I could have cared less. At the time, following local tech business wasn't on my radar. I had no money to invest in stocks, so what did I care?

"He was a big deal in the investment community," Brian said. "In fact, I was an early investor in his company."

"You must have made a lot of money then," I said.

"I did. Yes, ma'am. Your husband was a heck of a brain, wasn't he?"

"The biggest brain," I said. "Competitive and cutthroat, but incredibly generous too."

"He had that reputation," Brian said. "I'd have liked to meet him."

I wondered what Garth would have thought of Patrick had he met him. They were similar in some ways. Their capacity for adventure and competition was similar. Garth was a gentler soul than my late husband with less ambition and without an ounce of pretension. Patrick always cared what people thought of him. Having grown up poor, he'd always made sure people knew how smart and ultimately powerful he'd become.

"He liked the spotlight," I said.

Patrick had a larger-than-life personality and used social media copiously. Our staff knew a lot about him and were excited when he asked to meet the chef so that he might compliment her. I didn't like to go out to the dining room. Staying in the kitchen suited me just fine. But when Patrick Wilder asked for something, he got it. I went out to greet him, expecting to dislike him. Like my grandfather, I had a natural distrust of the wealthy, especially ones who lived so much in the spotlight as Patrick had. To my surprise, we had an immediate attraction. Dressed in a vintage tweed jacket and black glasses and self-confidence off the charts, he'd immediately started flirting with me.

"Was that difficult for you?" Sam asked. "Married to someone in the public eye?"

"A little, yes. I hated going places with him. People always stared at us. In Seattle, high-tech moguls are like movie stars."

Garth had gone quiet. He traced the pattern in the granite with one finger.

"I'd have loved the attention," Brian said. "I wish everyone knew how rich I was."

Garth's head snapped up to look at his father. "Dad, that's terrible."

"Is it?" Brian laughed. "If it is, then I'm guilty. I always want to tell people how clever I am to have started with nothing and turned out like this."

"I understand what you mean," I said. "You should be proud of your career. But the celebrity and admiration aren't as good as you might think. When people know, they treat you differently."

"That's exactly what I want," Brian said.

I knew he was joking, but if he'd only known half of what I'd endured on social media, he wouldn't have found the idea attractive. "Social media is full of trolls, just looking for a way to let out all their rage. I got hammered after his death."

"You've never told me that," Garth said.

"I don't like to think about it. I put it all behind me when I came here."

"What did they do?" Garth asked.

"People on the internet were not very nice to me." I hadn't told Garth how bad it had gotten. The mean tweets and posts on social media about me had been devastating. As if losing Patrick and the baby hadn't been bad enough, the online trolls had come after me. The narrative made me seem evil, like I'd married him for his money and was happy he was gone. None of which was true.

"What do you mean?" Brian asked.

"False rumors about me marrying him for his money and things like that." I lifted the pot to look at my chicken. Steam rose up and brought the scent of wine, garlic, and onions.

"Is that why you moved here?" Sam asked. "To get away from all of that?"

"Yes, that's exactly why. His death made people even more

curious about me. No one cares about any of that here. I returned to being just me. That's why I went back to using my maiden name. I shut off all social media. Which is why I didn't know how close the fire was. If your son hadn't come for me, who knows what would have happened."

I looked up from the stove to see Sam watching me. "How frightening all of it must have been."

"Brandi—that's my best friend—told me to come here. I lived with her for a few months while I looked for a house. I've never looked back."

"That was a wise choice," Sam said.

I hadn't expected her to be sympathetic and intuitive. She was not at all what I'd expected from a woman who'd run away from her own family. Had I misjudged her?

"She opened the kitchen store in town." Garth did nothing to disguise the pride in his voice, which made me uncomfortable. What would his parents think of all this? Would they have us married off before morning? Knowing I was getting in too deep and yet not being able to stop myself, I had the niggling feeling of guilt.

"And you know what else?" Garth asked. "All the proceeds from the store go to feeding the homeless."

"Garth," I said quietly. "They don't want to hear about that."

"We do," Sam said. "What a wonderful thing to do."

"I didn't think y'all had homeless people here," Brian said.

Garth laughed. "Only those of us who lost our houses in the fire. These are homeless in Denver mostly."

"Seattle, too," I said. Why had I said that? I sounded full of myself. I despised boastful people. Especially since all this wealth was Patrick's, not mine. "Never mind. I don't mean to sound like I'm bragging."

"There's no reason to be ashamed," Brian said. "You care about people. We need more like you in the world."

"She's like the patron of Emerson Pass," Garth said. "I know she does more than she tells me about."

"Garth, stop. You're exaggerating." I gave him a look before turning away to fiddle with the burner.

"Fine, I'll stop," Garth said. "But that doesn't make it false."

Outside, night had come, prompting the outside lights on the patio to flicker to life. At the end of the long room, the gas fireplace burned brightly. For a split second, I imagined us all here at Christmas. We'd have a tree that reached the ceiling, twinkling lights, and stockings hung over the fireplace. Maybe my mother would come.

I put a screeching halt to those thoughts. I was letting myself get carried away. Or was it that my heart was finally healing?

"Speaking of patrons," I said, hoping to divert the conversation. "Garth does a ton of pro bono work for battered women."

It was Garth's turn to seem embarrassed. "No big deal. I mean, it's the least I could do, really. These women—they don't have a chance."

"Honey, what a great thing you're doing." Sam wrapped her hands around the stem of her wineglass. "Despite having me as your mother, you've become such a good man."

"You were a great mother," Brian said.

"Until I wasn't," Sam said.

No one said anything for a moment.

"You're here now." Brian exchanged a glance with Garth in their secret, silent language. As different as they were, the men knew each other in that way people do who have fought a war together, or survived tragedy.

"Mom, we can't go back, only forward."

"Not that I've always been good at that," I said. "But it's really the only choice we have, isn't it?"

Brian smacked the counter. "Well, let's not waste another moment of tonight. We're all here together in Garth's beautiful home. I say we open another bottle of wine. Life's too damn short to spend all of it crying into our glasses."

"I couldn't agree more," I said.

Brian was up and crossed over to the counter to open another bottle of wine. A few minutes later, he had us laughing with a story from his childhood.

I watched him, impressed by this man's resilience. He was in the middle of a new, probably nasty divorce, and yet here he was entertaining us. Garth was much more like his mother, sensitive, which made them vulnerable to the world. They felt emotions so deeply.

That was the thing with Garth. The way he loved me scared me the most. I held his happiness in my hands. I didn't like it. With Patrick, I'd felt that if anything had happened to me or to our relationship, he would've been fine. This man before me now was an entirely different breed. His heart beat outside his own chest. I had the power to break that tender heart.

Who was I to have such power? I was a woman pining for a ghost. Here was the very best kind of man—a man most women would do anything for. I was selfishly taking what I wanted from him with no idea of the future. I'd never in my life been ashamed of my actions toward another person. I'd thought of myself as a good person, unselfish. The patron of Emerson Pass. All my charities and giving to those less fortunate. Yet here I was hurting the best person I've ever known. No one could look at themselves in the mirror and not see the truth. He deserved better. Every moment I stayed here in this house, and in his bed, led us closer to the eventual pain I'd cause him when I had to leave.

If I had to leave.

Maybe I could stay.

Forever.

13

GARTH

In the middle of the night, I jerked awake from a sound sleep. Something wasn't right. I reached across the bed for Crystal but found only cold sheet. I sat up, wincing from the dull ache in my ribs. A three-quarter moon hung low in the sky, lighting the room. Crystal, her head bowed and knees drawn to her chest, sat in the armchair next to the window. Long strands of her hair, almost silver in the moonlight, hung over her face as she silently sobbed.

"Crystal?"

She yanked her head upward and looked at me. "I'm all right. Go back to sleep." Her voice sounded eerily normal, given her obvious emotional state.

"It's cold. Come to bed."

She hesitated for a moment before unfolding from the chair and padding across the floor to climb in next to me.

I couldn't bring her to me because of the cast between us. Drawing her close must be done with my words, not my touch. I knew from past experience that I was better with touch. "What's going on?" I asked gently.

She didn't answer. I heard only the drawing in and out of her breath. After a few more seconds of this, she finally answered. "I couldn't sleep. All the bad thoughts started coming. Chasing me—calling out to me to listen to them. To relive all the regrets. Do you know how that is? When it's dark and the morning seems far away and that nothing will ever be all right ever again?"

"I do."

"I had a miscarriage after Patrick died. It was my fault that I lost the baby." She put a cold hand on my chest.

I lifted up a few inches to put my arm around her shoulders. "How was that your fault?"

"After Patrick died, I was in a very bad place. I didn't know I was pregnant. I asked God to let me sleep and not wake up."

I sucked in a breath as if someone had sucker punched me. Did she think God took the baby from her because of the wish of grieving widow? I thought about what my mother had said earlier about Christopher's death. She'd said she felt it was her fault. Was this the plight of all women once they were mothers? All their thoughts led to and from their child? Every bad outcome was somehow their fault? I chose my words carefully. "I can understand how you arrived at that conclusion. But I don't think God would punish you for a moment of darkness. Not when you were in so much pain. He understands that you were grieving for your husband."

"How do you know?" she asked, not in accusatory way, but as if she truly wondered.

"I just do."

"I should've been stronger for the baby. I gave in to the sadness, let it consume me. There are studies that show stress can cause women to miscarry."

"You were grieving. Even if it did harm the baby, it's not something you could control. The husband you adored died suddenly. There's no other way through that but to feel sad."

"It was a double blow. Losing Patrick and then the baby."

"I'm sorry." Such inadequate words for such a profound feeling, but it was all I could think to say.

"Today, watching your mother, I could see so much of myself in her."

"In what way?" I asked.

"How trapped inside herself she is. How guarded and regretful. The weight of the past pressing down on her tiny body."

My eyes stung as I took in what she said. Crystal was right. My mother's movements were laborious, like those of a much heavier woman.

"I'm so sad for her." She rolled to her side and touched my face. "I can see how much she loves you."

I took Crystal's hand and pressed it to my mouth. "I don't know about that. She loved my brother best. Sometimes I think she wished it were me that died."

"No, a mother would never think that."

I didn't argue with her even though I knew she was wrong.

"Tonight, when I was lying here in the dark listening to you breathe, I felt as hopeless as I ever have."

"Why?"

"When I met Patrick I thought he would make up for my lack of a father. Like I was finally whole. I know it sounds strange. It was as if he made up for all the love I missed growing up without a father. When I lost him, it seemed like too much of a coincidence. I wasn't supposed to have the kind of love most girls or women get. To try simply tempted fate. The moment I believed I'd found my family in Patrick, he was snatched away."

I thought about that for a moment. She'd come to the conclusion that any man she loved would leave her, one way or the other. Thus, she couldn't allow herself to love me for fear it would all end the same way. She would be alone and grieving.

"Does that sound ridiculous?" she asked.

"Actually, no." Hadn't I felt the same way about women? First, my mother. Then, my wife. Both left me. Why, then, was I willing to give my whole self to Crystal when she couldn't do the same? Knowing that she wasn't able to return my feelings and would eventually leave me, was I setting this up on purpose to prove my greatest fear to be true? I could not be chosen. I could never be a woman's first choice. My mother had chosen my dead brother over the one who lived. Crystal was now choosing her dead husband over a live, breathing man who wanted her. Was the human mind that much of a saboteur? Was *my* mind that much of a saboteur?

"What're you thinking?" Crystal asked. "I can hear your mind churning."

"I was wondering if you'd had a father and if my mother hadn't left, if we'd be here like this?"

She went perfectly still. "Do you mean if we hadn't suffered those losses, we'd be able to love each other?"

"Maybe it's even more complicated than that for me," I said. "Like have I fallen for you to prove to myself that my worst fears are true?"

"Which are?" Crystal asked softly.

"That all women eventually leave me. I'm always second place."

"Second place?"

"My mother preferred my brother to me. You wish Patrick were here instead of me. I've been blind to it until just now. I'm repeating a pattern. One so ingrained that I didn't even see it."

Her breath caught. "Is that what you think is happening? That I've chosen a dead man over you? You're second?"

"My brother and Patrick are the chosen ones even though I've been here all along just waiting for you both to love me." Tears leaked from the corners of my eyes. I wiped them away and wished I could turn over on my side, away from Crystal.

"Garth, I'm sorry," she whispered. "I'm sorry I've hurt you. I don't want you to think you're second best."

"You can't force yourself to love someone just because they love you."

"Or think they do anyway. Do you think you just wanted to win me? Maybe you don't really love me?"

Was she right? Had I fabricated all these feelings? No. I loved her. My heart wouldn't ache this way if my feelings weren't real. Despite how damaged I was, I loved this woman. I'd do just about anything to have her in my life. "I don't think anything. I love you."

"You're not second best. Not to Patrick or anyone else," Crystal said.

"But to you? Am I second best to you?"

"No, it's just that you're different. This thing between us is not how it was with Patrick."

"How?"

"My feelings for you crept up on me. With him, it was all a whirlwind. With you, it's been a slow build."

"Maybe that's better," I said as hope flooded me.

"You've become the first person I want to call when anything good or bad happens."

"Same for me."

"Don't let go," she whispered. "Hold me until I fall asleep."

"I won't." I'd never let go if she wanted me to stay. God help me, did I have a chance?

The next morning, I woke late to a bed without Crystal. I lay there for a moment, remembering the talk during the middle of the night. Had I dreamed all of it?

I sat up and reached for my crutches. The light outside the window was dim. A cloud cover must have come in while I was asleep.

Crystal came out of the bathroom, showered and dressed and looking way too pretty. "Morning," she said.

"Morning." How could it feel awkward when we'd shared such intimacy last night? In the light of day, there was no place to hide.

"Your mom's here already. She's in the living room with your dad watching television." Crystal rushed toward me, threw her arms around my neck and kissed me, long and hard, leaving me breathless.

"What was that for?" I asked.

"For last night. For listening. For not letting go."

I put my weight on one crutch and pulled her against me. "Do it again."

She did. By the time we pulled away, we were both breathless.

We were interrupted when Crystal's phone buzzed from the dresser. She hustled over to take a look. "It's a text from my mom. She wants me to come to breakfast at the lodge. She says it's urgent. That's weird."

"Go ahead. I've got my dad to help if I need anything."

She nodded as she tucked her hair behind her ears. "Garth, don't give up on me."

"Never."

"All right, then. I'll see you later." She gave me a peck on the mouth. "I'll call you later."

I waited until I heard the front door slam before I bumped out to the front room on my crutches. They were sitting on the couch watching football on the flat screen my dad had hung. Dallas was up six points over Los Angeles.

"I should've known you had an ulterior motive for getting the television hung yesterday, Dad."

"San Francisco plays tomorrow," Dad said. "It was either this or watch it down at the bar."

My father was a diehard San Francisco fan even though he'd spent his childhood in Texas. When I was a kid, Mom had loved the Seattle team. I could vaguely recall watching the games as they good-naturedly ribbed each other. My mother had jokingly called us a divided home.

A sudden memory of my mother during a Sunday game came to me. My father had said something to make her laugh. He'd always been able to make her laugh. Until all the laughter in her dried up, replaced by tears.

"Is everything all right with Crystal?" Mom asked me. "She rushed out of here."

"Yeah, she's fine." I sat down next to her, then propped my cast on the coffee table. "Her mom asked her to come out for breakfast. Something urgent."

"She reminds me of me." Mom clasped her hands on her lap. "All closed up, as if that will help the pain."

"You've fallen for her hard, haven't you?" Dad asked.

I nodded. "Head over heels. I've never felt this before. I'm not sure I like it."

"Loving a woman takes courage sometimes," Dad said. "Especially a complicated one like Crystal."

I leaned my head against the back of the couch and looked up at the ceiling. "But I think I may have finally worn her down."

My dad's phone buzzed with a call he had to take. "I'll be back in a flash," he said. "A work thing. Won't take but a few minutes."

As if he needed to give my mother a time frame when she'd left us without warning.

After my dad left, Mom brought me a cup of coffee and a few pieces of toast. While I ate, we watched the game. My mind wandered, only half aware of the score. When the game finished, Mom surprised me by clicking off the television. She went to the bank of windows and looked out to the white fog so thick we could be in a cloud.

"It's strange to think how the view changes from one day to the next," she said.

"Kind of a metaphor for life, isn't it?" I used the crutches to get up and stand beside her.

"Yes, despite wishes to the contrary." She reached toward the glass but didn't put her fingers on the window. "Should we talk?" Wearing a bulky black sweater that hid her thinness, she looked better this morning than when she'd arrived yesterday.

"About what?" I leaned heavily on my crutches, suddenly tired. I vacillated between tension and fatigue around my mother. I could feel her trying. I was trying. All this effort was too much because we were strangers.

"I'm sorry for the way things have been between us," she said, breaking the silence.

I took in a deep breath. For a man who moved to Emerson Pass for a quiet, peaceful life, I seemed to have a lot of women who seemed hell-bent on making it otherwise. "It's all right. I'm fine."

"If it matters to you at this point, I regret leaving both you and your father. I had some kind of mental break. I'm sorry if I hurt you." Her hands shook as she touched the ends of her hair, a gesture I remembered from my childhood. Whenever she was nervous or frightened, her hands would not stay still. Even before my brother's death, she'd had trouble fitting into our suburban neighborhood. The other ladies on our block were constantly having parties of one kind or another: baby showers, Tupperware parties, happy hours with wine and cheese. She was always invited but never attended. I'd asked her once why she hadn't gone to a party thrown by my best friend's mother. She'd stared out the kitchen window and shrugged her shoulders. "All I do is try to think of something to say and then it's over and I've still not spoken. I decided to no longer torture myself."

Now I glanced over at her. "It's nice that you came."

"Even though we have nothing to say to each other?" Her eyes glittered with unshed tears.

"We might. Give it a few days," I said, lightly.

"I've waited too long." She backed away, brushing her knuckles under both eyes.

"Too long?"

"I waited too long to come back to you."

I didn't say anything. My throat ached too much to speak

even if I'd had anything to say. The assurance she needed was way down in the bottom of my gut, unable to come to the surface, pushed down by my hurt and anger.

"I wanted to," Mom said. "I meant what I said in the note. But then the days rolled by one after the other, and I wasn't able to muster the energy it took to raise a little boy. I had nothing to give you. I knew you were better off without me."

"Not true." My voice caught. No, I wasn't doing this. What right did she have to barge in here and make apologies and provide explanations after years of ice? I closed my eyes, seeing the note once more.

I'd come home from school that day, tired from the sadness that had weighed me down since Christopher left us. I was a little boy with no idea how to process grief; I was in a battle those days just to put one foot in front of the other. I hadn't known how to interpret the faraway look in my mother's eyes. I didn't understand that I'd already lost her before she physically left.

Dearest Garth, I have to go. Just for a little while. Until I can get my head straight. I love you no matter what. Love, Mom.

In her neat, symmetrical handwriting, she'd made a promise that she hadn't kept. She hadn't come back, not really, anyway. There were our awkward dinners, Christmas and birthday gifts. But she wasn't there when I needed her most. The first time I'd had my heart broken. The months leading up to and after my divorce, I'd needed her. I'd craved the love one can only get from a mother. My dad tried. God bless him, he'd done as well as he could raising a little boy on his own. Regardless, he was a man. We're not made like women, able to fix a skinned knee and a bruised heart with a kiss and assurance that everything would be better tomorrow.

That broken promise had defined and dictated so much of my life. I was the boy whose mother had left him. The son who lived only to be abandoned. She hadn't loved me enough to stay. As a child who missed his mother, how else could I interpret it?

From my adult eyes, however, I could understand depression and hopelessness. I saw her from the eyes of a man who witnessed his mother as a person, not his parent. She'd been a woman who could not see a way out of her darkness.

Maybe none of it mattered now. Perhaps to forgive meant also to forget. We were humans, fallible and broken. Not made for grief or loss but for love. What good would it do either of us for me to hold on to resentment and anger?

Still, there was a hard knot in my stomach. One that wouldn't allow me to soften. Since the trauma of my parents' divorce, I'd spent my time trying to be a man women wouldn't leave. Yet wasn't that what I was doing with Crystal? Falling for a woman I couldn't have? Was this a pathological behavior that could be traced back to the abandonment I'd felt as a child? If I could get her to stay, would that prove my worth? Prove that I was indeed lovable? That it wasn't just Christopher who was worthy of love?

Mom had wandered to the couch, where she sat. "Come sit with me. Tell me about Crystal."

I hobbled over and lowered myself down on the other end. "Do you really want to know?"

"Only if you want to tell me. I know I haven't earned that right, but I'd like to hear about your life if you want to share."

I let that sink in before deciding how to answer. She'd opened herself up to rejection and anger by coming here. I could meet her in the middle. Offer up part of myself. "I've fallen in love with her, but she's not ready." I explained how her husband had died and the circumstances surrounding the accident. "After he died, she found out she was pregnant. Then she lost the baby. There's so much hurt in her, Mom. I can see she has feelings for me, but there's this part of her that refuses to shed her shell and let me in. It's stupid, really. I know I'm going to get hurt." I hadn't expected to tell her so much, but it felt good to do so. "Then I got in an accident, which scared her."

"Brought up all those feelings of helplessness," Mom said. "I can understand."

"Right."

"Crystal sounds a lot like me." She moved her gaze to the windows. "Trapped in her grief. Unable to forgive herself for living when her husband died. Add a miscarriage and you have a woman afraid to love again."

"Is that how it was for you? You couldn't forgive yourself?"

She nodded, so subtly that had I not watched her so carefully, I would've missed it.

"What couldn't you forgive yourself for? Did you think Christopher's death was your fault?" I asked.

She looked down at her lap and said quietly, "It was my fault."

"He died of cancer. How is that on you?"

Her bottom lip trembled as she took in a deep breath, then let it out slowly. "Because he complained about the pain for months before I took him in to the pediatrician. I thought it was just growing pains. I always took you boys in for checkups and I thought we could ask the doctor about them then and she'd reassure us that aches and pains was just part of growing up. Instead, we found out he had cancer and that it had spread. If I'd taken him in early, we might have caught it in time. What kind of mother doesn't listen to her little boy when he tells her he's hurting?" Her voice wobbled. She clutched the delicate silver cross she wore around her neck.

"Mom, you couldn't have known."

"Motherly instincts should have clued me in to what was happening. I'm not fit to be a mother. I could see that clearly after we lost him."

The dawning of what this meant came to me in one of those moments of clarity. "Is that why you left me? You were punishing yourself?"

"I knew you'd be better off without me."

"I wasn't. I needed you."

"I'm sorry." Tears fell from her eyes. She wiped at them with the back of her hand. "I didn't know what I was doing. I didn't for such a long time. Your dad was such a good father. I knew you'd thrive under his care without me like a dark shadow in the house. I drove him to the bar with my depression. I was awful to him, directing my anger at myself toward him. Without me there, I knew he'd show up for you. He was always the type who stepped up whenever anyone truly needed him."

"He did well, but I missed you."

"I missed you. I still do. It's my fault we don't have a close relationship, and I'd do anything to make things better."

"You did the best you could. We all did."

"Thank you for that." She dipped her chin and her hair fell forward, covering her face. Her narrow, thin shoulders shuddered.

I got up and went to sit beside her. "Mom, you're here now. So am I."

She looked up at me and covered one of my hands with hers. "Yes, we are."

I'd forgotten how small she was. How hard it must have been for her to get in her car and come here, unsure of my reaction and wanting only to show up for me. "You were brave to come here."

"Thank you for not sending me away." She plucked a piece of lint from her pants. "There aren't an endless number of years left.

"I had breast cancer last year."

"What?" A dart of alarm pierced my chest.

"I had a full mastectomy and chemo. They got it all. I'm in remission. However, it made me realize I might not have a chance to make things right between us."

"Mom, why didn't you tell me?"

"What good would that have done? You have your own life."

"I could have come to help. Or at least sent you a card."

"It wasn't necessary," she said.

"Did you have anyone to help you?"

"I have a friend from work who helped. And my boss's wife. They were all I needed."

"I'm glad you're all right now." The familiar hurt had taken hold. Why wouldn't she want her son with her during such a horrendous ordeal? "I could have helped," I said again. "I'd have wanted to."

"It's never been about you or how much I love you."

"How did you know that's what I was thinking?" I asked.

"You're my son. I can read your face." A faint smile lifted her mouth, but her eyes were sad. "I was like a wounded dog. Licking my wounds and not wanting anyone to see me."

That's the way she was, I thought. Always running away.

Would this time be different?

14

CRYSTAL

My mom had asked me to come up to her room before breakfast instead of meeting in the restaurant. I knocked on the door and waited for her to answer. Seconds later, she yanked it open, grunting as if it were heavy. "Come on in."

I followed her inside. "Mom, aren't we going downstairs?" She wore black leggings and an oversize sweatshirt. Her hair was pulled back into a ponytail. She obviously hadn't showered or put on makeup. In fact, she looked as if she hadn't slept.

"I'm not hungry." She plopped in the armchair. The shades were drawn. An empty wine bottle was on the mantel above the fireplace. I pulled up the shade and turned on a lamp. With better lighting, I could see that her eyes were red and her skin blotchy. She'd been crying.

"Did you have that whole bottle of wine yourself?" I asked.

"Maybe," she mumbled.

"Mom, what's going on?" My mother never had more than a glass.

"I had lunch with Jack yesterday."

"What did he do? Did he make you cry?" How dare he. I

139

knew exactly where I was going after this. He'd get a piece of my mind.

"There's something I need to tell you."

I shivered. Why was it so cold in here? I flipped the switch on the gas fireplace before sitting next to my mother. "What happened?"

"It's about Jack and me in high school. There's more to it. Something I didn't tell you. Something I should have told you." Her entire body shook. I'd never seen her this upset.

"Mom, you're scaring me."

"So much time went by—the years just roll on one by one until it's too late."

"Too late for what?" I had the sensation of falling into an endless black hole.

She tightened her grip on the arms of the chair as if she were on a scary ride at an amusement park. "Jack Vargas is your father."

I laughed. "Very funny, Mom."

"It's the truth. I didn't know I was pregnant until it was almost time for him to come home. I got a letter from him. He told me he'd gotten a girl pregnant and had to marry her. I didn't tell him about you. Instead, I ran away to Seattle and never told a soul who your father was. After a while, it was as if I'd made him up. You were mine and mine alone."

I stared at her as the room tipped. This was impossible. Jack Vargas was my father? "How could you lie to me?"

"I had to."

"Did Nana and Pop know?"

"They knew I was pregnant but not that it was Jack's baby. I lied to them too."

"Why would you lie? I don't understand."

"Because he was very clear about one thing. He was going to marry Malinda. He said it was the right thing to do."

My mind was reeling so quickly I was dizzy. On trembling

legs, I got up from the chair and went to stand by the fireplace. "But that would mean Brandi is my sister."

"Your half sister."

"Why now? Why tell me now?"

"Because Jack asked me directly. He asked me if you were his."

"What? Suddenly you had to tell the truth? After lying to everyone all these years? I can't believe this." My voice cracked. I wrung my sweaty hands. Air. I needed air. "If he suspected this, why didn't he ask you before now?"

"He said it hadn't occurred to him until recently. One day a few months ago you made a certain expression or gesture—I can't remember now what he said it was—and he saw his mother in you. He dismissed the idea but it kept nagging at him. When he heard I was in town, he decided to ask me for the truth. He thought I would say no—that it was only a coincidence."

I fell deeper into the black hole as I tried to hold on to a sense of reality. My cheeks were wet with tears. Why had she allowed him to marry Malinda? He'd belonged to my mom. "Why would you let him marry her? He didn't even love her."

"Because I was young and stupid and hurt. I'd thought that he and I were soul mates. When I found out he cheated—it wrecked me. I had to get away, honey. I'm so sorry. You deserved better, but I didn't know what to do."

"*You* deserved better."

"I know that now. But I was eighteen years old then. And really scared."

"What did he say? When you told him."

"He was stunned, of course. Like I said, he'd suspected it but didn't really think it could be true."

"Does he want to…" I trailed off, unable to ask all the questions tumbling around in my mind. *Would he want anything to do with me?* Or was his anger at my mother too strong to want a relationship with me? Did I want a relationship with him? What did this do to Brandi and me? My dearest friend in the world had also been lied to by the woman who was like a second mother to her.

"You have made a mess of things," I said. "For all of us."

"I know I have. But Jack wants a chance to know you better. In spite of his shock and anger, he was happy to learn the truth. He saw it as a good thing…you, that is. Not the lies."

"You took all that time away from us. We'll never get that back."

The sadness in her eyes changed to fury. "Don't you think I know that? I did what I thought was best. For all of us. I let her win. For that I'm regretful. But I knew how strong I was. I could take care of you by myself. If I told him, what would he have done? A man like that? Two women? Two babies? I couldn't make him make an impossible choice. I loved him more than that."

I sank onto the end of the bed. What was I to do now? Another wave of anger consumed me. "Were you going to keep this a secret from me forever? What would you have done if he never asked you?"

"I didn't expect him to ask me. I thought we'd have a quick lunch and that would be the end of it. But he had an agenda. When he said that about his mother, I knew it was too late to lie anymore. You do look like her. I've always seen it and was surprised no one else ever did. When I first started letting you come here I worried about that, but then no one ever noticed."

"Is he going to tell Brandi? You've lied to her all this time. She's fragile right now. The baby. God, Mom."

"He's going to tell her."

"Well, isn't that convenient for you? You're off the hook, once more. With no repercussions for your lies."

"You think I'm off the hook? He broke my heart and I had to raise a baby by myself. So you be really careful about who you're accusing of what. He's the one who cheated on me and got another girl pregnant. Don't forget that part of the story."

My mother's anger jolted me out of my own. This was the rage of a woman scorned. She'd never gotten over him. I softened, thinking about her broken heart at age eighteen. I'd still been a child at eighteen. But I remembered quite clearly how grief and betrayal had made Brandi grow up overnight.

"Mom, what do we do now?"

She sighed, as if relieved by my gentler tone. "I don't know. If you think about it, nothing's really different between you and Brandi. You've always acted like sisters."

I thought of her as my sister. Had I known the truth on some level?

"Do you think Brandi will ever forgive me?" Mom asked.

"I don't know what she'll think." I looked down at my hands. What if Brandi saw me as complicit somehow? What if she blamed me? Would she see me as a threat to her relationship with her father? *Our father,* I thought. *My father.* "When is Jack telling her?"

"As we speak."

My heart skipped a beat. I said a silent prayer. *Please God, take care of Brandi and that baby. Don't let this harm them.*

"I have to go now," I said. "I need some to time think."

"I understand." She rose out of the chair and reached out to me. "I'm sorry, honey."

"I know you are, but that doesn't make this all right."

For the first time in my life, I rejected a hug from my mother and left without another word.

As I got in my car, a text came through from Brandi.

Holy crap. Can you come over?

I wrote back that I'd be there in a few minutes. As I drove away from the lodge, the enormity of my mother's confession washed over me. What was I supposed to do now? Would this disrupt my friendship with Brandi and Trapper? What about Jack? Would he wish he'd never known?

The more I went over all the details in my head, the more convinced I was that this was partially my fault. How had I been so stupid to just accept my mother's explanation of a stranger and a one-night stand? I should have done one of those DNA tests and figured out the truth earlier. How had I not suspected Jack was my father once my mom told me about their relationship in high school? Numbers had never been my strongest subject, but even I could do simple math.

By the time I'd reached Brandi's, I was sick to my stomach. The repercussions of this on all of us would now begin to unfold. A sense of dread weighed me down as I crossed the yard to their front door. Normally, I would just walk in without knocking, but for some reason I felt like a stranger. Should I knock or ring the doorbell?

Trapper saved me from the decision. He pulled me into a hug. "How are you holding up?"

"I'm all right. How's Brandi?"

"She was surprised. No doubt about that. Then she decided that she's known all along."

I smiled. "I thought about that too. How we instantly bonded when we were little girls." The first summer I stayed with them, my grandmother had arranged for Brandi to come over to the house so that I might make a friend. I was shy and quiet, but so was Brandi. However, the minute we met, we'd started talking and playing together. That had not stopped.

I followed Trapper into the house. The scent of coffee brewing filled the kitchen. "You want coffee?" Trapper asked.

"No, I'm jittery enough."

"She's waiting for you upstairs. Go on up," Trapper said.

Anxious to see her, I practically sprinted up those stairs. I tapped my knuckles on the door.

"Crystal, is that you?"

"Yes, can I come in?"

"Get in here," Brandi said.

I crept into the room feeling a bit like a dog with my tail between my legs.

She was dressed in a white cotton nightgown and had her hair twisted into a braid. "Don't look like that. This is a happy day."

"Happy? Or confusing?" I sat next to her on the bed as the questions tumbled from my mouth. "I can't believe she lied all this time. How are you? Are you upset? Mad at me? Mad at Mom? How was Jack? Is he as angry as me?"

"Slow down. I'm not mad at anyone, especially not you. You and I are innocent."

"I guess we are. For some reason, I feel like I did something wrong. Like this is all my fault somehow."

"You did nothing wrong. As far as Dad goes, I'd say he's more in shock than anything. He feels a lot of guilt about his part in it."

"The cheating?"

"Right. And that your mom had to raise you all alone when my mom didn't. He feels like a bad guy, which he's not used to."

Without the cheating, there would be no Brandi. Had that occurred to her? "One thing I don't understand, though. You're older than me. I don't understand the math."

"I was six weeks premature."

I stared at her, shocked. "You were? How did I not know this?"

"It was a quirk of my mother's. She never wanted me to tell anyone for fear they'd think there was something wrong with me. You know how she is."

"So that makes sense, then," I said. "We were conceived not that far apart but you came early." I glanced out the window as another detail occurred to me. "I was late by two weeks. They had to induce my mom."

"Which makes us two months apart."

"How could this have not occurred to me?" I asked. "I feel like an idiot."

"If so, then we both are." Brandi chuckled. "It seems like we might have suspected after we learned they'd dated in high school. I blame my pregnancy hormones. They're making me dumber than usual."

"I have no excuse," I said. "Other than blinders. I've spent all my life trying to forget about the idea of a father."

"To protect yourself," Brandi said. "Which is completely understandable."

"Is it weird to think your dad has another child?" I asked.

She nodded her head vigorously. "That he had another child was shocking enough, but that it was you? I was so bowled over when he told me that I went utterly speechless. Do you know how they say that, but no one really is? I was."

I inspected her closely. For damage. Anger. But there was nothing. Just her clear, kind eyes staring back at me. The best friend I'd been able to count on for as long as I could remember. *My sister.* That would take some getting used to.

Brandi reached for my hand. "I know you're angry right now. You have every right to be. I'm sure your mother did what she thought was best."

"She said she loved him too much to make him choose," I said. "I mean, he'd already promised your mother he'd marry her."

"That was without knowledge of you," Brandi said. "I wonder what he would have done had he known? Think about how different our childhoods would have been if he'd chosen you and your mother."

"It would have been an impossible choice." Although I still reeled with anger, I could imagine how scared and young she was at the time.

"I understand why your mother did what she did."

"You do?" I asked.

"I made a similar decision when I found out I was pregnant. You understood why I did what *I* did at the time. Maybe you can give your mom the same grace you gave me."

I hadn't thought of it that way. Brandi had gotten pregnant at the end of their senior year and instead of telling Trapper, she'd let him leave to pursue a hockey scholarship. The baby had not lived, which made it easier for her to keep it from him. For ten years, all the time they were apart, he didn't know that Brandi had given birth to a baby that hadn't lived. He'd been able to forgive her, and now they were in their own happily ever after. Could I forgive my mother the way he'd forgiven Brandi?

"I hadn't thought of it like that," I said. "But think about all those years we lost. We can't get that time back."

"The same could be said for Trapper and me. We choose not to think about it that way. We think only about all the years we have left."

"You're both better people than me," I said.

Brandi laughed. "You're the best person I know."

"I try, but I'm not sure."

"Sisters. Can you believe it?"

"Not yet, no. Nothing's sunk in all the way yet. Will it be weird for you? For you to share your dad with me?"

"Honestly, no. He's the best dad in the whole world, and I'm glad for both of you that you have a second chance."

"Do you know what this means? I'm going to be the baby's aunt."

"You were always her aunt. Only now it's official." She touched the sleeve of my blouse. "Tell me what's going on with Garth."

"It's a mess." I proceeded to tell her about the last few days, ending with the question that had been on my mind ever since. "He asked me if I thought we'd have had a chance had his mother not left or if I'd had a father."

"Interesting. What do you think?" Brandi asked.

"I think this morning seems like a long time ago now."

"Can I ask you this? Where do you want to be tonight when all of this starts to sink in?" She put up a hand. "Don't think. Just answer."

"I'd like to be with Garth."

"Don't you think that's your answer?"

15

GARTH

Dad and I were out on the patio wearing winter coats and smoking cigars when Crystal arrived. We'd come out to enjoy the fire pit and fresh air. I'd been grateful for Dad's company as his ebullient personality distracted me from worrying about what came next in my life.

"Hey guys," Crystal said.

"Everything okay?" She'd obviously been crying.

My dad stood and led her over to one of the chairs. "Hey, Mouse. You seem a little puny."

She sat and pulled her coat tighter over her chest. "I'm all right. Shocked but all right."

"I can see that on your face," I said. "Is it something about your mother?"

"She told me who my father is."

I lurched forward. "No way."

"Remember how I told you that she and Jack were high school sweethearts?" Crystal asked.

Oh God. I knew what she was going to say. The other day, when I'd seen them together, an odd feeling had come over me. "He's your father, isn't he?"

"How did you know?" she asked. "I had no idea."

149

"After you told me about their relationship in high school, it crossed my mind because of the math. I quickly dismissed the idea. I didn't think your mother would have kept that from either of you."

"She did."

I hated to hear the bitter tone in her voice. "Does Brandi know yet?" What would she think about all this? God, the repercussions of Jennifer's lies were far-reaching. I didn't want to think about how this might derail us. Another person she'd trusted had betrayed her. Not by dying this time, but by a terrible secret. Would this make it even harder for Crystal to trust me?

"Yes. I just came from talking with Brandi. She was surprised. A few days ago we didn't even know our parents dated in high school, and now this. We're already like sisters, so this doesn't really change anything." She started to cry. "But can you believe we never knew? All this time, we've been super close with no idea who we really are to each other."

Dad poured Crystal a glass of whiskey from the bottle on the side table next to him. "Have a drink. You've had a shock."

She took a tentative sip. "I can't believe this."

"Have you heard from Jack yet?" I asked.

"No, not yet. I have no idea how to approach him. There's no playbook about how to suddenly think of someone as your father that has been just your friend's dad all these years. He might not even want to be part of my life. I mean, he can't just automatically feel something for me simply because we share DNA."

"If he wants to be part of your life then he will be," Dad said. "If not, you'll still go on and do whatever comes next in yours."

Given my mother's surprise visit, I had to wonder if he was directing that to me.

"Listen, kids, I'm going to let you two talk," Dad said.

"Thanks, Dad." I gave him a grateful smile.

"Appreciate it, Brian," Crystal said.

"Not a problem." Dad leaned down to give Crystal a quick kiss on the top of the head. "You hang in there, Mouse."

After he disappeared into the house, I motioned for Crystal to come sit with me. "Come here. Let me warm you up."

She crawled in beside me. I covered us both with one of the blankets we'd brought out with us.

"I said I wanted answers. I guess I got them," she said.

I kissed her temple. "But this was a heck of an answer. Are you okay?"

"I'm better now I'm here with you."

"What do you need from me? What can I do?" I asked. My very male way of wanting to fix everything had kicked into full gear.

She snuggled closer. I breathed in the scent of her hair. "This is exactly what I need."

"I'm glad." I looked up at the sky. The stars were hidden by cloud cover.

"There was no one else I wanted to go to."

After my mother's shocking revelation about having had cancer, I'd been anxious to speak with Crystal. "This was the day for mother bombs," I said. "My mom had cancer last year and never told me. That's one of the reasons she's here. She knows the time we have isn't forever and wants us to be closer."

"How do you feel about that?"

"Is it too trite to use the word *healing*?"

"Not if that's what it gave you," she said.

"I feel for the first time that we might actually have a relationship."

She barked out a bitter laugh. "How ironic, since my relationship with my mother just blew up."

I couldn't think of an antidote to soothe her. Her mother had lied to her about something so fundamental. How could Crystal ever forgive her?

"All my life, I wanted a father," Crystal said. "My mother

knew that. And she lied to me, over and over. Every day was a lie."

"Did she explain why?" Jennifer Whalen was a good person. She'd obviously had a reason that made sense to her.

"It was because he told her he planned on marrying Brandi's mom. My mother thought they were moving to Seattle together, and then he tells her he's cheated and gotten another girl pregnant. Mom didn't want to put him in the position to have to choose. So she left. Did everything on her own. And lied to me my whole life."

"I can understand how she felt like she had no choice but to go it alone."

I felt her stiffen. "You can?"

"Don't mistake me," I said. "I understand your side of it absolutely. However, think about it from your mother's perspective. It must have been such a hard blow. To learn that he'd cheated and gotten her pregnant too. That kind of betrayal would make anyone do what they had to do to survive."

"I still don't understand." She began to sob. "She robbed us of all those years. I was here every summer, for heaven's sake. I was at their house and all this time I had no idea he was the father I so desperately wanted. We can't get those years back. What if you're right—if I'd known my dad, maybe I wouldn't be so messed up. Maybe I wouldn't be so confused about everything."

"There's no doubt our missing parents had an effect on us," I said. "The more time I spend with my mother, the more I understand what happened. Seeing them as people and not just our parents is a rite of passage."

"I don't want to," she said. "I want to be mad. At least for a while."

"You have every right to be."

She relaxed against me.

"I'm sorry. What can I do?" I asked.

"Just be here with me."

"If you need me, I'll be right there by your side. You can count on that."

She put her head on my chest and cried as if her heart would break. I would have done anything to ease her pain. I was helpless. All I could do was hold her as tightly as my bruised ribs would allow.

When she finally stopped crying, I asked her what she would do next. "Will you see Jack tomorrow?"

"What choice do either of us have? We have to confront all this head-on. Especially because of Brandi. It's not like we can email each other before we agree to meet. I've known him almost all my life."

"From what I've seen, Jack is a good person," I said. "He might see his own part in all of it and be able to get past feelings of anger and regret and see what a remarkable opportunity it is to have a relationship with you now."

"Thinking of him as my father? Will that ever seem real?"

"I'm not sure. I'd guess that someday this will seem normal. Isn't that how it is when we're adjusting to a new reality? At first, it's hard to understand or accept, but after a time it becomes the new normal. For now, give yourself some time to let it all sink in. Everything will look better in the morning after a good night's sleep."

"What if it doesn't?"

"I'll still be here. Whatever happens next, I'll be here when you wake up and when you come home."

16

CRYSTAL

I was in the back office of my shop finishing up some paperwork when I heard Jack Vargas's voice coming from the front. My stomach turned over. *This is it. The time has come.* I would have to face him.

Ironically, at the same time, a text came in from my mother. *Can we talk?*

I couldn't respond. Not yet, anyway. For the first time in my life, I was ignoring her calls and messages. Some children had had rebellious streaks growing up. I'd been as compliant and flexible as my mother's clay. However, we'd never experienced this kind of rift. I wasn't sure I could get past the betrayal. The lies that had piled up one after the other compounded over time. I'd had a father I could have known. We would have had a real relationship instead of only a connection through Brandi.

Think of it from his perspective, I told myself. *I'm sure he was as nervous as I. It's not every day you find out you have another daughter.*

I took a deep breath and walked out to the front.

"Hi, Jack."

"Crystal, hey." He shifted, rocking on one foot and then the other. He wore his usual khakis and conservative button-down shirt. Had there ever been more of an "opposites attract" than my mother and Jack Vargas?

"I'm sorry to drop by unannounced," he said.

"It's no problem." My voice sounded shaky and dry and not at all like myself. Actually, I felt like a child standing here in front of the father I'd yearned for all my life.

"Brandi said I would find you here."

Conscious that Mindy had picked up on the weird vibe between us, I suggested we take a walk. Soon, the whole town would know my mother's secret.

Jack agreed. "Grab your coat and hat, though. It's cold today."

I flushed with pleasure. He'd suggested a coat. This is what it would have been like to have him in my life. At that thought, a whole new fury enveloped me. *Don't think about all that now. Focus on Jack.* Working this out with my mother didn't have a place in the moment. I'd been robbed of thirty years. I wouldn't let her steal a moment more.

"Hang on two seconds," I said. "I'll be right back." I got my coat from the office along with a cap and gloves. Seconds later, we walked out to the sidewalk. Snow had finally stopped falling, replaced by sunny weather with temperatures in the low twenties. Our streets were clear, thanks to the snowplows that had come through earlier. One of Brandi's employees had shoveled the snow in front of both our shops. Most of the other businesses had done the same. Anyone who owned a store in Emerson Pass knew shoveling snow came with the job description.

"Are you hungry?" I asked. "We could get some lunch."

"Sure, I could eat." We agreed to go to the bar and grill. I hoped, although I knew it was futile, that we would not run into anybody we knew.

Frosty air stung my cheeks. Bits of fallen snow drifted from the rooftops and trees to dance in the breeze. Thanksgiving was a week away, and the shops had started to decorate for the holidays. Soon twinkling lights would make the main street of town look like a fairyland. We'd keep the lights until the end of February. They brightened the dark days of the deep midwinter.

As we walked toward the bar and grill, we made small talk. He asked about my business. Was it doing well? Did I find it too time-consuming, in addition to my charity work? He seemed genuinely interested, so I shared with him my plan to sell the shop to Mindy. "She's been saving up enough for the down payment. I bought it only to keep myself busy when I first moved here. Now that I'm helping families and businesses rebuild, I don't really have the need for a distraction."

"Brandi said you insisted Garth's house be rebuilt first."

"He needed one more than I do. I have Brandi. She and Trapper have been incredibly generous. Taking us in—the refugees of Emerson Pass."

"You're a blessing to Brandi. Especially now."

"I never had siblings growing up." I pressed my gloved fingers against my mouth, self-conscious that I'd stated the obvious. "You know that. Anyway, it's been fun to live with them. Like a family. I always wanted that." *Like a family?* What was wrong with me? Would my social blunders continue all through lunch? "I don't know why I keep saying stuff like that."

To my surprise, Jack laughed. "I know, this is weird. There's really no handbook for this kind of thing, right?"

"Right."

"Can we just agree to do the best we can?" Jack asked.

"I can agree to that. It's so strange. All of this. I can't wrap my mind around any of it."

"I know. I feel the same way." Jack glanced at me. "It's hard to think about all the years I've known you and yet didn't know who you really are to me."

Who I was to him? What would that evolve into? Would we always feel as awkward as we did right now?

"Brandi told me you girls had a good talk."

"I thought she might feel weird about all this. As far as I can tell, she's happy."

"That's my girl."

A twinge of jealousy hit me then. *My girl.* She'd always been his girl. When I'd been desperate for a father, she'd had him. *No, don't be unkind and petty.* Brandi was innocent in all this. No matter how we sliced this open, she and I were blameless. Nothing would or could break our bond. Sisters or best friends? Really, what was the difference? None, when it came to Brandi and me. As long as I kept myself in check.

We were almost to the bar and grill. I was breathless, as if we'd run here instead of strolled.

Jack held the door open for me. "In you go."

I liked the gesture. *In you go* had such a dad vibe to it. Would it have been as meaningful to me yesterday, before I knew he was my father? I might not have even noticed. Now he was my dad, and his words had made me feel cherished. How strange.

A few minutes later we were seated in a booth next to the fireplace. We'd beaten the lunch crowd. Vintage Vince Gill crooned through the speakers. Soon, the bar and dining room would fill with hungry skiers, fresh from the slopes, and drown out the music.

We each ordered a salad and a cherry Italian soda. When the server walked away, I turned back to Jack. "Do you always order a cherry Italian soda? Or did I give you the idea?"

"I always order one when I'm here. They're especially good, don't you think?"

"I do." I smiled, pleased that we had this in common. "What else do you like? What do you like to eat?" Under the table, I rubbed one of my fingernails with the pad of my thumb. "Garth teases me that I have an obsession with food and drink."

"How could you not? It's your job, after all."

"Some women remember what they were wearing during certain events. I always remember what I had to eat."

Jack chuckled. "My mother was that way. You remind me of her."

"How so?" My heart leaped in anticipation. "My mom told me you said I look like her."

"You do. Now all I can see when I look at you is her. I don't know how I didn't notice the resemblance all those years.."

"The truth never occurred to you? Until recently, that is?"

"I know, it's crazy. Especially when you think about how much time you spent with Brandi when you were younger. I guess we all have blinders about things we can't conceive of. I would never have thought your mother would keep a secret like this."

"How are you feeling about…that part?"

"Shocked, obviously. I feel terrible that I didn't know. Your mother and I are both responsible for that."

"How is it your responsibility? You didn't know about me."

"Yes, but it was my mistake that led to her decision. Had it not happened the way it did with Malinda, she wouldn't have had to run away." He tilted his head, watching me. "You're upset with her?"

"Furious."

"No one could blame you for that. However, I hope at some point you can forgive her. We all do the best we can with what we have."

I teared up, move by the kindness of his words. This was a good man. A man who would have been tortured given the choice between two women and two babies. My mother was right about that.

"Where do we go from here?" I asked.

"I suppose we get to know each other in a whole new way. You've been Brandi's best friend for a long time. I've always thought you were a special girl. A woman, I mean. I was grateful for your friendship with Brandi as well as for your mother's presence in Brandi's life. As you know, Malinda was a difficult person. *Is* difficult. She's not dead." His mouth turned upward into a half smile that did nothing to disguise the hardness in his eyes at the mention of her name.

"She was difficult." My cheeks warmed. Why was I talking about Malinda? "It's really none of my business. But it always bothered me, the way Malinda treated Brandi."

He let out a sigh. "Me too."

The server delivered our sodas. Jack set aside the straw and took a sip from the plastic glass. Was he like me and against straws?

"No straw?" I asked.

"They should have reusable ones."

"That's exactly what I think," I said.

"My mom and I have always been close, even though we're very different. This, though. I don't know how to get past the lies. Brandi pointed out that my mother's situation and decision were similar to the one she'd made herself at eighteen."

"True."

"Somehow it's different when it's your mother. There were so many times when I was young that I wished for a father." I grabbed a napkin to wipe underneath my eyes. "When I think of everything we missed, it's hard to reconcile. She lied to us both for thirty years."

"I'm sad about all of the missed years, too," Jack said. "But as my wise daughter told me this morning, there's no point in being bitter about the past. We're here now. We have many years left to spend together."

"Let's start with a cherry soda," I said.

———

After lunch, Jack and I strolled down the sidewalk along Barnes Avenue. Thin winter sunlight warmed the top of my head and made the snow sparkle. As we neared the park, Jack gestured toward the gazebo. "Stop for a minute?"

I agreed, wishing for more time with him. Lunch had gone too fast.

We walked over to the bench that faced the statue of

Alexander Barnes. We all knew the story. Alexander had made an abandoned mining town into a community. He'd invited merchants and tradesman from all over the country to come and open businesses, providing loans and encouraging them to bring their families. His wife Quinn, whom the high school was named after, had been the first schoolteacher of Emerson Pass. Her legacy of education for all, regardless of religion or race, had been carried forward for generations.

"What a love story," I said. "Quinn and Alexander."

"This whole town was founded by the idea that we're greater together than apart." Jack brushed the snow from the bench with his gloved hand and waited for me to sit before joining me. "I always thought people from here were more likely to fall in love with each other than from other places. Like our ancestors lingered around playing Cupid."

"It does seem that way. What do you know about our family?" I asked. Our family. Yes, it was mine now too.

"Lizzie and Jasper came with Alexander Barnes from England." Alexander Barnes had been a British lord but had given it all up to come to the American frontier to strike out on his own. "Lizzie was his cook and Jasper his butler."

"My mom said Harley and Merry worked for them, too."

"That's right. Until they started breeding horses. I'm fairly certain Alexander gave them the money to get all that started."

"I'm trying to be like him." I took my sunglasses out of my jacket pocket and put them on to protect my light eyes from the glare. "I'd like to do something important with my life."

"You're doing that now. All your charity work's making a huge difference."

"I hope so. I'm not sure." I paused for a moment as a sparrow sang from the tree above us. Sparrows were special to Brandi and Trapper, reminding them of the little girl they'd lost.

Jack poked at a tuft of snow with his boot. "When I lost my parents, Brandi was only a few years old. I felt pretty alone. My marriage was unhappy. I was barely keeping up with work while going to school at night. I couldn't sleep even though I was exhausted. The only way I could fall asleep was on the floor next to Brandi's crib."

The image of him watching over baby Brandi made me want to weep. For him and his loveless marriage. For me and my fatherless childhood.

"I'm sorry," he said. "That was a stupid thing to say."

"No, it wasn't. I don't want you to feel like you can't talk about what it was like with you and Brandi. Just because I didn't get you doesn't mean you have to apologize for being there for her."

"I don't know if this will make things better or worse. But I want you to know that I was very much in love with your mother. I wanted to marry her and grow old together. I messed up. I can't ever make that up to you. That being true, I'd sure like to try."

I blinked away tears. "To be honest, I can't imagine you with my mother."

He chuckled. "Why not?"

"She's such a free spirit. You're so steady and safe."

"*Boring* is more the word."

"I like boring. I wish Patrick had been a little more boring. Maybe he'd still be here."

"But would you have fallen in love with him if he wasn't exactly who he was?"

"Probably not." The qualities that had attracted me were the very ones that caused him to head out in the helicopter that day. "I'm more like you. He made me more adventurous and joyful. I loved that about him."

"What was it like growing up with your mother? I bet she kept you entertained."

"She's the most fun of anyone I've ever known. The most ordinary thing would turn into a hilarious adventure. She was always supportive and encouraging about whatever I wanted to do or be. Almost too much. I could have come home and told her

I wanted to join a traveling circus and she would have said what a delightfully eccentric thing to do and could she come too?"

Jack laughed. "I could see her following the circus."

"She was always impeccably dressed, but not at all like the other mothers with their jeans and sweaters. Did you know she worked at a department store before her art took off?"

"No, I didn't."

"Instead of buying clothes at the shop, she went to thrift stores and found the most beautiful things. Everywhere we went, people flocked to her. After her work started to take off and the art community opened up to her, she became kind of famous. We moved downtown and she was always having these parties with arty types—theater actors, painters, opera singers. You name it and they were at our apartment."

"They must have been interesting."

"Looking back, yes. But I liked my summers here with Nan and Pop better. I preferred the quiet and nature and my Nan's way of making everything simple. My happiest memories were of my summers here. I can remember laying out on the grass and watching the sky and feeling that this was where I belonged."

"I watched the sky when I was young too. I don't know why I stopped," Jack said.

"Life happens and you forget that peace comes from watching a cloud move across the sky."

"Or the way the stars shine on a night in July," Jack said. "Your mother and I used to go down to the river on summer nights. We'd spread a blanket out and just take in the stars. She would tell me that she wanted to travel all over the world and have an unusual life. Everything seemed possible for us back then."

"That sounds like her. I just wanted to be like everyone else. My mother wasn't like anyone else. Ever."

Jack nodded as a smile broke out over his face. "I loved that about her. She never cared what people thought about her. My mother called it dancing to your own music."

"She certainly did that. *Does* that."

"I wasn't that way, as I'm sure you can picture." He chuckled as if remembering something funny. "She made me more adventurous. Better, too. Not so afraid of everything."

"What were you afraid of?"

"Not being good enough, mostly. Then when my parents died and I was left alone with Malinda, I grew more and more isolated. I focused on work and Brandi, and the rest just sort of fell away. I accepted that my life with Malinda wasn't as I wished, but we had Brandi. I told myself that was enough. I wish I'd been braver."

"You wanted Brandi to have a secure family."

"Yes, but in hindsight, she was raised by two people who didn't love each other. I'm not sure that was the best choice."

In the sunlight, I detected the fine lines around his eyes and mouth. Still, he was young. There was a lot of his life left for love. "Have you been dating at all since your divorce?"

"No, I'm not ready. I don't think, anyway."

"When do you know if you're ready?"

"Are you asking about me or you?" Jack asked.

"Both, maybe." I shoved my gloved hands into the pockets of my jacket. "I didn't plan on getting involved with Garth. There's something about him that I can't resist."

"Do you love him?"

"I didn't want to, but yes. I told myself it was just for fun. It morphed into something real. The minute something good or bad happens, my first instinct is to rush to him and tell him everything. I can't seem to walk away. Yet I'm scared. To lose him or to keep him and then lose him."

"Think about it this way—if you walk away from him, you're guaranteed to lose him. If you give in and let yourself love him then your chances of keeping him are that much better."

"That's logical…" I trailed off.

"I sense a *but* coming. Is there a reason why you think you shouldn't get to have a second chance at happiness?"

My eyes stung with unshed tears. "I've been punishing myself."

"For what?" Jack asked, gently.

I explained about the baby and my despairing plea to God. "I feel like I caused the miscarriage by giving up on life."

"No, no. That wasn't your fault. You'd lost your husband very unexpectedly. God understands. We all despair at different points of our lives."

"That's basically what Garth said." I looked upward, trying to describe what it was that was holding me back. "I feel if I move on that I'm betraying both Patrick and the baby. Like, why should I get to have a new love and maybe even a family when he's dead?"

"Because you're still alive. That's the only criterion."

Was that true?

"Isn't life hard enough?" Jack asked. "Without making ourselves feel guilty and unworthy of love just because we're imperfect and have moments of weakness?"

"I guess so." I choked up as he pulled me into a fatherly embrace. "Is this what it's like to have a dad poking into my business?"

"You'd have to ask Brandi." He let me go but cupped my chin. His glove felt rough against my skin. "All will be well if you go with your heart. That one's from my dad."

I wished that were true. Sometimes things weren't well.

"Do you have a picture of your parents?" I asked, changing the subject.

"Sure." He reached into his jacket pocket and took out his wallet. "This is a photograph of my parents on their wedding day. They were twenty years old here. Sunny and David were their names."

I studied the black-and-white photograph, searching for myself. His mother was almost as tall as David and skinny like me. Her eyes might be similar to mine as well.

"Do you think you look like her?" Jack asked.

"A little. The tall and skinny part, anyway."

"She often complained about being too thin and feeling awkward and gangly."

"That's how I felt growing up too. During my brief stint as a runway model, I met girls who were just like me. We commiserated about never having had a date in high school. We looked better walking down the runway than wearing an actual prom dress."

"You became a swan, no matter how you look at it."

I warmed with pleasure at the compliment. "My mom said you noticed just recently that I looked like Sunny?"

"That's right. I always thought you looked just like your mom but one day over at Brandi's you made this certain gesture with your hand and I swear it was exactly like my mother. I pushed it aside as a fanciful notion. I hadn't even planned on asking Jennifer about it."

"Why not?"

"Like I said, I'd dismissed the idea. But as we were sitting there, it just kind of slipped out. I knew the minute I asked that I was right."

"I wish she'd told us the truth," I said.

"Don't be too hard on her. Holding a grudge can't go side by side with love."

"Will you be able to forgive her?" I asked.

He looked over at the statue of Alexander Barnes before answering. "I can and will forgive her, especially considering my part in everything. I hope in time you'll be able to do the same."

"I can't imagine this anger is going away anytime soon."

"I can understand that. But life's too short for fussing. Another thing my mother used to say. Call your mother. Have dinner with her. She's hurting."

"How can you be so forgiving?"

"Because I loved her, and yet I hurt her very badly. It's important we take responsibility for our part in any scenario."

"I'm hurting Garth." Shame flooded through me. "Even though I love him."

"Sometimes the ones we love the most are the ones we hurt the worst."

I'd go to Garth, I thought. Tell him how I feel. Make this right.

He patted my leg. "Come along now. We'll get you back to work."

I sighed with pleasure as we rose to our feet. "This wasn't as weird as I thought it might be."

"Agreed." He tucked my arm under his and we walked back to my shop that way. Just a father and daughter out on an ordinary day for lunch. Life was too short for fussing.

GARTH

On my patio that evening, Crystal and I snuggled together under several wool blankets. Stars twinkled from their inky sky. A sliver of a moon hung just above the mountains. From somewhere below came the howl of a coyote.

Crystal shivered. I pulled her closer. "I had lunch with my dad today." She sucked in a breath that made a whistling sound. "My dad. How weird is that?"

"And great. Right?"

"Yes, he's great. We had a really good talk."

"Great."

"We talked about a lot of things, including you."

I braced myself. "Yeah?"

"I've come to understand something better. Your accident, almost losing you, scared me. You know that."

"I do."

"But it also woke me up. If I didn't love you, I wouldn't have been so terrified. I'm ready to embrace my feelings for you. There's nothing wrong with me getting on with things. I've been an idiot."

My heart raced. Were her words real or was this a dream? "What are you saying?"

"I'm saying that I love you. I want to be with you today, tomorrow, and for all the days after that."

"Are you sure?"

"I'm sure. I was lying to myself in order to stay detached and therefore safe," Crystal said. "I don't want to be that way. My dad said his mother used to tell him that life was too short for fussing."

"Fussing?" I laughed. "Like a baby?"

"I think she meant, making things harder than they have to be or focusing only on the difficult parts of life."

"Sometimes life is hard, though. We can't just wish them away."

"I know. But there's also a point when it's time to embrace whatever's next. You're my next. I've been running from you for long enough." She shifted to look up at me. "I don't want to run anymore. I'm sorry for how hard I've made this."

"I *do* understand. More than you know. My divorce was like a death in a way. I didn't want to fall in love with you and have you leave me—or what was once love become anger and indifference. From the first night together, I sensed that whatever this was with you was big. Bigger than I wanted. I didn't feel ready to take this all on."

"Me either. Yet, here we are."

I stroked her hair. "Here we are. It's occurred to me that we're not really in charge of any of this."

"True. I remembered something Nan told me once. She said that when I found the right person, I might feel very, very scared. I was to take that as a sign."

"A sign of what?"

"That he was the right one." She lifted her mouth to kiss me. "And that's you."

I closed my eyes as a wave of emotion overwhelmed me. A

phrase echoed through my mind. *She loves me. She loves me. She loves me.*

She caressed the side of my face with her thumb. When I opened my eyes, she was there, staring straight into my soul. "What do you think?" Crystal asked. "Are we ready for this big thing between us?"

"I am. I've been ready from that first night."

"You saved my life and now we're forever bonded?" Crystal asked, teasing. "Or am I forever in your debt and must commit to a life serving you?"

I laughed. "We both know that's not going to happen."

"Depends on what you want." She trailed a finger down the side of my neck to my collarbone. "I have two skills. Cooking and nightly activities. They're yours if you want."

"Be careful. This cast is only on my leg."

She threw her head back in laughter. If I could spend the rest of my life making her laugh, I'd never want for anything else.

18

CRYSTAL

A few days later, I'd just come down from serving Brandi her lunch when Jack knocked at the back door. I waved for him to come in. Since I'd been staying here, I'd become accustomed to Jack coming and going. Today, however, his visit felt different. I was his daughter too.

"What brings you by?" I asked.

"I found this in a trunk of my parents' old things." Jack carried an old hatbox with him, which he placed on the island. "They're letters exchanged between Lizzie and her daughter Florence during the 1930s. I thought you girls would enjoy reading them."

I thought about all that for a moment. Brandi had shared some of the letters exchanged between Lizzie and her mother. I'd enjoyed them as fiction and a peek into the past. Now that I knew I was related to Lizzie, they had a whole new meaning. "Lizzie belongs to me too."

"She sure does. Have you ever wondered where your love of cooking came from?"

"No, I never did. Nan used to let Brandi and me make cookies and quick breads at her house. I thought that might be the reason we both fell in love with baking and cooking. We had such fun on those days. Now I can see that we have Lizzie flowing through our blood."

"The older I get, the more intrigued I am with the past. Isn't that funny? When I was young, I thought only of the present and the future. Ambition and doubt and worries—how best could I provide for my family and was I a good enough husband and father. Then, perhaps as a way to better understand my own life, I've looked to the past."

I pulled the hatbox closer. The color had once been purple but had faded to a dusty lavender. I expected it to smell moldy. Instead, I caught a hint of cinnamon. "I wonder what Lizzie smelled like?" I asked, thinking out loud.

"Cookies, maybe," Jack said. "Like Brandi."

"I've always associated ice cream with Brandi," I said. "Not just because she's sweet."

"Because of the first day you met?"

I peered up at him, surprised he remembered. "Yes." My eyes filled. "If I'd only known who you two really were to me."

"I've been thinking about that too," Jack said. "Wondering how I didn't know."

"Right? Doesn't it seem like we would have sensed a connection?"

"I was a mess that day. You looked so much like your mother when she was that same age. I was flooded with all these memories of growing up with Jennie. God, I was crazy about her. My whole childhood I'd bragged to everyone that Jennifer Whalen would marry me someday. That day we saw you, I wanted to ask about your mom. I had a hundred questions. However, I knew better than to bring any of it up with your grandmother. She wasn't too fond of me for obvious reasons."

What had she said when I asked if she'd known the boy who'd broken my mother's heart? *Not as well as I thought I did.*

"Nan told me that a boy had broken Mom's heart. I had no idea it was you."

He rested his backside against the sink. "I wish it hadn't been me."

"But then we wouldn't have Brandi."

"Right. It always circles back to that."

"I thought you might like to read some to Brandi as a way of distracting her."

I smiled at him, touched. "She'll like that."

"I love that you girls are interested in the past. Even if you're only humoring me. My ex-wife hated when I talked about my family. It irritated her."

"A lot of things irritated her," I said, not joking.

"Sadly, true."

"Brandi says Malinda's called a few times but their conversations are stilted and awkward. I thought the baby coming might help break the ice, but it hasn't. Have you heard from her?"

He shook his head as he headed toward the coffee maker. "No, not since the divorce was final. It's better this way. We can't have civil conversations. Not yet anyway. I wish it didn't have to be that way for Brandi's sake. Malinda is who she is." He paused to pour himself a cup of coffee.

"Do you think Brandi will ever forgive her?" I asked, thinking of my relationship with my own mother.

"I hope so. Her attitude might change once the baby comes." He brought his coffee with him to lean against the sink. "Becoming a mother or father has a way of changing the way you look at your own parents. People become less critical once they experience the terror of holding the fate of a little person in your hands and how easy it is to make mistakes. At least, that's how it was for me."

Knowing I had nothing generous to say about Malinda, I kept my mouth shut. "Have you read any of the letters?"

"Yes, there's some good stuff in there. Florence was Lizzie's daughter. The letters are back and forth between them when Florence was a young woman. She writes about when she first meets her future husband, Robert and of their work later in Castaway." He hesitated, abandoning his coffee cup by setting it in the sink. "Like you, Lizzie lost a baby. She talks about it some in the letters to her daughter. I found them particularly moving. And I thought…"

"They might help me?"

"That's right." He looked down at his shoes before gesturing toward the upstairs. "How's our patient?"

"She's a little cranky about being in bed yet another day."

"She never was one for sitting still." He pushed his hands into the pockets of his khakis. "Have you talked to your mother?"

"Just a text or two," I said.

"Maybe take her to dinner tonight?" Jack asked. "I'm sure she's hurting. This has to be a nightmare for her."

"What about for us?"

"We gained something, kiddo. We have the chance to know each other. She might feel like she's losing you."

"Maybe." No wonder my mother had loved him so much. "You're a good person, Jack."

"Nah. No better than most." He brushed aside my compliment with a wave of his hand.

I cleaned up the kitchen while he was upstairs and started the dishwasher. After that was completed, I looked over at the hatbox. Were there secrets in those letters? Ones shared between mother and daughter? None would be as large as the one my mother had kept from me. Jack was right, though. I couldn't let too much time go by without a reconciliation. My mother had always been there for me. Besides Patrick, she'd been the most important person in my life. I needed to find a place within myself that could forgive her. I was grateful that I now knew the truth. I needed to focus on that part.

And Garth. Just thinking of him made my body tingle with longing.

I opened the lid of the box. Jack had arranged the letters neatly in piles with a rubber band around them. I picked up one of the groupings and realized they'd been put together by decades on the date stamps. How clever, I thought. Like me, he was a detail type of person. I appreciated that quality. For the ninth or tenth time since I learned the truth, I thought about what a strange pair my mother and Jack must've been.

I would save the letters for later. I needed to deal with the living right now, not the dead.

I texted my mother asking if she would like to meet me for dinner that night.

She wrote back almost instantly that, yes, she would very much like to have dinner.

We agreed to meet at the lodge at seven. She promised to make a reservation. That in itself was an olive branch, I thought, as I set the phone down. Reservations were not really my mother's thing. I always made the arrangements. She was in charge of fun once we got to wherever we were going.

Thinking of life without her made me feel ill. Repairing the damage between us might take work, but we would mend our relationship. There was no other choice. Not for me. Not for her. It had always been Mom and me against the world. I could not let that go even after this kind of betrayal. Family was family. We took each other as we were, flaws and all. My love for my mother had been the through line of my life. Pride and anger and fear kept us from the love we all craved.

I had to find a way to move past all this and start the next chapter of my life. Garth and I had a future mapped out. I wanted my mother part of it all.

My mother was already seated in a booth in the lodge's dining room when I arrived. She stood as I approached. We quickly embraced.

"I'm so glad you texted," Mom said. Dark smudges under her eyes told me that my mother had not been sleeping well. A twinge of guilt nudged at me. I'd caused her sadness with my lack of empathy.

"It's good to see you," I said as I slipped into the booth.

I focused on the abstract painting hanging on the opposite wall, avoiding eye contact. What did we say to each other now? I knew it was up to me to initiate the conversation, but I was empty of thoughts.

"You're a good girl to meet me," Mom said, breaking the silence. "You've always been such a good daughter. Better than I deserved."

"Don't say that." I had always been a good daughter—responsible and steady. We'd made a good pair. She reminded me the only way to soar was to fly. I'd grounded her enough to keep her from crashing. "This doesn't take away all the good."

"I can't tell you how sorry I am," Mom said.

A server came to take our drink order, saving me from having to come up with a response. I asked for a bottle of chardonnay and a basket of bread. I'd been too nervous to eat earlier and needed something to soak up the alcohol. I'd been vacillating all day about what to say to my mother. I couldn't seem to stop careering between anger and a longing to have her wrap me in her arms and comfort me as she'd done when Patrick died. This time, however, the person who usually gave me support was the same person who had caused the problem.

"I've missed you," Mom asked. "Are you all right?"

My heart softened at the sound of such tenderness in her voice. "I'm still reeling, but I'm getting used to the idea. I've spent some time with Jack. It's been nice."

A small muscle in her cheek twitched. "Good for you." She took a menu and stared at it as a tear traveled down her cheek, making a path through her makeup.

"Mom, don't cry." I reached over and took her menu. "We'll get through this."

Her face crumpled as more tears came. "Do you think you

can ever forgive me?" She opened her purse and took out a package of tissues to wipe her cheeks.

"You're my mom. It's always been the two of us, facing all the good and bad together. Knowing the truth doesn't change any of that. Nothing would ever change how much I love you."

"I wish there was something I could do to make it up to you," Mom said. "To Jack too."

"He's surprisingly forgiving. In fact, he blames himself."

"He was always that way. Selfless."

"He knows he broke your heart."

Her gaze flickered toward the wall behind me. "That's generous of him."

"It must have been so very hard to leave here, all alone, knowing he was with someone else."

"You have no idea," Mom said.

"I lost Patrick, so I know what it's like to be without the one person you loved more than anyone else. The betrayal, though. I would've have been devastated in a whole new way had that been the case."

"Thinking about him with her—I can't really describe the particular kind of hell that was. Then, when I met Brandi, I tried to forget that I'd ever loved him. I had you. That helped."

"But it still hurt, didn't it?"

"I'll never get over it. Or him. The only way I could go on was to pretend like it never happened. I'd thought he loved me as I did him. I was wrong about, that, obviously."

"Why do you say that?"

"A man in love doesn't cheat."

"He was young. Teenage boys don't always think with their brain. He told me he loved you very much. Malinda was a mistake. A youthful indiscretion, as they say."

"That mistake cost me everything I wanted." The anguish in her voice broke me.

"Mom, I'm so sorry that happened to you."

She dabbed at the corners of her eyes. "I'd like to think he loved me like I did him, but it's simply not true. No amount of alcohol would ever have caused me to betray him."

"Men are different."

The server arrived with our bottle of wine and made a big show of opening it and having me taste. I wasn't in the mood. Normally, I'd have enjoyed it all, but tonight I didn't feel much like eating, which wasn't like me, but I ordered the angel hair pasta with fresh tomato and garlic in olive oil. Mom ordered a bowl of chowder.

"What did you and Jack talk about?" Mom asked after the server hurried away to another table. I hadn't noticed until now but the dining room was lively tonight. The skiers had arrived. In a few weeks the holidays would bring even more.

"This and that. He brought me a batch of letters from his family."

"Lizzie and Jasper," she said under her breath as if trying to memorize a fact.

"How did you know?"

"Those of us who grew up together here always talked about which family of the first settlers we were descended from. It was a thing. We're descendants of Harley and Merry. They were the horse people."

"Nan told me everything she knew about our family," I said.

"Right. Of course she did." Mom smiled as her gaze drifted upward. "My parents were very proud of the Depaul legacy."

"It's a gift to know about those who came before us. Most people have no idea about their families."

"I used to think they were all looking after us," Mom said.

"Jack said he thought they were like Cupid, ghosting around matchmaking."

"Wouldn't that be wonderful if it were true? I'd have had Jack all this time if they granted those kinds of wishes."

"He said he thought the two of you would marry and grow old together."

"He did?"

I nodded as I buttered a piece of bread. "He has a lot of regret and remorse for what happened. I think he loved you, Mom. I don't know if that makes things better or worse."

"Nor do I."

The server brought our meals, presenting them with the customary fanfare of an upscale restaurant. We smiled and thanked him, but our hearts weren't in it. After he left, my mother picked up her spoon but didn't dip it into her soup.

"Honey, I've been thinking. What would you think if I moved here?"

Her question surprised me so much that it took me a second to answer. "Here? Isn't it too small for you?"

"That wasn't what kept me away." She ducked her chin and reached for her water glass.

"Right. I can see that now." I studied her for a moment. "Wouldn't it be hard to be here, though? Jack and I are going to have a relationship."

"That's exactly what I'm worried about. You'll be here with Jack—the greatest father in the world. What would you need me for? Pretty soon, you'll stop calling or inviting me places because you'll have perfect Jack."

"That's ridiculous. You're my mom. Nothing changes that. I have enough love for both of you." I'd never heard my mother jealous before. Strangely, it touched me more than anything else she'd said tonight.

"I never had to share you. Being a single mother was hard in some ways but in others it was easier. I can remember friends complaining about differing parenting styles with their spouses. I could raise you however I wanted. Now there's a new person in your life. One who might turn you against me."

"Jack wouldn't do that."

"Not on purpose. But you'll have a family here with Brandi and Jack and her children. I'll be off in Seattle doing whatever it is I do, too far away to really be part of things."

"Isn't Seattle where you belong? Where your people are?"

"*You're* my people. You're the only person who matters to me. I want to be here and part of the day-to-day of your life."

"You'll always be part of my life. There's no reason to feel insecure or jealous."

"Jealousy? You can't imagine how I burned with jealousy when he told me he was marrying her. I felt this rage I'd never felt before. The darkness of it scared me. I knew that staying away from him and Malinda was the only way it wouldn't consume me. I had to go toward the light, so to speak. And now, here I am again. About to lose the battle because of Jack."

"Oh, Mom, I'm sorry." My stomach ached at the raw emotion in her voice and expression. I'd loved Patrick that way, all-consuming and breathtaking. If he'd cheated on me I would have been devastated. To find out he'd gotten another woman pregnant would have made me want to die. Thinking about it this way gave me new insight into my mother's decision. I could see how her only choice was to run away. The pain would have been too much otherwise.

"It's all right now," Mom said, tightly. "All of it was such a long time ago. None of it matters except you. I just want you to be all right. That's all I ever wanted. I know you got a raw deal getting me as your mother."

"No, that's not true at all." My mother claiming that it was all such a long time ago and that none of it mattered was also very clearly not true. No one spoke of something that supposedly didn't matter as she had tonight. How was it possible that thirty years later, the pain was still fresh?

"The other mothers of your little friends growing up were always so conventional—so normal—and you were stuck with me."

"No one had a mom like you, that's true. But those kids were the ones missing out. You're the most fun and the most interesting of all of them. I wouldn't trade you for anyone."

Mom's eyes filled. She dabbed under them with a new tissue. "That's kind of you to say, honey."

"Are you serious about moving here?"

She nodded. "I've been thinking about it all day. What do you think about the idea of me opening an art gallery? We could display my work and others. If I sell my condo in Seattle, I can probably buy a building here."

"Mom, you don't need to do that. I can fund a gallery if that's what you want."

"You've already been so generous. I can't ask you to do that. Not after all this."

Patrick and I had bought a condo for her in downtown Seattle, moving her from the smaller one she'd lived in for almost two decades. Her views from the twenty-first-floor windows looked out to the Puget Sound. She'd set up her pottery studio in one of the bedrooms. I had no idea how much income she generated through her work, but she'd never asked me for anything. Patrick had wanted to open a gallery for her when he and I had first married, but she'd refused, worried that he would feel taken advantage of.

"Let me do this for you," I said. "Patrick would want you to have a gallery if that's what you want. Or I can buy you a house here. Whatever you want." I gazed across at her. "What *do* you want? To stay in Seattle? Or to come here?"

Her eyes flickered. "You don't want to know the real answer to that."

"I do."

"What I want isn't something I can have."

The torment in her voice stabbed me in the gut. "Mom, are you talking about Jack?"

She ignored my question. "I thought I could buy that building behind the bar and grill. You know the one? I could live upstairs and have the gallery downstairs."

The building she referred to was one of the oldest in town, built in the early 1900s. If I remembered right, Alexander Barnes's office had been there. Over the years, it had had various incarnations. The most recent had been a haircutting salon run by a trio of sisters, but that had closed last spring. They'd moved to a different facility with more reliable heating and water. "It would need an overhaul. To make it livable as a residence." I didn't know when my own house would be built. The contractors in town and the ones we'd brought in from Cliffside Bay had their rosters full through the summer.

"Maybe I can find a rental until then," Mom said.

"We can look around tomorrow." I didn't have much hope of finding anything. With all the people who'd lost homes, rentals were hard to find. When Jamie Wattson had lost her inn, where she'd lived in one of her rooms, she'd moved into Brandi's old apartment above the bakery. If not for that, Mom might have been able to move there. The inn was scheduled to open again in the spring, but all work had been halted once the snow started to fall.

"When I rebuild the Lake House, we could have a cottage built for you. I don't like the idea of you living in some drafty old building."

She rested her chin in her hand as she looked across at me. "We can decide all that later. The most important thing is that you understand I'm serious. I *will* be moving here."

My mind had sped ahead by then to holidays and family gatherings. Would Mom and Jack be able to be together without resentment and hostility? Jack would be able to put the past behind them, but would Mom have that same ability? She clearly still had strong feelings for him. "Mom, as long as you don't get hurt again. That's all I care about. I'm afraid seeing Jack all the time will cause you more pain."

"It will hurt. Especially when he gets married again." Her voice broke. She paused for a few seconds before continuing. "Which will happen sooner than later. A man like Jack doesn't stay single for long."

Married again? I hadn't even thought about that. She was right. He was a catch. The single ladies of a certain age would be circling soon. Or maybe even some of the younger ones.

"But listen to me, honey. I'll be all right as long as I know you forgive me."

"I do. I'd love to have you here in Emerson Pass. It's a dream come true. Please, let's just move past all of this and embrace a new beginning."

"One in which I can be honest with you and myself," Mom said.

Yes, I thought. Honesty. I needed a little of that myself. I had fallen for Garth. Denying it had only hurt him and me.

I closed my eyes for a second as a wave of emotion swept over me. As I'd thought about special occasions and family events, I'd seen Garth by my side. Goodness, I was in trouble. I wanted to be with him. He was the one I belonged with now.

Outside the lobby, I slipped a few bills into the valet's hand before getting into the driver's seat of my car. Under the awning, the cement was dry, but snow had begun to fall while I was inside having dinner.

"Be careful out there. It's starting to dump," the valet said before closing the door and running to get the next car.

My spirits were high after such a productive talk with my mom. For the first time since I learned of her deceit I felt sure we would be able to repair the damage to our relationship. It had felt good to air it all out, as my Nan had done with her laundry in the summertime. I could still see the way the sheets had flapped in the breeze, collecting the scents of flowers and grasses. Tonight, I felt a bit like one of those sheets after the sun had dried all the dampness that had weighed it down.

As I pulled out of the lodge driveway and onto the street, the valet's prediction proved correct. Snow did indeed dump from the sky with flakes so thick the windshield wipers strained under the effort. I cursed under my breath and tightened my grip on the steering wheel.

Although this was my third winter in Emerson Pass, driving in the snow still scared me. I wanted to get home to Garth. He'd already texted several times to ask me to let him know when I was on my way home. He was worried about the weather and rightly so. I'd take it slowly, I told myself. My car was good in the snow. That's what it was made for.

The lodge was down a long road a few miles from downtown. By the time I rolled onto Barnes Avenue in the heart of town, the roads were blanketed with at least three inches of snow. The plow would not be out for another hour, if that. They liked to wait for a break before bringing out the equipment.

That morning, the workers had hung the twinkling lights in the trees that lined downtown. Despite their cheery glow, my gut clenched. The street was bare except for my car. All the storefronts were dark except for the bar and grill. Had everyone else gotten word of the storm? I'd been so preoccupied, I hadn't paid any attention to what the weather was supposed to do.

I turned on music to keep me company. As long as I drove carefully, I'd be fine. After what seemed like an hour I passed through town and turned right onto the road that would take me up the southern mountain to Garth's house.

Garth. I'd forgotten to text him. I used the voice command to send a note to him. *On my way but the roads are bad. Headed up the mountain now.*

I chugged up the winding road. Five minutes later, I had only a mile more to go before Garth's driveway. My snow tires gripped the slick road. They were doing their job. I would make it home soon. Just minutes from now, I'd be in Garth's arms.

A pair of deer came out of nowhere, bolting into the road. I slammed on my brakes. Too hard. The car careered and slid. Next came the sound of metal crumpling and glass breaking. The airbag opened and thrust me back into the seat. Pain shot through the middle of my body. Garth. I had to get home to Garth. Then, blackness.

19

GARTH

I stood at the window watching the snow fall, growing more panicked by the second. A text had come from Crystal just minutes before that she was on her way up the mountain. The snow was the icy kind that would stick to the roads and make them slick. I'd been worried all night. A feeling of dread had clung to me, despite the enjoyable evening I'd spent with my parents. We'd put together a puzzle in front of the fire and had hot apple cider and popcorn. I'd basked in the glow of their company and the warmth of the room.

Now, however, I was frantic with worry. If I could have driven, I would have rushed out of there, but I couldn't ask my dad to go. Then I'd be worried about two people instead of one. I should have warned her not to go out to the lodge. She should have come straight home. Now she was stuck out in this. The forecast had predicted another storm, but not until midnight. Obviously, it had come early.

She hated driving in the snow. All the years in Seattle with barely any storms had not prepared her for this kind of weather. If I could have paced, I would have done so. Instead, I could barely hobble around.

My dad and mom were in the kitchen putting away dishes

from our dinner. I limped to the kitchen, then leaned on my crutches. "I heard from Crystal. She's on her way up the mountain. She should be here any minute."

Mom peered out the kitchen windows to the driveway. "I don't see any lights. When did she text?"

"Like two minutes ago," I said.

"She'll be here, son," Dad said.

The minutes ticked by and still no Crystal.

"She should've been here already," I said.

Dad nodded, looking uncharacteristically worried. "She might've gotten stuck. I reckon I'll go out and look for her."

"I'm not sure that's a good idea," Mom said.

"She said she was just headed up the mountain when she texted," I said. "Maybe she had an accident."

Dad was already putting on his jacket. "I'll call you as soon as I see her. If she's in a ditch, I'll bring her home."

I watched from the window as my dad's car disappeared down the driveway. He was good in the snow after all of the years driving me to and from ski practice. If anyone could find her, it would be him.

I wandered into the living room. Chilled with fear, I stood near the fireplace hoping to get warm. Her brow furrowed with worry, Mom moved around the room, straightening pillows and folding a blanket. I'd seen that expression before. Too many times. One night shortly before Christopher passed, I'd watched her from the doorway of my brother's bedroom. She'd had the same look on her face then as now.

"I have a bad feeling, Mom. I've had one all day."

"She may have just run into a little trouble and gotten stuck in the snow." My mother's reassuring words did not match her concerned tone.

"Slick spots can come out of nowhere," I said. "But what are the odds that we'd both have a bad accident within weeks of each other?"

"You're right. I'm sure she's fine," Mom said. "Any minute now your dad will bring her home."

For the next quarter of an hour, we sat in silence. I watched my phone, willing it to ring or buzz with a text from Crystal or my dad.

Despite being ready, I jumped at the sound of my phone. "Dad?"

"Take a deep breath. Brace yourself. I found her. Her car had spun off the road and smashed into a tree. She's alive but unconscious. The paramedics are on their way."

I froze as a jolt of terror went through my body. "Are you sure she's breathing?"

"Yes," Dad said.

"Can you tell if she's broken anything? Or if she's suffered any kind of internal injuries?" My voice was a higher octave than usual.

"I can't see anything wrong with her. Try not to worry."

Famous last words.

My heart pounded in my chest. A ringing started between my ears. "What do I do, Dad?" I held my breath waiting for his answer.

"Start praying. As hard as you can."

Through the phone I could hear the sirens. "Dad?"

"I'll stay with her. Don't worry. I'll keep her close."

"Call us as soon as you get to the hospital. Or when you know something."

"I will. I'll be in the ambulance with her. I'll hold her hand for you." My dad sounded as though he was crying, which made me feel as if I were hurling off the side of the mountain. I wanted to stay on the line, but Crystal needed him more.

After I hung up, I turned to my mom. Her fingers were gripping a bit of my shirt. I hadn't noticed until now.

"What's happened?" Mom asked

"It's what I thought. She's had an accident." I told her as much as I knew. "Dad says he'll stay with her." I'd never felt more helpless in my life. She needed me, and here I was with a broken leg. Stuck.

As I sat there with my mom waiting for news, I understood for the first time what Crystal must've felt the night of my accident. I could see now how it had jolted her out of the cocoon we'd spun around each other and into the bad place of fear and insecurity. She'd thought I might die on her.

This is what it felt like on the other end. Waiting and worried, fearing the worst.

My mom took my hand and held it between her own. They were soft and dry. I'd remembered the feel of them all these years. How they could soothe a headache or sore throat by the simple placement of them on my forehead. Tonight they were cold. She, too, was afraid. I could see in her eyes that she was convinced this would not have a happy ending. We didn't get those in our family, after all.

"I hate that I can't be with her."

"Your dad was always good in a crisis. He'll take care of everything." She removed her hand from mine. "I always panicked and lost my head if you guys ever fell or got hurt." She smiled as a faraway look came to her eyes. "Did I ever tell you about the time the two of you unlocked the gate and started walking to the park?"

"No, I've never heard that one."

"You were four and your brother was two. We'd just had a new fence and gate put into the backyard so you guys could play and I wouldn't have to worry about you wandering away. One summer night, right after we put the fence in, you boys were outside playing. Your father was still at work, and the phone rang. I figured you were safe, given the new fence, so I went inside to answer it. I was only on there for about two minutes—it was a sales call and I hung up right away. Anyway, I went back out to the yard and lo and behold, the gate that was supposedly childproof was wide open. I let out a scream and then dashed through the gate to the sidewalk. We lived in a busy neighborhood back then. Our street was quiet, but one of the main thoroughfares was only a block away. I looked one way and then the other, and there you two were at the end of the block marching toward the park. Just then, a woman exited from the bus and quickly saw what was going on and put herself between you and the street. All night long all I could think about was what could've happened to you two if that woman hadn't been there at the right time. I felt like the worst mother in the world."

"I have no memory of that."

"I'm glad. You could add it to another in the long list of mistakes that I've made."

"You had every reason to believe the gate was impossible for little kids to open," I said.

"I don't know if any kid could have opened that latch. You and your brother were always clever that way."

"How come you never say Christopher's name?" I asked.

"I don't?"

"No. Never."

"I didn't realize," Mom said. "I think about him every single day. I wonder what he'd be like as a man. Would he be married by now or have children? What would he have decided to be? Would you two be best friends?"

"I think about all that too. Playing scenarios in my head. What if he'd lived? Would you and dad have stayed married? Would we all celebrate holidays together? I also think about what it would have been like if it had been me and not Christopher."

"What are you saying?"

I shook my head, instantly sorry I'd said anything. "Never mind."

"Do you think I'd have preferred it to be you?"

I kept my gaze on the fire. "Sometimes. It seems like it would have been better."

"Why would you ever think such a thing?"

"Because you so easily left me." The words plopped out of

my mouth before I could stop them. "Christopher died, but you left me by choice."

She reached out and put her hand briefly on my cheek. "Oh, my beautiful boy. Is that what you've thought? I'm sorry you've lived with that idea all this time. I wouldn't have wanted either of you to get sick. I loved you the same. Leaving was about me, not you. I'll keep saying it until you truly believe it to be the truth. Nothing that happened was your fault. Please, you have to know that." She wrapped her arms around me and kissed the top of my head as if I were still a little boy.

"Don't leave again," I whispered. "Please."

"I won't. I promise. Not until the good Lord takes me."

That was the crux of it all, wasn't it? There would be no choice after all was said and done. We would all leave the world at some point. What we did with the time we had here was all we could control.

"I don't want to lose her, Mom." Tears blinded my vision. I closed my eyes and let my head sink toward her.

She stroked my hair. "I know you don't. It's all going to be all right."

Damn, I wished I could believe her.

20

CRYSTAL

I traveled through a long black tunnel. Patrick stood before me, dressed in his black-and-red skiing outfit. "What are you doing here?" I asked. "Are you back from your trip?"

"No, I won't be coming back." He peered at me from behind his glasses. "You know that."

"No, that's not true. I've had the worst dream. You were killed when the helicopter went down."

"That's what happened. I'm sorry. I didn't mean for it to happen that way. I had no intention of dying." He grinned and adjusted his glasses. "I know you're mad at me. But it *is* true that I'm in a better place. I always thought that was just something people said."

"But I don't want you to be gone. I need you here."

"That's not true. You never needed me. You're strong on your own. You always were."

"I don't want to be. I want you to come back."

"It's not possible. You need to live again. Waiting around for a ghost is no way to live your life."

Words tumbled from my mouth. "That's easy for you to say. You're dead. Why should I listen to you? You're the one who left me. Why did you have to go on that trip?"

"Because I was living. When we're alive, we should do the things that make us happy, even if it's risky."

"But what about the people you leave behind? Did you ever consider that? Did you ever consider my feelings? What it would be like to get the call that you were dead?"

"I'm sorry I hurt you." He moved closer, reaching out as if to take my hand. I jerked away.

"Hurt me? That doesn't even come close to what you did to me."

"He's good, Crystal."

"Garth?" I asked.

"Yes. You could be happy again with him. There's no reason to die with me."

"He needs someone who can love him. I'm not that person."

"Only you would argue with a dead person." Patrick laughed. "You've always been stubborn and loyal to a fault."

"I promised to love you forever. In front of God and everyone."

"Only until death do us part. You can let go now." He began to fade. At first it was just a slight loss of color, but he gradually faded into nothing. I called out to him, crying. But he did not return. I stared into nothing but blackness. I was so very cold. Sharp pains rocked through my body. I was dying. How had I not known that? Patrick was already dead and I was headed there too.

No. Not yet. Not now. *I want to live. I want Garth and babies and flowers in the springtime.* I wanted to meet Brandi's baby. And cook Thanksgiving dinner. *I'm not ready. Let me go back.*

A voice spoke softly into my ear. "Hang in there, Mouse. Come back to us. We all need you." The voice belonged to Brian. What was he doing here? Could he pull me back to life? I tried to answer him, but the blackness came again.

21

GARTH

Mom and I both fell asleep on the couch waiting for a phone call from my father. He finally called around 3:00 a.m. Bleary-eyed, I reached for the phone. "Dad?" I held my breath, waiting.

"It's good news. She's out of surgery. Doc said she came through great and should make a full recovery. She's resting. You can come see her in the morning after she wakes."

I breathed a sign of relief. "Are you coming home? The snow stopped."

"I'll be there in a few minutes," Dad said. "How's your mom?"

"She's here with me. We both fell asleep on the couch."

Mom had stirred at the sound of my voice. She rubbed her eyes. "What is it?"

"Crystal came through the surgery fine. Dad's on his way home."

"Thank God," Mom whispered.

"Y'all go to bed," Dad said. "You'll need your strength for tomorrow."

After we hung up, I turned to Mom. "You need to get some sleep."

"I think I'll just stay here on the couch if you don't mind," she said.

"There's no way you're driving back to the lodge. But will you be warm enough out here?"

Mom nodded, then rubbed her eyes. "Sure. I'll grab a blanket and pillow from the guest room."

I nodded and yawned myself, then hobbled off to my bedroom. After brushing my teeth, I didn't even bother to undress, falling into bed more exhausted than I'd ever been in my life. Now that the adrenaline of worry had ceased, I'd crashed. I was asleep within minutes.

I woke around seven the next morning to the scent of coffee. Even with the hassle of wrapping my leg, I managed to shower and shave. After dressing in a sweater and pair of oversize sweatpants my dad had picked up from the clothing store, I went out to the main room. I'd expected to see my mother still asleep on the couch, but she must have gotten up and gone back to the lodge. I was starting to gain momentum with my crutches and moved quickly across the room to the kitchen. My eyes were scratchy from lack of sleep, but I wanted to call Crystal's mother and tell her about the accident and reassure her that Crystal was all right.

I didn't have her cell number, so I called the lodge and they connected me to the phone in her room.

"Hello." She sounded sleepy, as though I'd awakened her.

"It's Garth Welte. Is this Jennifer?"

"Yes. Is something wrong with Crystal?"

A mother's instinct. They always knew. "She's all right, but she slid off the road last night. My dad found her, and an ambulance managed to get up the mountain to get her and take her to the hospital. She had some internal injuries, but the surgeon said she came through really well. She's resting now, but I'm hoping we'll hear from her when she's well enough to use the phone. She'll be in the hospital for a few days."

"Can I see her?"

"I'm not sure yet. As soon as I get word, I'll send my dad out to get you if she says she's feeling well enough to see us."

"Thank you. It's so kind of you to call."

"I'm sure you'll hear from Crystal when she wakes. I didn't want you to be completely in the dark."

"I really appreciate your thoughtfulness. My poor girl. She's been through so much."

"I know she has. I'm trying to make sure that the times ahead are good. Last night, I was scared I wouldn't have the chance."

"I can't think about it," Jennifer said.

"We don't have to. She's going to be fine." I promised her I'd call the minute we got permission to visit, then hung up. Then I called Jack, followed by Brandi. They took the news similarly to Jennifer, grateful that she was all right, followed by thoughts of what might have happened. I assured them that I'd call the moment I knew anything else. Jack said he'd be ready to head over whenever she was awake and receiving visitors.

Nothing sounded as good as a fresh cup of coffee. Thankful that my dad had already made a pot, I poured a generous amount into a mug and put a few pieces of bread in the toaster.

I drank my coffee standing on my one good leg while supporting myself with one crutch. The day was clear and sunny with a sky so blue it was hard to believe that a blizzard had come through last night. At least a foot of snow covered the patio.

My toast popped up, and I buttered it the best I could with my clumsy hands. I'd just taken a bite when I heard voices coming from the guest room. My dad's low voice, followed by Mom's higher-pitched one. My stomach lurched. They were in there together. I looked over at the couch again. There was no evidence of anyone having slept there. Had she moved into my father's room after he came home? I was still contemplating this and vacillating between disbelief, horror, and joy when my father appeared. His hair was damp and his face clean-shaven. There was absolutely no evidence of a sleepless night. Upon closer inspection I came to the conclusion that if anything, he looked better rested than yesterday. Which made no sense, as we'd all been up half the night.

"Good morning. Did you get some sleep?" Dad asked.

"A little. You?"

"A little." Dad gave me a goofy grin before going to the cabinet and pulling out two coffee mugs. They weren't even going to try to hide it?

"Was that Mom's voice I heard in your room?"

Another adolescent grin crept over his face "She was awake when I got home. I convinced her she'd be more comfortable sleeping in the bedroom with me."

I cringed. "Dad, don't say anything else. Please, not another word."

"You asked." One shoulder lifted before he burst out laughing.

"This is not funny."

"Your expression is funny," Dad said. "Don't be worried. We just talked and slept. We used to be great friends, you know."

"What does all this mean?" I set my crutches more firmly under my arms.

"Nothing at all, other than we had a lot of catching up to do. And we're both here to be with you."

I couldn't help but feel a bit crestfallen. I'd hoped maybe they'd have remembered what they once had together. "Oh, okay."

"Son, it's perfectly natural to wish your parents would get back together."

"And you're not?"

"If it were up to me, we'd still be together. Would I love to win her back? Heck yeah. But a lot of time has passed. A lot of hurt on both sides."

A throbbing pain at my right temple started. "I don't want you hurt again."

"Don't worry. I'm a big boy." Dad set his coffee cup aside and looked at me. "Whatever happens between your mom and me has nothing to do with how much she loves you."

"I know." I nodded, feeling suddenly very miserable. "I wish Crystal would call me."

He clapped a hand over my shoulder. "Have a little faith, kid. Everything will come together."

I wanted to believe him, but right now I was tired and dispirited. The emotional turmoil of the last few weeks was starting to catch up with me. What if Crystal had changed her mind? Who knew what being in an accident would do to her?

Just then, as if an answer to prayer, my phone buzzed. It was a text from Crystal.

Please come visit. I miss you.

I smiled at the phone before looking up at my dad. "Can you take me to the hospital? Crystal wants to see me."

"You got it." He grinned again, and this time I joined him.

22

CRYSTAL

My eyelids felt as if they were glued shut. With great effort, I opened them. Hospital room. I was alive. Despite the pain coming from my middle, joy surged through me. I'd made it. God had heard my prayers. I was back. Happy tears gathered at the corners of my eyes. I wanted to live. Really live.

What had happened? The car had slid from the road. I could remember hitting the tree and the sound of the crash. After that, nothing. Had Brian found me? Where was my phone? I needed to call Garth and my mother. I tried to sit up, but the pain worsened so I stayed still.

A nurse hustled through the doorway. Her name tag read Elsie. Stout and sturdy with a pageboy haircut, she reminded me of a Dutch boy in the children's story my mother used to read to me. He'd plugged a hole in a dike with his finger and saved his village.

My mother. Did she know? Had anyone thought to call her?

"Are you awake and ready for some breakfast?" Elsie asked.

"What happened to me?"

"You busted up your insides when you slid off the road."

That explained the pain. "What's busted?"

"Your liver was damaged. The surgeons repaired it, and you'll be good as new in no time." Elsie's communication style was a robust as her build. No nonsense. No coddling.

"My liver?"

"Internal injuries. A few tears and such, but the doctors fixed you right up." Elsie picked up my wrist and took my pulse.

"Was there a man with me?" I asked. "When I came in?"

"Yes, he found you after the crash. The father of your boyfriend is what he told the admitting nurse."

Garth must have sent Brian to look for me when I hadn't shown up at the house. I'd heard his voice.

"Can I have visitors?" I asked.

"Suit yourself." She opened a drawer next to the bed. "Here's your phone if you want to make some phone calls. I'm going to order your breakfast. Oatmeal or eggs?"

"Oatmeal," I said weakly as I took the phone from her. Glancing down at it, I could see there were a dozen missed calls and texts from Garth around the time of the accident. He must have been frantic. I knew that feeling all too well. My mother had called several times this morning, as had Brandi. Garth must have called them first thing to tell them what had happened.

I called my mom first. She answered right away, sounding breathless. "Crystal, are you all right? Garth called and told me about the accident."

"Hi, Mom. I'm totally fine." I filled her in as best I could about the details of the accident and surgery.

"Can I come see you?"

"The nurse said I could have visitors. Garth's on his way over now."

"Garth's sending his dad out to get me and bring me later," Mom said.

"That's great, Mom."

Brandi called right after I hung up. First, she scolded me for driving in the snow. Then she started to cry and said how grateful she was that I was all right. "If I'd known, I wouldn't have slept a wink last night."

"I'm sorry. I was so distracted with all this stuff going on with my mother that I didn't pay any attention to the weather."

"When can you get out of there?" Brandi asked.

"They say I'll be in here a few more days."

"I wish I could get out of this bed so I could come take care of you."

"I don't want you upset. Stress is not what you need right now. Although if you weren't on bed rest, I'd beg you to come take care of me." I lowered my voice. "I have a scary nurse named Elsie."

On cue, she came in with a breakfast tray of gluey oatmeal, thin orange juice, and a piece of wheat toast made soggy from the few paltry melon slices. I mouthed a thank-you, but Elsie didn't seem to notice. She hustled out of the room.

"Dad's on his way over to see you," Brandi said.

I brushed my hair away from my face. "My mom's coming over too."

"Oh, goodness. As if you need the stress of that whole inter-action. I'm sorry, sweetie."

"They're going to have to get used to seeing each other if they want to be part of my life. You won't believe what my mom told me last night. She wants to move here."

"You're kidding." She paused. I could practically hear her little mind churning through what that meant. "Crystal, what if they got back together? For real. Think about that."

"It's impossible. There's no way." I halted, remembering what my mother had said about her lingering feelings for Jack.

"What is it?" Brandi asked. "I could hear you thinking something."

"Don't get carried away, but I think my mom's still in love with him," I said.

"Holy crap. I can't believe I'm missing all of this by being stuck in this bed. If I could be around my dad when she's there, I'd be able to tell if he felt the same."

"Honestly, though, even if he did, how could he ever forgive her for what she kept from him for thirty years?"

"I don't know about that. Look at Trapper and me." She continued without taking a breath. "It would be awesome. We'd be a family. He'd be so happy if he were with someone like your mom. Someone who didn't criticize everything he did."

She sounded so genuine and excited. I shook my head as if she could see me. "You're dreaming, because it's not going to happen."

"Well, at least we have each other, no matter what happens with them. Now listen, you kick them all out if you need to rest. Dad called me after hearing from Garth. He was beside himself and said he was going to the hospital right then. I had to beg him not to go and wake you up. I told him you needed your rest."

I looked up at the ceiling, overcome with emotion. This was what it was like to have a father. A caring, protective father. The feeling of being cherished was silly, because he couldn't actually keep me safe. However, knowing he wanted to gave me a sense of peace.

I'd taken a few bites of the gluey oatmeal when Elsie returned. "What's the matter? Not to your liking?"

"It has a strange texture," I said.

Elsie pursed her lips in an expression of disapproval. "You need to eat to get your strength back."

"This isn't going to give me my strength back." I held up a spoon of a glob of the gelatinous oatmeal.

She ignored me. "You have two very insistent men in the waiting room anxious to see you."

"Can I?" I asked, meekly. Elsie made me feel as if I were back in elementary school and had to ask permission to use the bathroom.

She pointed at the orange juice. "Drink that up, young lady, and I'll let them in."

"Citrus makes me itchy."

She gave me a stern look before shrugging. "All right, but I will expect you to eat a little more at lunch than you did for breakfast. You don't have enough meat on your bones to last a day without food."

"Would it surprise you to learn that I'm a chef?"

Her eyebrows shot up. "No offense, but I don't ever trust a skinny chef."

"Nonsense," I said. "But I'll do a better job on my lunch, I promise."

"Good then. I'll get your visitors. Only two at a time, mind you." She gave me a self-satisfied smile and bustled out of the room. Given the hard-heeled nature of her gait, it was a good thing she wore shoes with a thick rubber sole.

While I waited, I thought about my vision of Patrick. Had I been in the in-between place that Garth thought he'd gone to, or had it just been a dream? Could Patrick have known I was torn between him and a living, breathing man and come to set me straight?

I didn't have any time left to consider all the possibilities because just then Jack and Garth arrived. Jack held a bouquet of flowers and entered first. Garth followed, using his crutches.

My heart felt lighter just looking at them. "Hey, guys." I pushed the tray with my breakfast to the side.

"Hey there," Garth said as he drew close and kissed me on the cheek.

"Jack, you didn't have to bring flowers," I said, secretly pleased.

"These are from Garth," Jack said as he set them on the table next to the bed. "Carried in by the guy without the broken leg."

"Thank you. They're pretty." I smiled up at Garth. His familiar scent was like home. "But mostly I'm glad to see you both."

Jack leaned down to kiss my forehead. "I brought you a cookie from the bakery." He sneaked it out of his pocket. "Peanut butter."

"That's my favorite."

"Brandi told me," Jack said. "Mine too, by the way."

"How are you feeling?" Garth stood next to the bed leaning on his crutches. He seemed as though he wanted to touch me but was afraid I'd break.

For the first time since I woke up, I wondered how I looked. By the expressions of concern on their faces, I must have appeared much rougher than I actually felt. "The drugs are good. I'm feeling no pain." I held up my hands. "They put me all back together again. I can still whip up a meal in under ten minutes."

Garth smirked, clearly not amused. "Whether you could cook for us or not is not what we're worried about."

"I know, I was only teasing," I said. "I'm sorry I worried you. Both of you."

"The nurse said you can probably come home the day after tomorrow." Garth smoothed the sheet next to my hip. "But the doctor has to approve your release."

"I can't wait to get out of here," I said. "Don't tell Elsie, but the food is terrible."

Jack brushed strands of hair off my cheek. "You'll have to take it easy, you know. All this looking after everybody else needs to be put on hold for a while."

"I'll be good, I promise."

"You should keep Brandi company," Jack said. "You two can watch movies all day."

"That's a great idea," Garth said.

"We'll see." There was no way I was going to stay down for long. I had things to do.

"I'll leave you two kids alone for a few," Jack said. "I need a cup of coffee. You want anything?"

"No, thanks," Garth said.

"Elsie probably won't let me have coffee," I said.

After Jack left, Garth perched on the side of the bed while balancing with one arm on his crutch. His gaze moved to the IV in my arm. I glanced down at the purple bruise around the needle entry. "It doesn't hurt."

"Looks like it," Garth said.

"Bruises on fair skin look worse than they really are."

He leaned closer and brushed my cheek with his knuckles. "You scared the hell out of me. For the first time, I understood what you must've felt the night of my accident. When you didn't show up after texting me, I totally panicked. It was awful. That feeling of helplessness. Then I had to send my dad out there to find you, hoping I was just overly worried. Instead, my worst fears came true. I never saw it from your perspective. I didn't think about how scared you must've been. I'm sorry for not *trying* to understand better."

"This fear of losing people I love was here before your accident."

"Yes, but I brought it all back to the surface," he said. "I didn't understand until last night how it felt to be the one left worrying about the fate of the person I love. It about killed me waiting to hear from him after sending my dad out there. I wanted to go myself. To rescue you. But I couldn't. All of which made me understand for the first time exactly how you feel. I get it now. When my leg heals, I won't be going back to skiing. I don't want you to ever feel the way I did last night. That awful, helpless dark place where I bargained with God to let you live."

I stared at him in shock. Give up skiing for me? "No way." Skiing made him alive. That's what I'd learned after all this. There was no reason to be on the earth if you denied yourself all the pleasures that life had to offer. Even the risky ones.

"I love to ski, but I love you more." His mouth set in a firm line. "I never want you to feel like I felt last night ever again."

"No, you're not giving up skiing. If you do, then you're basically giving up the idea of living fully. Last night when I thought

I might not come back to the world, I wanted nothing more than to have one more chance. Living with all these boundaries and rules is not the answer. We're not safe. Not ever. Anything could happen to us at any time. We can't deny ourselves what we really need or want just because we're afraid tragedy is around the corner. I'm still afraid to lose you. That will never change, because I lost someone I loved so much. I know exactly how awful the other side of love can be. I'm always going to be worried the phone will ring with the darkest news of all. Even so, I have to let myself have hope that I won't ever get another call like that. Do you understand? We have to ski. Or whatever it is we're passionate about."

"I do understand. But do you understand that I'd do anything for you?"

"Yes, I do. You will ski again. In fact, you can teach me. Bunny slopes only. In fact, I might never leave the bunny slopes."

"If that's where you want to be, then I'll be there too." Garth kissed my mouth gently, careful to avoid touching the rest of me. "I'd stay on the bunny slopes with you for the rest of my life if that's what you want."

"When I was unconscious, I had a dream about Patrick. Like you had with Christopher."

"You did?" I couldn't quite read his expression. If I had to guess? Threatened. Which was the opposite of what I wanted.

The dream had changed me. I knew now without any doubt that Garth was my path. Patrick had known that I needed him to tell me it was all right to let go of him. "I don't know if it was a dream—" I couldn't bring myself to say the words.

"Or the in-between place?" Garth asked.

"Right. Does that sound insane?"

"Not to me. Not after what happened with my brother."

"It seemed so real. He was wearing the ski outfit he had on the morning he died."

"What did he say to you?"

What a loaded question. But I had to answer. How could I describe to him exactly what had transpired? "He set me free."

"Oh." He looked toward the window. The light streaming in through the window made his eyes the color of cinnamon tea.

"What is it?" I wrapped my hand around his wrist. His face was newly shaven, revealing his silky skin. I ached with love. This man had become my world. My second chance at happiness.

He turned back to look me. "I don't know what that means. Did you have to have his permission?"

"No, not exactly that. I needed to feel as if it's all right to love again. Why does that hurt you?"

"I want you to love me so much that everything else falls away. Including your late husband. I know, I sound awful—petty and jealous—over someone who isn't even here."

"No, you don't. I understand what you mean."

"Do you really? Because it's important to me that you truly get what I'm saying. I'm helplessly in love with you. That you need permission from him makes me feel small. Insignificant."

"I don't want you to feel that way." I touched his face. "I'm helplessly in love with you too. I don't know why I've felt guilty, but I have. Like I was still bound to him."

"And now you don't?"

"I'm ready to move on. I woke up grateful be alive and wanted nothing but to see you. To have you by my side each and every day."

"That's all I want." Garth brought my hand to his mouth and kissed each finger. "I want you to be my wife. No one else will do. Will you marry me?"

My tears blurred his face, making him appear as a beautiful watercolor. "Yes, I'll marry you."

He kissed me again and then again. "I'll do my best not to die on you."

"I'd appreciate that," I said. "And I'll do the same." I stared up into his warm brown eyes. "How did this happen? How could I love you this much?"

"I don't know. All I know is that you've made me the happiest I've ever been." Tears slipped from the corners of his eyes.

I caressed his wet cheek. "Me too." For the first time, guilt didn't disguise the truth. Garth was here, living and breathing and loving me. I loved him in a way unique to the two of us. "We're an us," I said out loud.

Garth's face lit up, shining so brightly I could not see anything but him. "We are."

Nothing would ever take away the memories I'd made with Patrick. Now I would make new ones with Garth.

I had an image of the bald eagle soaring overhead. Like me, soaring to new heights.

"The strangest thing happened. My mom slept in my dad's room last night," Garth said as he adjusted the hospital blanket over me.

"No way."

"Yes. I left the two of them in the living room when I went to bed. Dad said they were only catching up as old friends, but I don't know. Is it possible that my brother was right?" His thumb caressed the back of my hand. "I've already gone down a dangerous path in my mind. Sunday dinners and that kind of thing."

"Wouldn't that be nice? But you're right to be cautious." Still, I had hope. The loneliness that had shrouded Garth's mother when I first met her had dissipated during the week we all spent together. Had old wounds been healed right before our eyes?

"I used to pray so hard when I was a kid she would come back," Garth said.

"I know about that kind of prayer." I'd done the same,

wishing for my father to magically appear. Had God finally answered our prayers?

Jack showed up in the doorway. "Are you up for another visitor?"

"Sure." My mother followed him into the room. "Hi, Mom."

Mom rushed to my bed. "Oh, honey, look at you." She placed cool fingertips on my arm. "How are you?"

"I'm a little banged up, but I'm the best I've been in a long, long time." I reached for Garth's hand. "We're both good."

Mom looked from one of us to the other. "I'm glad to hear that."

Jack beamed. "Happy for you kids."

"Where's Brian?" I asked my mother.

Mom gestured toward the hallway. "He and Sam are in the lobby. They wouldn't let all of us come in."

"I hope you won't get in trouble. Nurse Elsie said only two at a time," I said. "I'm not sure why it matters."

"I sneaked your mom in like contraband," Jack said. "Hopefully, Nurse Elsie won't bust me."

"You're brave to risk it," I said. "She already scolded me that I didn't eat my breakfast. Plus, she said she doesn't trust a skinny chef."

"What a thing to say." Jack brows knit together as he rocked back on his heels.

"Especially to someone in a hospital bed. She was always skin and bones no matter how much I fed her," Mom said to Jack apologetically.

"She looks just right to me, Jennie," Jack said. "You obviously did a great job."

Jennie? I'd never heard anyone call her that before.

"I haven't been called that since the spring we graduated from high school," Mom said.

"I was the only one allowed to call her that," Jack said to me. "She hated it."

"Not when you said it." The way Mom looked at Jack made

my stomach drop. For them, there was no second chance. Not after a thirty-year betrayal. But the way he smiled back at her had me questioning my own reasoning. Could the mountain air do the trick on them too?

I wanted so badly for my mother to be happy. All the missing pieces about her had come together since I learned the truth about Jack. She'd never found anyone who compared to him. Even after he broke her heart, she still loved him.

"I need to scurry off to check on Brandi," Jack said. "Trapper's out all day and asked if I'd feed her some lunch."

"That's supposed to be my job," I said.

"You'll get back to it soon enough," Garth said.

"Will you come back to see me?" I asked, unable to keep the yearning out of my voice.

"I'll be back this afternoon. From now on, I'll always come back," Jack said as he leaned over to give me another kiss on the top of the head. There was something about that gesture that made me feel like a little girl.

It occurred to me just then that tomorrow was Thanksgiving. "Oh my gosh, we have to get me out of here before tomorrow. I can't be in here for Thanksgiving. It's my favorite holiday of the year."

Garth's brow furrowed before he answered. "How about if we save Thanksgiving until you get out of here?"

"But I won't be able to cook," I said.

"You can supervise," Mom said.

Jack nodded. "We'll prop you up in a comfy chair and you can call out instructions."

Wait? Did this mean that Jack was joining us for Thanksgiving dinner?

As if I'd asked the question out loud, Jack answered, "Brandi has asked that we all go to their house for Thanksgiving. She doesn't want to miss out on the fun but promised to stay on the couch as long as she can come downstairs."

"All of us?" Mom asked softly.

Jack looked over at her and gave her a gentle smile. "The *whole* family. That's the way we're going to do it from now on."

My mother burst into tears. "Oh, Jack, thank you."

"The gratitude goes both ways, Jennie. You didn't have to share your girl with me. I don't know that I deserve it, but I'm grateful."

"I think we've all talked about who deserves what way too much," I said. It was true. Garth's mom. My mom. Jack. All of them certain that redemption could not be theirs. "Let's simply be thankful for what's happening right at this moment and stop apologizing for the past."

"I'm in," Jack said.

"Me too," Mom said.

The small muscles in Garth's face twitched as if he were trying not to cry. But me? All I could do was grin.

23

GARTH

My mother and father arrived together at my house two days before Christmas. They hadn't said much about what was happening between them, other than my dad had been "staying" in Bozeman since they'd left Emerson Pass a week after Thanksgiving. I'd asked him a few times about what was going on between them, and he said they were happily dating and having fun together.

Thus, it was a great surprise when at breakfast on the morning of the twenty-third, my dad popped a bottle of champagne. Crystal and Mom were already seated at the dining room table. Crystal had made waffles and bacon and now that my cast was removed, I could help her. I'd never been so happy to say goodbye to anything in my life. I was now in the process of rehabilitation and growing stronger by the day.

I'd told my dad the night before that I planned on officially proposing to Crystal on Christmas Eve with a ring. Trapper had asked if we could come to their house so that Brandi could join in the fun. It would be a merry crew of Trapper, Brandi, Jack, Jennie, Dad, Mom, and of course Crystal and me. I planned to surprise her with the ring.

"I have something to toast," Dad said as he poured us each a glass.

I brought the ladies their glasses and sat next to Crystal. My mother and father were on either end of the table. Dad stood and held up his glass. "Your mother and I have an announcement."

I looked over at Mom. She was beaming, her eyes fixed on my father.

"Sam, do you want to tell them what we've done?"

"No, you do it," Mom said.

"Your mother and I got married last weekend in Vegas."

My mouth dropped open. "You got married?"

"Eloped," Mom said gleefully. "We already had one wedding. We didn't need another one."

"But aren't you still married to wife four?" I asked.

"Not as of last Friday. We got married on Saturday." Dad smacked the table. "We couldn't get to that chapel fast enough."

"But how could this happen?" I blinked rapidly, hoping this wasn't a dream. "I mean, after all this time apart?"

"When we were here together last month, we started talking and talking," Dad said. "And we figured out we wanted to keep talking."

"Your dad came to Bozeman and basically never left." Mom smiled at my father. "That's how our courtship was back in the day. A whirlwind. Your father doesn't hesitate when it's something he wants."

"I missed her for twenty years. When fate brought us back together, I seized the chance to see if I could win her back."

I didn't know what to think. Married. My parents were officially back together. Christopher had been right. My accident had caused all this to happen.

"Congratulations," Crystal said. "I'm happy for you both. Will you stay in Bozeman?"

"I'm taking Sam to all the places we wanted to go when we were young and didn't have the money," Dad said. "But we're going to buy a home here. Your mother quit her job. She's officially retired. I quit all the boards I'm on and am ready to enjoy the rest of our time here to the fullest."

"That's wonderful," Crystal said.

At the same time, I said, "Dad, here in Emerson Pass? Really?" I couldn't believe my ears.

"We don't want to miss anything," Mom said. "You're our children, and we want to be near you."

"Maybe there will be grandchildren, for example," Dad said. "We'd hate to miss a moment with them."

"God willing," Crystal said as she glanced upward.

"Here's to you two," I said, finally recovering enough to speak coherently. I lifted my glass and we all toasted.

Then we dug into Crystal's delicious breakfast as my dad and mom told us about all the places they wanted to visit. *What a turn of events*, I thought, as I helped myself to several pieces of bacon. All because of an icy road. One just never knows what is around the corner. Life could change for better or worse in an instant. What was there to do about it, really? As Crystal and I had learned and accepted, all we have is the moment. We'd vowed to make the most of each one with the people we love without worrying about the future. In the end, I understood better than I ever had that when love arrives, open to it without fear. The unknown will always have the power to frighten us. We must go out into the storm anyway.

On Christmas Eve, we all gathered at Trapper's house. Before dinner, I asked Jennie and Jack to accompany me outside. The three of us bundled up and went out to the firepit. Trapper had turned it on for me, knowing I wanted to tell Jack and Jennie that I was proposing to Crystal tonight. I didn't need their permission. Crystal and I were grown-ups, and both married before. However, I wanted to start out on a respectful note with my in-laws.

"What's up?" Jack asked.

"I have a feeling." Jennie's eyes sparkled.

"At dinner, I'm going to propose to Crystal," I said. "I wanted to let you know before I did it. I'm hoping neither of you have any objections?"

"Even if I did, which I don't, I wouldn't get in your way," Jennie said. "My daughter has never been as happy as she is here with you."

"What about with Patrick?" I had to ask. Would I ever stop being jealous of a ghost?

"They had a deep love," Jennie said. "But they weren't equals like you two are. Plus, there's a way she looks at you with so much love and respect. I've never seen that particular look in my girl's eyes before. Don't spend any more energy worrying about whether she loves you as much or if you're as good for her as he was. You are. Just as you are."

"I don't know what it was like between her and Patrick," Jack said. "Frankly, it doesn't matter. You're here. Crystal's here. And you two make a great team. You're obviously best friends as well as being passionately in love. A man can't ask for more. It's time to let go of that chip on your shoulder."

"The guy was a billionaire," I said. "And a genius. I'm so ordinary."

"Each of us has something special to offer the world," Jack said. "What you have is just as good as the next guy."

"I've always been second place," I said. "Or I felt that way, regardless if it were true."

"Not this time," Jennie said. "You won her reluctant heart. No small feat."

"You're good to her and for her," Jack said.

"You brought her out of a bad place." Jennie glanced up at Jack before returning to me. "Bit by bit, you thawed her out and breathed life into her."

Jack nodded as he squeezed my shoulder. "I agree. Whatever's in your wallet has no relevance here. Your character is what counts. You're a good person who, as far as I can tell, always puts my daughter first. I'll be proud to call you son."

My throat ached from the myriad of emotions that his words gave me. "I can promise both of you that I'll do my very best every single day to show up for her."

"That's all we ask," Jack said.

I hadn't realized I actually did need their approval. "Thank you. Both of you. I wish I didn't think about all this and if I'm good enough, but I do."

"No one can blame you," Jack said. "Heck, I feel that way about the guy too. I mean, what does she need me for?"

"What's in your wallet has no relevance," I said, repeating back the words of encouragement he'd just given me. "You're everything she wanted and needed."

"Thanks, bud," Jack said. "Welcome to the family." We shook hands.

"Come here," Jennie said as she held out her arms. "Give me a hug."

I did so. "I know you'll take good care of my girl's tender heart," Jennie said. "That's all I care about."

Crystal showed up at the French doors and beckoned for her mother. "What's going on out here? Are you guys having a family meeting without me?"

Jack laughed. "You could say that."

"I'll expect a full report later," Crystal said, laughing. "Dinner's almost ready. Mom, would you come in and light the candles?"

"You got it," Jennie said.

After she left, I glanced over at Jack. He'd gone quiet. His hands were inside his jacket pockets as he gazed down at the fire. The slump of his shoulders troubled me.

"Anything I can do?" I asked.

He raised his eyes to meet mine; the sadness in his eyes confirmed what I'd thought.

"You know that way Crystal looks at you?" Jack asked.

"Jennie used to look at me that way. Until I broke her heart. Don't ever break my baby girl's heart."

"I won't. I can promise you that."

He smiled. "You know what? This time I'll be there to walk her down the aisle. Thanks for giving me that opportunity."

We were silent for a few minutes, watching the fire. A few lazy snowflakes tumbled from the white sky. Was it possible that Jack's feelings for Jennie had been resurrected? "Jack, if there's anything still left in your heart for Jennie, you should tell her."

"I'm not sure there's any hope that either one of us can let go of the past. We've agreed to be friendly for Crystal's sake, which is our priority. There's a lot of damage there between us. My fault, all of it. But I'd be lying if I said I didn't have a giant hole in my heart. We were like you and Crystal back then. Made for each other."

I didn't say anything further. Sometimes, things are obvious to the observer before they are to the observed. The story of Jack and Jennie wasn't finished. My parents had come back together because the foundation of love was still there even though they'd made mistakes. Forgiveness of each other and of themselves had come at last. Miracles could happen. I'd witnessed more than one over the last few months. They needed a little time and a little help from God, but they'd find their way back together.

"Come on inside, kid," Jack said. "Let's go help your bride."

"Yes sir." As we reached the glass doors, I tugged on the sleeve of his jacket. "Miracles happen. Don't give up the faith that one could come your way."

Jack gave me a sad smile. "I'll keep that in mind."

Later, we all gathered in Trapper's dining room. Jennie had decorated the table with fir boughs, silver lights, and white roses. The flickering flames of candles interspersed cast the room in a golden glow. A feast was displayed on the buffet, including a prime rib and Yorkshire pudding that Crystal had made using Lizzie's recipes. At Dad's request, my mom had brought a green bean casserole with crispy onions on top as we'd had for every holiday when I was a kid. In addition were a garden salad made colorful with cranberries, and ruby red lettuce salad and a sweet potato casserole.

Brandi, who had gotten permission from her doctor to come downstairs for dinner with us, sat at one end of the long wood table and Trapper at the other.

Jennie was seated across from Jack, looking elegant in a sparkly red dress. My mother had on dark blue velvet and a pearl necklace and had already taken her seat next to Jennie. They had their heads together chatting quietly. I had a feeling they were discussing how soon they would become grandmothers.

Brandi glowed in a black sheath that displayed her ever-growing baby bump. We were all grateful for the baby who remained nestled in her mother's womb where she belonged. She just needed to hang in there until the first spring wildflowers bloomed in the meadows.

I escorted a flushed Crystal to her seat. She'd worn an apron for most of the day over a green cashmere sweater and white jeans but had taken it off for dinner. Her hair was up in a twist, showing off her slender neck. I'd have rather nibbled there than have the prime rib, and I love a good slab of meat. My stomach fluttered when she looked up at me. "Merry Christmas," she said to me.

"Merry Christmas," I whispered in her ear. "I can't wait to take you home and get you under the mistletoe."

"I hope you hung it over the bed," she whispered back.

Having decided to stay at my house instead of rebuilding Crystal's, during the month of December we'd fully embraced the idea of nesting. Together, we'd made my house a home. As

Crystal had done to my heart, the furnishings and decor had softened all the hard edges.

It had occurred to us today that her property could very easily house two cottages. One for my parents and one for her mother. If they wanted, the land was available. We planned on putting the offer into their stockings tomorrow morning.

For the umpteenth time that night, I checked for the ring box in my inside jacket pocket. Still there. Trapper knew the plan. As soon as the champagne had been poured, I would fall onto one knee. We'd made sure Crystal was seated on a corner.

My dad and I filled everyone's glasses with champagne before taking our seats.

"Thank you all for being here and Merry Christmas," Trapper said. "Before we start to feast on Crystal's amazing dinner, Garth had a little something he wanted to say."

I stood as Trapper sat. I had a speech planned in my head and hoped nerves wouldn't derail me. "I wanted to thank everyone at this table for being insanely supportive in what seems on the surface to have been a hellish year. Strangely enough, that's not the case. The fire and all that followed brought me the most important thing, far more valuable than any object could bring—love. I have two new friends in Brandi and Trapper, when before we were only acquaintances."

Trapper gestured toward me with his glass and nodded. "Cheers, bud."

I turned to Brandi. "Thanks for letting me invade your home during a time that should have been a honeymoon phase for you and Trapper."

Brandi patted her belly. "I think that ship has sailed. Anyway, there's nothing to thank us for. We loved having you guys here."

"This is Emerson Pass," Trapper said. "No one is left out in the cold. Friends become like family. Our door is always open, should you need us again."

"As is mine," I said.

Next, I addressed my parents. "Mom and Dad, thank you for

coming to take care of me. I had no idea of what was to come, but I couldn't be happier."

My dad actually teared up, which made me almost do the same. I kept it together long enough to look over at Jennie. "Jennie, thank you for giving me the greatest gift of all. Bringing your daughter into the world." I glanced at Jack. "And thanks for making her so happy these last weeks."

I dropped to one knee in front of Crystal.

"Are you doing this now?" Crystal asked, looking somewhat horrified. Too late to back out now.

"I am."

She whipped around to look at her mother and then Brandi before returning to me.

"I would never have thought that losing my home would bring me the best thing that's ever happened to me. A scary night for both of us, but that was the beginning of us. The fire brought you into my life, and for that I will be forever grateful." I took the box from my jacket and lifted the lid. "Crystal, will you be my wife and make all my dreams come true?"

"Yes," she whispered.

With a shaking hand, I slipped the ring on her finger. It was a solitary diamond, not very big but all I could afford. If she wanted something else, she could pick it out later. Adjusting to the idea of her wealth was a work in progress. "Will you accept this ring and my promise to put together an ironclad prenup in case you decide to run off with the pool boy?"

Everyone laughed. "We have a pool boy?" Crystal asked as she brought the ring up to the light.

"Not yet," I said. "But someday we might."

"I'd recommend against that," Jack said. "Given the prenup."

Crystal sobered as she returned her gaze to me. "It's me who is grateful to you. You saved my life that night and you breathed life into me in the months that followed. Every day I think I can't love you more, but I do. I look forward to a long life together."

Only I knew how loaded that statement was. She was betting

on a long life with me even though she understood more than most how quickly that dream could be snatched away.

"Kiss her," Brandi said.

"Yes, kiss the girl," Jennie said.

I did so, lingering to take in the taste and scent of her. Then I rose to my feet to take my seat next to her, where I belonged.

"Shall we eat?" Dad asked. "I'm starved and can't wait for some of that green bean casserole."

My mother rolled her eyes. "It's embarrassing next to Crystal's gourmet meal."

"But I love this stuff," Dad said.

"So do I," Jack said. "My mom always made it too. Just looking at it makes me think of her and all the happy times we had together around a table such as this."

"That's sweet, Jack," Jennie said.

For the next thirty minutes, we all shared favorite Christmas memories and favorite holiday traditions. My mother was quiet for the most part until Jennie asked her if she had a favorite memory.

"It's of my boys on Christmas morning when they were five and seven," Mom said. "I'd never understood the meaning of the line 'sugarplums danced in their heads' until that time in my life. They came tearing down the stairs that morning and the looks on their faces when they saw what Santa had brought."

"Big Wheels," Dad said softly. "Do you remember, Garth?"

I nodded, recalling the way we had torn around the cement patio on those three-wheeled pieces of plastic day after day as if we were racing in the Indy 500. I ached for that time and my brother. Yet the memory gave me joy. "I always wanted to race. Christopher preferred to pretend he was out for a country drive."

"That seems like yesterday," Mom said in a trembling voice. "I used to keep one eye on you from the kitchen as I cooked or cleaned. If only I'd known then what I know now, I would have put the dishcloth down and gone outside to watch you boys. Soak it all in."

The rest of us had gone quite still, forgetting for a moment that we were supposed to lift our forks to our mouths or drink from our champagne glasses.

"Time is such a whisper, isn't it?" Jennie asked. "Gone by way of the wind."

"Yes," Mom said. "And no one knows that to be true more than a mother."

"Except maybe a father," Jack said.

Under the table, Crystal slipped her hand onto my lap. I covered it with mine.

"Here's to *this* moment." Brandi's eyes were glassy with unshed tears as she picked up her glass. "And making more memories together as a family."

"Here's to sisters and parents and children," Crystal said. "And babies yet to be born."

"To all who came before us," Brandi said. "May the memories of those we've loved and lost be always close to our hearts and minds. They are still here because we love them." She raised her glass. "To my little bird who I lost on the day of her birth."

"To Ava Elizabeth." Trapper's voice caught as he gazed back at his wife.

"To my Nan and Pop," Crystal said.

"To Christopher," Mom said. "My baby."

"To Christopher," my dad and I said at the same time.

"To Patrick," Jennie said. "May he rest in peace knowing how much good his fortune is doing in the world."

Crystal leaned her head against my shoulder. I squeezed her hand.

"To my mom and dad, Sunny and David." Jack smiled. "And to all of us sitting around this table, blessed to be reunited."

"To miracles," Dad said. "For bringing my family back together."

And then, in a miraculous fashion, each of us around that table echoed the exact same phrase. "To miracles."

"Everyone, eat." Trapper waved a fork at us. "We have presents to open."

I brought Crystal's hand to my mouth for a kiss. She leaned more heavily against my shoulder. A sense of great peace came to me. The years to come would unfold as they should. Trust and faith would guide us through good times and bad. Love, too. Always love.

The Pet Doctor, starring Breck and Tiffany is next! Will Breck ever get the courage to ask her out on a date or will the friends have to do a little matchmaking? Grab The Pet Doctor Here!

Keep reading to for bonus content! Letters from Lizzie and her daughter Florence from the historical series will give you a peek into the past. Enjoy!

THE LETTERS

A week after Christmas, I sat next to Brandi on her bed. I was still supposed to be taking it easy, but Brandi was bored out of her mind, so we'd compromised by spending the day together reading through the letters in Lizzie's hatbox. Brandi liked me to read them to her so she could close her eyes.

"Read the first one," Brandi said.

Dearest Florence,

It's hard to believe you've been gone for two weeks already. The summer flew by, didn't it? Here you are in your fourth year of college. I don't know how it is I have a young lady for a daughter.

I'm happy to hear you and the other girls have settled back into the boardinghouse. Mrs. Reed sounds like a true terror. As much as you might not like her, I'm glad she's such a stickler for the rules. That's just what you girls need to keep you out of trouble. I'm sure Sally was mortified to get locked out, but good for Mrs. Reed for keeping to the rules. Your father approved. He did not approve of you and Gwen rescuing her by lowering a sheet out the window. I'm going to have to edit out certain passages from your letters or I fear his heart won't take it. Letting you go to university was a big leap for him.

Your father and I miss you very much. However, hearing about your adventures and your studies makes us both smile. We are so proud that you were able to go to college. Where we came from, someone of our class would never have been able to do so. No matter how smart you were. Your father would have enjoyed school. I, on the other hand, prefer to do things with my hands.

With all of you children off to your own lives, Quinn, Merry, and I have been busy with what we hope are good deeds for the community. The dance we put on at the community center was very successful. We were able to raise a lot of funds for the new school. It's hard to believe how quickly Emerson Pass has grown in the last five years. Sometimes I don't like it. However, this is what Lord Barnes has wanted and worked for all these years. A thriving community!

I should probably close. I have dinner yet to make for Quinn and Alexander. They are throwing a small dinner party tonight for the newly elected mayor and his wife. He's a little slick for my taste. A wee bit full of himself, as my mother used to say.

Anyway, my darling girl, I miss you terribly but I'm so very, very proud of you. Write when you can. Stay out of trouble.

Much love,

Mum

Dear Mum,

Thank you much for your latest letter with all the news from home. I look forward to getting one in the post every Friday. I'm still home-sick, but your newsy letters make me feel like I'm home. Please tell all the others hello from me and that I'm counting the days until Christmas.

I've met someone, Mum! He's utterly charming and very hand-some. Dark brown hair that curls slightly around his ears. Which he hates. Isn't that funny? His eyes are dark brown, almost black. He has the most terribly long eyelashes. I met him at the football game. He was sitting right below us and kept turning around pretending like he was looking for someone. I knew it was really to catch glimpses of me. He's from Maine and studying to be a doctor. He says he's always wanted to visit Colorado. I told him if he's patient he might get an invitation.

He's called Robert Vargas and I'm completely smitten. Enough to actually contemplate introducing him to Father. Or maybe not. Thinking of that day makes me cringe. I can't imagine what Father will say to him, other than to threaten him slightly. Father's so very English still, and worried about rules. (Don't show Father this part of the letter.)

Sally and Gwen both approve even though he's from a poor family. He's at college because a rich man named Wesley Ford sent him to university. It's a long story but I'll try and summarize. When Robert was only a baby, his father died. All alone with an infant, his mother found a group home in Castaway Maine that helped widows or unwed mothers to find work and a new life. Mr. Ford and his wife Luci run this home. Without them and their organization, who knows what might have happened to them? When Robert's mother died a few years back, this same Mr. Ford paid for Robert to attend school. He's studying to be a doctor and wants to help people like Mr. Ford helped him.

He works at the soda and coffee shop across from school to help with his rent and food. The girls and I have started studying there in the afternoons. It's the kind of place where all the kids come and go all day long. The owner won't let us stay unless we order something. Sally and Gwen always order a coffee. I keep to my afternoon tea like at home.

There are more and more people in line at the soup kitchens. I feel so terribly sorry for the men. They're downtrodden and hopeless. I can see it in the slump of their shoulders. Every night I pray that President Roosevelt will lead us out of this soon.

Must run. Meeting Robert at the library this afternoon. He likes to study there because it's quiet. He says he can't understand how the girls and I can study at the soda shop.

I'm all about Robert, aren't I?

Love,

Florence

Dear Mum,

I can hardly wait to see you and Father and all the rest of them.

Robert's nervous to meet Father, of course, but determined that he ask for my hand in person.

Robert's been offered a job in the small town of Castaway, Maine, working at the facility for unwed mothers where his own mother went when she was pregnant with him. Can you believe such a thing could happen? They need a doctor to deliver the babies. A doctor who won't snatch the child away unless the mother wants to put them up for adoption. A couple called Wesley and Luci Ford run the operation, along with some other helpers. If you recall, Phillip was Robert's benefactor. Anyway, they offer rooms to any young woman in trouble and while they're waiting for the babies to come, they're trained for different jobs, including seamstress, cook, teachers, even nurses. It's not exactly what I thought of when Robert said he wanted to be a small-town doctor. I thought he'd be like Theo, but it's admirable that he wants to help women who have such similarities to his own mother.

There's one thing I haven't told you about Robert. He's of Italian descent. His mother and father came from Italy to Ellis Island before he was born. My dearest hope is that you and Father will welcome him even though he might not be what you imagined for me. I know you had your heart set on me marrying a local boy, but this man is the one I want.

Love,

Florence

Dearest Florence,

I've never missed you as much as I do now. It was such a wonderful time, having you and Robert here. I hope it didn't feel too rushed, having the wedding in such a spontaneous fashion. However, as you said, with Robert's mother no longer alive, there was really no reason to wait after your father gave Robert his permission. I was secretly hoping Robert would fall in love with Emerson Pass and decide to stay here. Theo was quite serious about offering him a job. He told me to tell you once again that any time you want to move back here, the job offer is open to Robert.

You looked absolutely stunning on your wedding day. How serendipitous it was that Annabelle had a bride cancel at the last minute, leaving a dress almost perfectly sized to you. I suppose God had a hand in all of it.

You'll all be getting married one after another now. I only have to close my eyes to conjure the long days of summer when you were all small and playing in the water. Merry and Harley's Henry has his eye on a young lady in town called Lillian. She's taken a spot teaching the younger grades and comes from somewhere back east. With Jack in the army, who knows when he'll come back to us. It seems all of you have grown up so fast.

The only things that stay the same are the love between us all. Quinn and Lord Barnes are as smitten as they ever were. I suppose the same is true for your father and me, though you'd never know to look at us. It appears that English training will never leave him. I don't mind, and I hope you don't think his lack of demonstrative showing of affection means he doesn't love you. He's just the stiff upper lip and all that.

I'll count the moments until you come visit again. Your father said Robert hinted about bringing you back to Emerson Pass when the time is right. Robert wants to pay Phillip back for all he's done for him first. I can't blame him for that.

Dear Mum,

Thank you for sending the extra money. I hate to admit it but we needed a few items to set up a proper house. We're renting a cottage with walls so thin I can hear the waves crashing on the shore. It seems I can never get warm no matter how much I stoke the fire.

Robert is settling in at work with Wesley Ford. He likes it very much and says looking after the pregnant women and delivering their babies suits him just fine. We had a long talk the other night about coming home. He knows how homesick I am. But it's not time yet. He's promised me that after a baby or two come we'll head home. Until then, he feels he owes Mr. Ford.

I've learned since coming here that Robert's mother was pregnant with him when she lost her husband. She found her way to Castaway and was taken in by the staff. She had him and was apprenticed to a baker in town. Robert has no memory of this, obviously, as he was an infant. *They moved to a town farther south where she worked at a bakery shop until her death when Robert was sixteen. Phillip's wife Luci told me the story. She keeps track of all the infants born under the care of the Castaway Home.*

Luci asked if I'd like to work with her at the home. She says I have a gift with people and that she'd like me to help train the girls who would like to find domestic positions like cooks, maids, and housekeepers. I guess I do know a bit about those positions. Poor Father. I know he would hate the lack of formality in our training. I'm afraid I'm an American, quite sure that everyone should be counted as important as the next despite being poor.

The longer I'm here, the more impressed I am by the work they're doing. How many women have they saved? I can't count that high. Phillip's mother's plight was the impetus for the entire organization. She passed just a few years before we arrived. I'd have liked to hear her tell her story of being an unwed mother and having her children taken from her against her will. At least there was a happy ending. But that's a story for another day.

I love you, Mum, and miss you terribly. Kisses until we meet again. Florence

Dear Mum,

I'm writing to you as I'm grinning like a child in a candy shop. Robert and I are expecting! I didn't imagine it would happen this soon in our marriage. We're both delighted, of course, but nervous too. Were you that way? All I do is daydream these days and wander about the house in a daze, so happy but forgetful.

Robert is hoping for a son. I secretly want a daughter. Either way will be fine, of course. I only hope that he or she will be healthy. Robert says it's absolutely heart-wrenching when they lose a baby. It's the only time he's regretted being a doctor. I won't even allow myself to think of such a tragedy.

I do hope you'll be able to come and stay when the baby is born. I know Maine is far away, but maybe you and Father could take the train here and then stay for a few weeks. Surely Lord Barnes would allow

you a month off? I long for home but Robert's work is of such impor-
tance here in Castaway. No one else will deliver these poor women's
children. I've been working closely with Luci to get the mothers and
babies off to the right start. Just this week I'm working with a young
woman name Maddie. I'm training her to be a cook, using all your old
recipes that I know like I know the back of my hand. After she's ready,
we'll find her a job in a house like the one Lord Barnes provided for us.

I've gotten letters from several of the girls we've helped. One
apprenticed under a tailor here in town and by the grace of God, they've
fallen in love. He's adopted her child and they're all very happy.

I've already written Quinn to thank her for the paints. I've been
using them like mad trying to capture the sea in all its varying shades
of gray and blue. Phillip and Luci gave me an easel for a birthday gift.
You can imagine me standing on the cliff with my hair blowing about
as I paint. Robert says he could watch me out there all day, but who has
time for that when your Castaway's only baby doctor?

I love you, Mum, and miss you bunches.

Florence

Dearest Mum,

It's with a heavy heart that I write to tell you I lost the baby. It was
too early to know the gender. I simply started to bleed. Poor Robert had
to rush me to the office where he delivers all the babies. At only sixteen
weeks along, there was no chance of a baby surviving. There was
nothing for me to see or hold. Robert said it was best I didn't see.

What he doesn't know is that I'd already imagined my son or
daughter a thousand times in my mind. I wish I could come home. I'd
just like to see my mummy.

Love,

Florence

Dearest Florence,

My heart is breaking for you. I've never talked about it much, but I
lost a baby when you were around three. I know how hard it is and
wish I were with you to put my arms around you and hold you close.

There's no greater sorrow than losing a child. Even our husbands, as much as they love us, can't know what it was like to have a baby inside you and how you fall in love the moment you know you're expecting. After I lost the baby (he was a boy born too early) I felt like I wanted to die with him. However, you were there, needing me, and I couldn't lie around sobbing forever.

Now you're all grown and yet you need me. I can't be there with you and I hate it. I'm sorry, darling girl. Perhaps it's time that Robert does what you need and brings you home for good?

Come home, darling. We're all here for you.

Love,

Mum

Dearest Mum,

I have much news. I'm pregnant! This time I've gotten past the eighteen-week mark and Robert thinks it's safe to plan for a baby. He knows how much I want to move back to Emerson Pass, and he's given his notice to Phillip.

Luci and Phillip understood perfectly that we needed to come home and be with our family, especially since a baby's coming. I've learned so much since being here. Practicing kindness and compassion even during my own periods of sadness have made me stronger. I suppose giving to others is really the only way to heal ourselves. Haven't you and Quinn taught me that all my life?

We're aiming to be home by Christmas. We'll have to stay with you and Father for a few months until we get our living arrangements sorted. Quinn wrote that we're welcome to build on their property whenever we chose to come home. She wasn't very good at hiding how much she wanted me home for your sake. Offering up property was a last-ditch effort, I suppose?

We've also corresponded with Theo, and he's only too happy to have Phillip come into the practice as a partner. He said Emerson Pass is growing so fast he can't keep up with all the babies. I'm excited to come home and be the town doctor's wife. I've grown pretty good at nursing, *having assisted Robert these last few years. I don't know if I'll have time once the baby comes, but we'll have to see.*

Regardless, it doesn't matter how we get there or where we live, I'm coming home where I belong.

Love,

Florence

Note from Tess - if you'd like to read the first novel in my Castaway Christmas Series and learn about Wesley and Luci Ford and how they came to Castaway, Maine download COME TOMORROW.

For more Emerson Pass, download the historical books in the series. Travel back in time to meet the original residents of Emerson Pass, starring the Barnes family.
The School Mistress
The Spinster

The first of the Emerson Pass Contemporaries, The Sugar Queen, starring the descendants of the Barnes family is available at your favorite retailer. Book three of the contemporaries The Pet Doctor is on pre-order for a release date of February 15, 2022.

THE RECIPES

Dear readers!

I asked for family recipes and you sent them. Thank you so much. This was way too much fun for my assistant and me. We enjoyed reading each of them, smiling as we read between the lines that so clearly conveyed the love the memories and recipes evoked from the sender. Although they weren't all appropriate for the time period that Lizzie would have been cooking, we decided to include them all!

I hope you enjoy them as much as we did. Be sure to email me at tess@tthompsonwrites.com if you cook any of the recipes and I'll include your note and photos in my newsletter.

Love,

Tess

Swiss Macaroni & Cheese sent by Teresa (Tee) Jacober

My father's parents were both immigrants from Switzerland way back when. In fact, my Grandfather only met my Grandmother when he was getting ready to board the boat to bring him to America - she was working in a small family owned eatery when they met and fell in love. He promised he would send for her once he was settled in America and he did. Not sure of the whole story but they ended up in Bakersfield, although I know my Dad was born in Pasadena. In

Bakersfield they opened a restaurant in an area of town known as Edison called Joe's Place. Sadly, due to numerous moves by all family members over the years I no longer have photos - but I have seen them.

This is not a recipe from their restaurant, but because my Dad was Swiss, Swiss cheese was the only cheese he would eat and my mom made the following Mac and Cheese version for him, which everyone in our family loved!

I don't really have true amounts so I am guessing but the ingredients are simple and to taste. These days I don't eat meat or dairy any longer, however typing this out makes me want to make and gorge on this just for old times' sake.

Swiss Macaroni and Cheese

1 Large Onion, Sliced into thin slices and separated

1 stick real Butter

1 lb elbow Macaroni

1 lb Swiss Cheese, grated.

Melt butter in a skillet and sauté the onions until golden and soft and silky.

Meanwhile cook the macaroni until al dente and drain. Immediately put Macaroni back in the pan and dump the grated cheese onto the hot pasta and stir until the cheese is melted and gooey and coating the macaroni. Once all combined, pour the butter and onions all over and mix again and serve.

Mom always served with Sourdough bread and butter as well as applesauce on the side. Enjoy!

Vanilla Crescent Cookies by Carol Corbin

Every Fall my mom would start baking dozens and dozens of cookies for the holiday season. All the favorites had chocolate in them. My mom would make this recipe specifically for me because I couldn't have very much sugar because of a blood sugar problem. Nor could I have chocolate because it gave me migraines instantly. This all started when I was only 13. Mom continued to do this every year until she passed five years ago when I was 61. Mom made special cookies for me for a whole lot of years.

Here is the very simple recipe:

2 cups Flour
    1/2 lb Butter
    1/2 lb ground pecans
    1/2 cup sugar

Cream butter & sugar, stir in flour, then stir in pecans.

Roll into little balls, smaller than a walnut, and bake at 350° until light brown. Approximately 12 minutes.

When cool, roll in 1/2 cup of powdered sugar.

Joe Frogger's Cookies by Christina Boyd

My father-in-law in Maine always made these Joe Frogger's Cookies at Christmas. When he died no one made them that first year. So I made them the next year and made sure to make enough to send to my mother-in-law. Usually I forget the rum because we often don't have it in the house when I start to make these. I guess that's my tradition.

Ingredients:
4 cups flour
2 tsp ginger
1/2 tsp cloves and nutmeg
1/4 tsp all spice
1 1/2 tsp salt
1 cup molasses
1 tsp baking soda
1/2 cup butter
1 cup sugar
2 Tbs rum
6 Tbs water
Stir molasses & soda together and set aside to foam.

Cream butter and sugar.

Mix flour and spices.

Add rum and water to molasses mixture, then combine all ingredients.

Cover. Refrigerate overnight.

Roll out 1/4" thick, cut into 3" rounds.

Bake on well-greased and floured pans are 350 for 10-15 minutes.

Cool before removing from pan.

Makes 3 dozen.

Baked Raisin Pudding by Lisa Sanetra

This dessert recipe was a great favorite of my late mother. We spent a lot of time in the kitchen together and to this day I think of her whenever I cook or bake.

Another enthusiastic participant in our kitchen adventures was our collie mix "Copper" who was always around looking for handouts.

1/2 cup brown sugar
   2 cups boiling water
   2 tablespoons butter
   1 cup flour (unsifted)
   1/2 cup white sugar
   1/2 teaspoon salt
   2 teaspoons baking powder
   1 cup raisins
   1/2 cup whole milk
   1 teaspoon vanilla
   Directions:

Combine brown sugar, water, and butter in a saucepan. Boil for 5 minutes. Pour into a buttered 2-quart casserole dish.

In a separate bowl, combine flour, sugar, salt, baking powder, raisins, milk, and vanilla; blend thoroughly. Pour over the hot mixture in the casserole dish.

Bake raisin pudding for 25 to 30 minutes at 350 degrees.

Easter Deviled Eggs by Susan Hill
Tie-dye eggs

Place boiled eggs, with shell on, in a zip bag (Lizzie will have to improvise)

Put a few drops of food coloring in the bag. Shake up the eggs, allowing the shells to crack. When peeled, they look awesome! You can have the kids help, putting 2-3 eggs in each bag, each with a different color.

How Did She Do That eggs

Boil and remove shells

Make several bowls of strong food colored water, each a different color.

Cut and remove yolk, rinse off any yolk residue. Put whites in the colored water and let sit until it reaches the color you want. Pat dry and fill with your favorite yolk mixture. *Always a hit!*

Cabbage Noodles by Jane Heuker Ring
This is one of my favorite potluck dinner dishes and is Hungarian or German. It always disappears quickly!

1 cup of Cream of Wheat
    1 onion
    1 stick of butter or more as necessary
    Shredded cabbage
    Egg noodles
    Sour cream as garnish
    Hungarian paprika as garnish

Sauté the Cream of Wheat and the onion in a stick of butter in a deep skillet.

When lightly toasted, add shredded cabbage. Sauté the cabbage. If more butter or a tablespoon of water is needed, go for it!

The more the cabbage is cooked and browned, the sweeter the cabbage gets.

In a separate pan boil egg noodles. Drain the noodles and add to the buttered cabbage.

Serve a huge scoop with sour cream.

You can also sprinkle Hungarian paprika on the sour cream to add color and flavor.

Buttered Pasta by David Cox

My family recipe is one my sister mandated when she was a pre-teen. My mother was not the world's best cook, something she herself acknowledged later in her life by telling my sister and I she wasn't going to invite us over to dinner anymore since we were both much better cooks than she. She preferred coming to our houses! Mom's spaghetti sauce was not great, and my sister insisted that when we had spaghetti, she just wanted butter on her pasta. Just butter.

Pasta

Butter

Boil pasta per package instructions. When al dente top with butter to each person's liking.

Steak Soup / Stoup by Beth Morrissette

I now make this in my Instant Pot because I can sauté then slow cook in the same pot...less cleanup! Nowadays for convenience, I use a 10 oz bag of frozen peas and carrots, and canned green beans and fire-roasted tomatoes. Family loves this classic beef/steak soup for delicious, easy, and quick lunches...and we call it Stoup. (Hubby doesn't much care for leftovers, but loves stoup warmed in the microwave.)

Steak Soup / Stoup

    1 lb beef sirloin steak, cubed

    2 ribs celery, chopped

    1 white onion, chopped

    1 cup chopped carrots

    1 cup green peas

    1-1/2 cups green beans, topped and tailed, cut into 1-1/2" pieces

    1-1/2 cups fire-roasted tomatoes, chopped

    40 oz beef stock

    1 tbsp Worcestershire sauce

    1-1/2 tsp each salt and black pepper

    For roux: ¾ cup each butter and flour

In medium fry pan, sauté beef cubes then remove from pan.

In same pan, sauté celery and onion in beef drippings until onion is slightly translucent.

Put beef, celery, onions, any pan fond and drippings into a large stockpot; add rest of ingredients except butter and flour, cover and simmer on low for 8 hours, stirring occasionally.

In medium fry pan, make roux with butter and flour, cooking until light brown. Stir into soup. Turn heat to medium-high and simmer vigorously another hour. Serve.

Beef casserole by Mary Allen

This is one of the first things I learned to make and was so easy with no extra dishes. The macaroni is flavored by the meat and corn. No extra dishes to clean and you have a starch, a vegetable and protein. I remember eating this when I was growing up and also when I first went out on my own. It isn't pretty but it is delicious.

1 lb. fresh ground chuck (80/20) Use the day you buy it.

    3/4 cup dry elbow macaroni

    1 can Del Monte cream style corn (other brands don't have enough corn.)

Put all three ingredients in glass casserole dish and mix well. Salt and pepper to taste.

Bake at 350 for an hour.

Graham Cracker Ice Cream by Marilyn Scolari

Hello, not sure what you consider a secret recipe? So many old recipes are now considered not healthy, but darn it, they still taste good. Here's one that I remember with fondness. I'd like to say how many servings, but would have to admit to eating the whole thing...

1/2 cup sugar
1 pint heavy cream
1 cup graham cracker crumbs
1 tsp. Vanilla

Combine and freeze in tray (yeah, remember when "ice boxes" had those aluminum freezer trays?)

When partially frozen, place mixture in a bowl and beat to thoroughly combine.

Put back in tray and freeze until firm. (Of course you can use any similar container)

This will be a bit soft and melts quickly so eat up fast!

Brown Sugar Pecan Rounds by Phyllis Sharrow

This is a recipe for my Aunt's cookies that she always had for us .. in a gold tin container. What a treat!

From Zia (Victorine Granberg, our aunt)

½ cup butter or margarine softened (1 cube)
1 ¼ cup brown sugar (packed)
1 egg (slightly beaten)

Mix butter, brown sugar and egg. Stir in remaining ingredients.

1 ¼ cup Gold Medal flour
1/4 tsp baking soda

1/8 tsp salt

½ cup chopped pecans

1 tsp vanilla

Drop dough by teaspoons, 2″ apart. Use ungreased cookie sheet.

Bake 12-15 minutes in 350.

Brownie Cake by Phyllis Sharrow

This is a brownie cake from softball days for my daughter...it's brownie height poured in a cookie sheet and a family favorite.

Put in mixing bowl:

2 cups flour

2 cups sugar

Boil together:

½ cup oil

1 cube butter

4 T Cocoa

1 cup water

Pour over flour and sugar

ADD:

½ cup buttermilk

1 tbsp vanilla

2 eggs

1 tsp baking soda

Put in well-greased cookie sheet.

Bake 20 minutes at 350.

Frosting:

1 cube butter

6 T Milk

4 tsp cocoa

1 box powdered sugar (16 ounces)

Grandpa Sam's Potato Latkes (Pancakes) by Cynthia Spencer

Ingredients:

6-7 medium potatoes, peeled & shredded

1 medium onion, finely chopped

½ tsp baking powder

½ cup flour

1 tsp salt

¼ tsp freshly ground pepper

2 eggs, warmed to room temperature

5 tbsp vegetable oil for frying

Preheat oven to 275° to keep latkes warm after frying until time to serve. Place large baking sheet in the oven. Line a 2nd baking sheet with paper towels.

In large bowl, whisk together the eggs, flour, salt, baking powder and pepper.

Shred the potatoes and onion, then quickly add to the egg mixture (to avoid potatoes discoloring).

In a large skillet, heat ¼" oil over medium-high heat until sizzles. Drop ¼ cup mounds of the potato mixture into the skillet and flatten into 3" rounds with spatula.

Cook 2 minutes per side or until golden brown. Drain on paper towel-lined baking sheet, then transfer to oven to keep warm.

Repeat steps 3-4 until all the batter is cooked, stirring potato mixture before adding each batch to the skillet. Add more oil to skillet as needed between batches.

Serve warm with applesauce and sour cream.

Mediterranean Baked Cod by Cynthia Spencer

This recipe works well with any firm white fish (halibut, red snapper, cod, etc.). I used Costco's

Spanish olives that are stuffed with jalapeño & garlic, which added wonderful flavor. Original

recipe called for more peppers. I traded for green beans & mushrooms.

Serve with rice and crusty bread to soak up the sauce.

5 tbsp olive oil (divided)

2+ lbs skinless cod fillets (easiest if precut into portion size)

Salt & freshly ground black pepper

1 - 2 sweet peppers, cut into thin strips

12 oz fresh green beans, cut in half

24 pitted green Spanish olives, sliced

1 medium finely chopped onion

1/2 lb sliced brown mushrooms

1+ tbsp minced garlic

2 cups canned tomatoes: drained & chopped

1 tsp dried oregano (or Italian spices)

1or 2 bay leaves

2 tbsp fish sauce (or 1/2 cup fish broth)

Red pepper flakes

1/2 lb feta cheese, crumbled

1. Preheat oven to 450 degrees

2. Coat bottom of a large baking pan with 1 T of the olive oil. Arrange fish fillets in the

pan. Sprinkle with salt & pepper.

3. In a large fry pan, toast the mushrooms in 1 T olive oil, then drain off excess water and

set aside.

4. Heat remaining 3 T olive oil in the fry pan, add the garlic, onions and green beans.

Cook a few minutes then add peppers, tomatoes, mushrooms, fish sauce and

seasonings. Stir and cook for about five minutes.

5. Spoon the sauce over the fish. Sprinkle the feta cheese over the sauce and bake for

about 15 minutes.

Yield: 8 generous servings.

Grandma's Sweet Noodle Kugel by Cynthia Spencer

Traditional German/Polish/Jewish baked noodle pudding.

Ingredients:

8 oz wide egg noodles

4 tbsp butter, melted

1 cup cottage cheese

1 cup sour cream

4 oz cream cheese, softened

1/2 cup Sugar

6 eggs

1 tsp cinnamon

1 small apple, chopped

1/2 cup raisins

Directions:

1. Preheat oven to 375°

2. Boil the noodles in salted water for 4 min, strain.

3. In large mixing bowl, combine noodles with remaining ingredients. Stir well to mix.

4. Pour into a large, greased baking dish (9 x 13) and sprinkle top with cinnamon & sugar.

5. Bake until custard is set & top is golden brown, about 30-45 min. OR bake 1 – 1.5 hrs at 350°.

Options:

• Add 1 tsp orange or lemon zest (or fresh juice)

• Add 1/2 tsp vanilla

• Add 1/2 cup chopped pecans

All Day Turkey Chili by Shannon Stubbs

(*I put it on before I go to work, when I get home its done.*) My husband doesn't like the texture of cooked onion. I leave it whole and fish it out later when it's time to eat the chili. I eat it with Fritos on top.

That's the family favorite at our house other than tacos. Because tacos are America's comfort food. Especially at the Stubbs house.

1 lb of dried pinto beans

1 can of crushed tomatoes

Chicken broth

1 lb of ground turkey meat salted and browned

1 onion

2 garlic cloves

1 tsp of hot sauce

1 tbsp of cumin powder

1 tbsp of chili powder

Water

Throw all ingredients into a crock pot cook for 12 hours or so.

Pirog by Donna Kosorwich

We used to enjoy a dish made by my father's Russian sister-in-law. I had asked her for the recipe a few times, but she never gave it to me. My Ukrainian grandfather said to her, "What for you no give her recipe? Big secret?" Well, she called me up and gave me the recipe, but without any clear measurements so over the years, I came up with acceptable ones to make this delicious dish.

It is a combination of Russian and Chinese ingredients, originally made with beef and pork, but for those that don't use pork, can be made with other ground meat like turkey or chicken combined with beef. I find that it tastes best with the original ingredients.

1 400 g (14 oz.) package Puff pastry

2 lb. combination of minced beef & minced pork (more beef)

1/2 package (150g or 5.3 oz.) vermicelli bean thread noodles (prepared as directed)

1 onion, chopped

2 hardboiled eggs, crushed

1 tsp. sugar

Salt, sprinkle a little over meat

1 tbsp + 1 tsp ground pepper

½ cup plus 3 tbsp soy sauce

½ breadcrumbs

2 tbsp vegetable oil

1 generous tbsp butter

1 egg, beaten

Sprinkle breadcrumbs under each sheet of puff pastry & roll out to fit bottom & top of large lasagna pan. Put first layer into lasagna pan. Sprinkle some pepper on top of puff pastry before putting meat mixture on top.

Fry onion in vegetable oil until limp, then add cold butter at end.

Add minced meats and cook until no pink is seen.

Add ground pepper and soy sauce.

Add cooked vermicelli noodles and mix gently until everything is evenly distributed.

Spoon meat/noodle mixture into pan over 1st layer of puff pastry.

Top with crushed hardboiled eggs, then second layer of puff pastry.

Make sure it covers everything and press edges down to go over meat mixture completely. Brush surface with beaten egg.

Bake for approximately 40 minutes until golden at 350.

Serve with green peas and other vegetables.

Pecan Pie by Pamela Fleming

This was my mom's pecan pie recipe. When she passed away, my dad made and sold many, many of these pies for family meals. He also sold them to people in town as well. He used pecans from trees in his yard. As you can see the recipe is well used.

3 whole eggs
   3 tbsp butter or margarine
   2/3 cup sugar
   2/3 cup dark Karo syrup
   Beat together and add:
   1 tsp vanilla
   2/3 cup pecans

Pour into a pie shell and bake at 400 for 10 minutes then reduce heat to 325 and bake for 30 more minutes.

Applesauce Cake by Mrs. Wosniski

This applesauce cake is from my aunt. She was from Italy in the 1800's.

½ cup Crisco or other shortening

1 cup sugar

2 eggs beaten

1 ½ cups well drained unsweetened applesauce

½ cup chopped (or cut into small pieces) well cooked prunes

1tsp vanilla

2 cups flour sifted together with

2 level tsp baking soda

1 tsp cinnamon

½ tsp cloves

¼ tsp salt

1 cup finely chopped nuts

Cream shortening and sugar.

Add beaten eggs, applesauce, prunes, and all dry ingredients that have been sifted together.

Add vanilla and nuts.

The batter will be very stiff and hard to mix, but continue to stir and mix until well blended.

Pour into greased and floured 9" cake pans.

Bake for one hour at 350 or until done when tested.

Nana's Blackberry Cobbler by Jamie Lovett

This recipe is so important to me because my grandmother and I would pick blackberries, and while we picked them, she would tell me stories. She made what could be a chore something I look back on with such fondness. After we picked them, we'd go back to her kitchen, and we'd make her amazing cobbler. And she always let me help! We would usually make homemade ice cream to go with it.

1 stick butter
  1 cup self-rising flour
  1 cup milk
  1 cup sugar
  4 cups fruit

Melt butter in a 4-quart baking dish.

Mix the flour, milk, and sugar together; then pour this mixture on top of the melted butter.

Take 4 cups of hot cooked sweetened fruit (peaches, blueberries, blackberries, or apples, etc) and spoon on top of the mixture in the baking dish. The fruit will sink and the crust will rise over the fruit.

Bake at 350 until the crust browns.

Hershey Pound Cake by Mary Staples

The recipe I'm sending is one my mom, Betty Garst, has made for at least 55 years. She found it through something Hershey put out. She made this anytime we went somewhere. Mom is now 93 and in assisted living, so longer able to make this but many continue her tradition.

Now for something special about the cake. My dad was a salesman and never met a stranger. On July 4th each year in our hometown of Roanoke Virginia, we celebrate with the local orchestra and a choir made especially for the event. Many bring picnics and enjoy family until the music begins. A new photographer for our local newspaper asked to borrow a chair to stand on to get a good picture of the crowd. Dad got to talking to her and found out she'd only been in town a few days and didn't know anyone. He talked her into taking a break and joining us for our meal. We ended our meal with Mom's cake. The young lady asked if she could take some pictures of the kids. Well, lo and behold, my daughter and 2 nieces were on the front page of the morning paper...in color, which was rare back in the mid 80's! That evening, our son and one of the nieces was in the paper. Several months later, my son was in a charity fashion show and that same photographer was taking pictures. The next day, he was in the paper. We've always said it was the cake that did it! And of course the hospitality shown by my very special dad who has been gone for 10 years.

2 sticks of butter at room temperature
  2 cups of sugar
  4 eggs
  ½ tsp salt
  2 ½ cups flour
  ¼ tsp baking soda
  1 cup buttermilk
  1 tsp vanilla
  6 Hershey bars
  1 can (16 oz.) Hershey's syrup

Cream butter and sugar.
  Add eggs and beat well.
  Sift flour, salt, and baking soda into the creamed mixture.
  Add buttermilk and mix well.
  Add vanilla, Hershey bars and Hershey's syrup and mix well.
  Bake in greased and floured tube pan at 350 degrees for 80 minutes (1 hour and 20 minutes).
  Do NOT open oven. This cake falls easily.
  Cool before removing from pan. Sprinkle powdered sugar on top.
  (Note: Put wax paper on bottom of pan to prevent sticking. Allow to cool 2 hours before removing from pan.)

Bailey's by Scott Erb
  1 cup heavy cream
  1 14 oz. can sweetened condensed milk

1 tsp. instant coffee granules

2 tbsp chocolate syrup

1 tsp vanilla extract

1 tsp almond extract

Combine all ingredients in a blender. Blend on high 20 – 30 seconds.

Store in a tightly sealed container in the refrigerator and shake well before using.

Tortilla Roll-ups by Betty Erb

8 oz. softened cream cheese

1 small can chopped green chiles

1 small can chopped black olives

½ cup shredded cheddar cheese

1 cup sour cream

2 tbsp minced onion

Mix all ingredients together and spread onto flour tortillas. Roll up tightly.

Place seam side down onto pan or platter.

Chill in refrigerator for several hours.

Slice into ½" to ¾" slices. Serve with salsa.

Diane's Oriental Salad by Betty Erb

3 oz. sliced almonds

4 tbsp roasted sesame seeds

6 strips of cooked bacon

½ cup chop suey noodles

1 head of lettuce

Onions to taste

Dressing:

2 tbsp white vinegar

4 tbsp sugar

1 tsp salt

¼ tsp pepper

½ cup oil
Blend well and pour over salad.

Thumbprint Cookies by Betty Erb
½ cup shortening
¼ cup brown sugar
1 egg yolk
1 tsp vanilla
½ tsp salt
1 cup flour
1 egg white, beaten
¾ cup finely chopped walnuts
Seedless raspberry jam

Mix shortening, brown sugar, egg yolk and vanilla.
Blend in flour and salt.
Roll dough into a balls.
Dip dough balls into beaten egg white.
Roll in nuts.
Press thumb in the center and fill with jam.
Bake at 350 for 15 – 20 minutes.

Betty's Stromboli – Betty Erb
1 tube of refrigerated French bread dough
2 cups (8 oz.) shredded mozzarella
1 tsbp melted butter
¼ lb thinly sliced salami
½ cup chopped roasted red peppers or pimentos, drained
1 tbsp grated Parmesan cheese

Preheat oven to 375.
On lightly floured surface, unroll dough and pat out to measure 14 x 12 inches.
Sprinkle mozzarella cheese over dough within ½ inch of edges.
Top with a single layer of salami and peppers.

Starting with the shortest side, roll up tightly; pinch edges firmly to seal.

Brush with melted butter, sprinkle with Parmesan cheese.

Bake 20 – 25 minutes until golden brown.

Let stand 5 minutes before cutting into 1″ slices with a serrated knife.

Serves 6 – 8.

Snickerdoodles by Mary Clifton

My great grandmother's snickerdoodle recipe is a family favorite.

1stick room temp unsalted butter

1 stick crisco.

1/2 cup sugar

2 eggs

2 tsp cream of tartar

1 tsp baking soda

1/4 tsp salt

½ tsp cinnamon

2 3/4 cups unbleached flour

Preheat oven to 375 degrees.

Cover cookie sheets with parchment paper.

Mix butter, Crisco, sugar, and eggs.

Blend in the dry ingredients.

Add cinnamon and mix well.

Pinch dough into small pieces and roll into small balls. It is easier if you roll all of the dough balls and set aside on wax paper.

Place 2 inches apart on cookie sheets.

These can be rolled into colored sugar at Christmas.

Bake 8 to 10 minutes.

Cool and move to wire racks.

Lasagna by Mary Clifton

I was taught to make this as a little girl by a close family friend. Originally it was made with 4 quarts home canned tomatoes.

Premade meat sauce

3 cans Cento crushed tomatoes

2 cans tomato paste

2 -16 oz cans tomato sauce

4 bay leaves

Parsley, chives, sea salt, black pepper, and Italian blend seasoning to taste.

4 garlic cloves

1 small onion diced

2 pounds freshly ground chuck and sirloin - 1 each.

Cook and drain meat.

Add garlic and onion.

Move to a well-greased Dutch oven.

Mix the tomato products and spices together with the meat.

Add the bay leaves and mix well.

Simmer 3 hours.

While simmering sauce, cook 12 lasagna noodles according to package directions.

Parmigiano Reggiano and Romano cheese

Grated mozzarella

Spray a casserole dish with cooking spray.

Place a layer of sauce on bottom.

Sprinkle with the grated cheeses.

Place 3 noodles on sauce and repeat sauce / cheese / noodles.

Cover and bake at 350 degrees 45 minutes.

Let stand a bit before serving. This makes sauce enough to freeze for later meals.

Shepherd's Pie by Gill Luongo

These are traditional English recipes from the late 1700's and early 1800's that we learned while stationed in England. We were very good friends with a British lady named Gill who married an Italian man named Nino. Gill generously shared her recipes with us.

MASHED POTATOES

3 lbs russet potatoes approx. 4 potatoes, rinsed, peeled, and cut

2 sticks unsalted butter cubed, softened at room temperature

1 cup whole milk warm

1 ½ tsps kosher salt or to taste

2 cloves garlic minced

LAMB FILLING

1 tbsp olive oil

1 medium yellow onion diced

¼ tsp dried thyme

¼ tsp dried rosemary

2 cloves garlic minced

1 ½ lbs ground lamb

½ tsp kosher salt or to taste

½ tsp ground black pepper

1 tbsp all-purpose flour

¼ cup sweet red table wine

3 tbsps Worcestershire sauce

3 tbsps soy sauce

3 tbsps tomato paste

½ cup unsalted chicken stock

1 cup diced carrots

1 cup fresh peas

TOPPING

1 egg beaten

⅛ cup parmesan cheese grated

Preheat oven to 400°.

MASHED POTATOES

Scrub the potatoes under running water with a vegetable brush to remove any dirt or debris. Peel and cut the potatoes into 1 to 2-inch thick chunks.

In a large stockpot, cover the potatoes with cold water and heat to a boil. Once boiling, turn the heat down to a simmer. Cook until the potatoes are tender in the middle, 20 to 30 minutes. Mine took about 25 minutes to cook through. Use a paring knife to check doneness by inserting the knife into the potatoes. When there is little resistance when inserting the knife, they are done.

Drain the potatoes in a colander and rinse under hot water for 10-20 seconds to wash away any excess starch. Place back in the pot.

Add the softened butter and mash thoroughly into the potatoes using a potato masher. Next, add the warm milk, and salt and fold in using a spatula.

LAMB FILLING

While the potatoes are cooking, heat 1 tablespoon of olive oil in a large skillet over medium-high heat. Add the diced onion to the skillet and sauté until the onion becomes soft and begins to brown around the edges, 4 to 5 minutes.

Add the minced garlic, rosemary, and thyme to the skillet. Mix into the onion and cook for another minute to release the flavors and aromas of the herbs.

Add the ground lamb and break into small pieces while cooking. Sauté until cooked through, about 8 to 10 minutes. Drain the meat and return to the skillet and sauté for another minute or two.

Sprinkle the 1/2 tsp salt, black pepper, and flour over the lamb and then mix into the meat. Next add the red wine, Worcestershire sauce, soy sauce, and tomato paste to the skillet and mix into the meat. Cook for a few minutes to allow the liquid to reduce.

Add the chicken stock and vegetables to the skillet, mix into the meat, and allow to come to a boil. As soon as the liquid begins to boil, turn the heat down to medium and allow to cook while the liquid reduces and thickens, about 10 minutes. Mix occasionally so that the meat doesn't burn to the bottom of the skillet.

SHEPHERD'S PIE

Evenly spread the lamb filling on the bottom of a baking dish. Spoon or pipe the mashed potatoes evenly over the lamb. Then, lightly brush the top of the potatoes with the beaten egg and sprinkle the parmesan cheese evenly over the top.

Place the baking dish on the middle rack of a preheated oven and bake for 25 minutes or until the peaks of the potatoes begin to brown.

Remove from the oven and allow to cool for 5 minutes before serving.

Ploughman's Lunch by Gill Luongo

Typically a Ploughman's lunch was packed and taken to the fields by men who worked the fields/farms.

Items included can vary according to preference, but a ploughman's lunch is always served cold, and generally includes crusty bread, butter and cheese, plus pickled onions and a relish or chutney.

The lunch may also include a selection of cold meats, ham, maybe a slice of pate or a slice of pork pie, hard-boiled eggs, and sometimes slices of apple or other seasonal fruit.

This lunch goes well with beer or lemonade.

Yorkshire Pudding by Gill Luongo

Typically served with roast beef.

1 ½ cups flour

¾ tsp salt

¾ cup room temperature milk

3 room temperature eggs, well beaten

¾ cup water

½ cup roast beef drippings (This can be from a roast prepared recently or one you made just prior to making this recipe.)

Mix flour and salt. Add milk and blend. Mix in eggs and water until the batter is light and frothy. Let rest for an hour or if making ahead for the next day, cover and refrigerate overnight.

If the batter has been refrigerated, return to room temperature before using. When the roast beef is ready to come out of the oven, ready the mixture.

Preheat oven to 400 degrees.

Pour drippings off roast beef and set aside approximately ½ cup. Pour drippings into a 9x12 inch baking dish and heat in oven until sizzling. Pour the batter over the drippings and bake for 30 minutes (or until the sides have risen and are golden brown). Serves 8.

Scotch Eggs – by Gill Luongo

6 hard-boiled eggs (or as many as you like)

Bulk breakfast pork sausage (enough to cover the eggs)

Flatten raw pork sausage and make a patty to surround each egg. Egg should be fully covered.

Deep fry until golden brown, or pan fry while making sure each side is well cooked.

Lena's Pie Crust by Katy McCollom

My grandma's name was Norma Porterfield. She was the strongest, smartest, kindest women I ever knew. She was an avid reader and instilled a love of books in her four daughters and many grandchildren. She painted, wrote, quilted, and inspired us all. I would love to honor her in your book! Thank you so much for the consideration. These are all family recipes written in my grandma's beautiful penmanship.

Brown bowl
>   2 cups flour
>   Pinch of salt
>   2 fingers full of Crisco
>   Water

Put flour and salt into brown bowl. Mix in Crisco until the consistency is that of cornmeal. Fill a water glass 2/3 full of water. Add water, a little at a time, until dough feels right. Drink the rest of the water. Roll out dough and put in pie pan.

Grandma Iola's Tea Cakes by Katy McCollom

1 cup room temperature butter
>   2 ½ cups sugar
>   4 eggs
>   4 ½ cups flour
>   1 tsp baking powder
>   1 tsp baking soda
>   ½ tsp nutmeg
>   ¼ cup of buttermilk
>   1 tsp vanilla

Cream butter and sugar.
>   Add eggs, beating mixture well.
>   Combine flour, baking powder, baking soda, and nutmeg.
>   Add to mixture with buttermilk.
>   Stir in vanilla.
>   Drop dough by spoonfuls onto greased cookie sheet.
>   Bake at 375 for 8 to 10 minutes.

Grandma's Chocolate Gravy by Katy McCollom

¾ cup sugar
>   3 tbsp cocoa

1 tbsp flour or cornstarch
2 cups milk
Butter
Vanilla

Mix sugar, flour, and cocoa together in a saucepan.
   Add milk.
   Cook over medium heat until mixture starts to thicken.
   Add butter and vanilla if desired.
   Let mixture cool and serve with hot biscuits.

Baked Corn by Shannon Dolgos
   Dorothy L. Doutt (1927-2015) - My Gram
   2 cans creamed corn
   4 eggs
   1 cup of milk
   1 cup sugar
   2 teaspoons baking powder
   4 tablespoons flour
   Grease pan. Bake at 350 for 45 minutes to one hour.
   1/2 stick butter
   1/2 cup sugar
   1/2 cup water
   2 tablespoons flour
   Cook in pot on stove top. Pour over corn after it is baked.

Zucchini Cookies by Shannon Dolgos
   Cream:
   3/4 cup butter
   1 cup brown sugar
   1/2 cup white sugar
   1 egg
   1 teaspoon vanilla
   Add:
   1 cup grated zucchini

2 cups flour

1 teaspoon salt

1/2 teaspoon baking soda

2 cups rolled oats

1 cup chocolate chips or butterscotch chips

1 cup nuts

Drop on ungreased cookie sheet, bake at 350 for 12 minutes.

Gobs (Chocolate Whoopie Pies) by Shannon Dolgos

Cream:

2 cups sugar

1/2 cup shortening

2 eggs

Add:

3/4 cup sour milk

1/2 cup boiling water

Sift & Mix:

2 teaspoons baking soda

1/2 teaspoon baking powder

4 cups flour

1/2 teaspoon salt

1 teaspoon vanilla

1/2 cup cocoa

Drop on ungreased cookie sheet. Bake at 400 for 5 minutes. Cool before adding filling.

Filling

2 cups powdered sugar

3/4 cup butter

1 cup marshmallow crème

1 teaspoon vanilla

1/8 teaspoon salt

White Gravy and Bread by April Willis

Fry bacon in a heavy pan.
  Drain and set aside.
  Add enough (2 tbsp flour) to bacon drippings to thicken.
  Add milk to make proper consistency.
  Stir with fork.
  Add salt and pepper.
  Tear bread into bites and ladle gravy over.
  Serve quickly with bacon on side.

Pie Crust by April Willis

2 cups flour
  1 tsp salt
  ¾ cup Crisco
  Fork it – combine using a fork.
  Add a little water and fork it.
  If ready, roll it out. If not, add a little more water, fork it then
roll it.

Swiss Steak by Alexis Lavoie

This is a recipe my mom would make for Sunday Dinners i just loved it and when it was cooking the great smell was something you had linger all thru the house. She would serve it with a veggie and mashed potatoes. Also my father would go early in the morning to the bread place where they would make bread on Sunday a.m. and you could buy it nice and hot and fresh most of the time. We got a large loaf of Italian Bread and served it with dinner. By the end of the meal not much was left.

1 tbsp oil
  1 tbsp butter
  1 1/2 lbs. meat (skirt steak or blade steak)
  2 oz white or red wine

3 tbsp flour

1 – 8 oz can tomato sauce and 1 can water

3 cloves

2-3 Bay leaves

¼ teaspoon celery salt

¼ tsp garlic power

4 thin slices lemon or if using juice, 1 tbsp

1 tbsp granulated sugar

¼ tsp pepper

Heat oil and butter in large skillet.

Brown meat on both sides and remove from skillet.

Reduce heat and blend flour with fat and gradually add water, tomato sauce, cloves, lemon, sugar, and all other seasonings.

Simmer until gravy thickens.

Add meat and simmer for 1 1/2 hours or until tender. Enjoy!

Rice and ground beef casserole by Keenalynn Pratt

My mom found this recipe in a newspaper years ago...

1 1/2 pound of ground beef

2 cans of Campbell's tomato soup

1 cup of water

Half a head of cabbage

1 cup of INSTANT rice

2 cups of favorite cheese. (I use sharp cheddar.)

Preheat oven to 350.

Cut cabbage (do not cook) in small bites and layer in a 4qt casserole dish.

Brown and drain beef then add uncooked rice and mix well.

Layer over cabbage.

Mix tomato soup and water together, then layer over meat.

Cook uncovered for 35-45 minutes.

Add desired cheese. Cook until melted (usually 10-15 minutes).

*Note: The original recipe called for onion (cook with beef) but we leave it out due to personal preference.

Butterscotch Breakfast Rolls by Wendy Tompkins

This is a recipe my Mom had, my girls and I make them often. It is about the only one I have that is in her handwriting. She passed away Mother's Day weekend in 2019...miss her so much.

2 cups flour
    ½ tsp salt
    1 tbsp baking powder
    1 cup light cream
    ¼ cup softened butter
    ½ cup brown sugar

Sift together flour, salt, and baking powder.
    Add cream and mix until dough follows fork around bowl.
    Roll out on a floured surface to a 6 x 12 inch rectangle.
    Spread with butter and brown sugar.
    Roll up like a jelly roll and cut in 1 inch slices.
    Arrange in a greased, round, 9 inch pan.
    Bake at 400 for 20 – 25 minutes.
    Invert on plate and serve hot.

MORE EMERSON PASS!

For more Emerson Pass, download the historical books in the series. Travel back in time to meet the original residents of Emerson Pass, starring the Barnes family.
The School Mistress
The Spinster
The Scholar (releases July 20, 2021)

The first of the Emerson Pass Contemporaries, The Sugar Queen, starring the descendants of the Barnes family is available at your favorite retailer.

Sign up for Tess's newsletter and never miss a release or sale! www.tesswrites.com

The Spinster

Her love died on a battlefield. He carries a torch for a woman he's never met. Can the tragic death of a soldier entwine the souls of two strangers?

Colorado, 1919. Josephine Barnes wrote every day to her beloved fiancé battling in the trenches of the Great War. Devastated when he's killed in action, she vows never to marry and buries her grief in the construction of the town's first library. But she's left breathless when she receives a request from a gracious gentleman to visit and return the letters containing her declarations of desire.

Philip Baker survived the war but returned home burdened with a distressing secret. Though he knows it's wrong, he can't stop reading through the beautiful sentiments left among his slain comrade's possessions. Plagued by guilt, he's unable to resist connecting with the extraordinary woman who captured his heart with her words.

When Josephine invites Philip to join her gregarious family for the holidays, she's torn by her loyalty to a ghost and her growing feelings for the gallant man. And as Philip prepares to risk everything by telling her the truth about her dead fiancé, he fears he could crush Josephine's blossoming happiness forever.

Will they break free from their painful pasts to embrace a passion meant to be?

The Spinster is the second book in the heartwarming Emerson Pass historical romance series. If you like staunch heroines, emotional backdrops, and sweeping family sagas, then you'll adore Tess Thompson's wholesome tale.

Buy *The Spinster* to read between the lines of destiny today!

The Sugar Queen

The first in the contemporary Emerson Pass Series , The Sugar Queen features the descendants from the Barnes family.

Get ready for some sweet second chances! To read the first chapter, simply turn the page or download a copy here: The Sugar Queen.

True love requires commitment, and many times unending sacrifice. . .

At the tender age of eighteen, Brandi Vargas watched the love of her life drive out of Emerson Pass, presumably for good. Though she and Trapper Barnes dreamed of attending college and starting their lives together, she was sure she would only get in the way of Trapper's future as a hockey star. Breaking his heart, and her own in the process, was the only way to ensure he pursued his destiny. Her fate was the small town life she'd always known, her own bakery, and an endless stream of regret. After a decade of playing hockey, a single injury ended Trapper Barnes' career. And while the past he left behind always haunted him, he still returns to Emerson Pass to start the next chapter of his life in the place his ancestors built more than a century before. But when he discovers that the woman who owns the local bakery is the girl who once shattered his dreams, the painful secret she's been harboring all these years threatens to turn Trapper's idyllic small town future into a disaster. Will it take a forest fire threatening the mountain village to force Trapper and Brandi to confront their history? And in the wake of such a significant loss, will the process of rebuilding their beloved town help them find each other, and true happiness, once again?

Fast forward to the present day and enjoy this contemporary second chance romance set in the small town of Emerson Pass, featuring the descendants of the characters you loved from *USA Today* bestselling author Tess Thompson's The School Mistress.

The Patron of Emerson Pass
She's afraid to take risks. He's an incurable daredevil. When tragedy throws them together, will it spark a lasting devotion?

Crystal Whalen isn't sure why she should go on. Two years after her husband's death on a ski trip, she's devastated when a fire destroys her quiet Colorado mountain home. And when she can't keep her hands off the gorgeous divorcé who's become her new temporary housemate, it only feeds her grief and growing guilt.

Garth Welty won't be burned again. After his ex-wife took most of his money, the downhill-skiing Olympic medalist is determined to keep things casual with the sexy woman he can't resist. But the more time they spend with each other, the harder it is to deny his burgeoning feelings.

As Crystal's longing for the rugged man's embrace grows, she worries that his dangerous lifestyle will steal him away. And although Garth believes she's his perfect girl, the specter of betrayal keeps a tight grip on his heart.

Will the thrill-seeker and the wary woman succumb to the power of love?

The Patron of Emerson Pass is the emotional second book in the Emerson Pass Contemporaries small-town romance series. If you like lyrical prose, unexpected chances at happiness, and uplifting stories, then you'll adore Tess Thompson's sweet tale.

Buy *The Patron of Emerson Pass* to rebuild broken hope today!

ALSO BY TESS THOMPSON

Cliffside Bay Series

Traded: Brody and Kara

Deleted: Jackson and Maggie

Jaded: Zane and Honor

Marred: Kyle and Violet

Tainted: Lance and Mary

The Christmas of Cats and Babies, A Cliffside Bay Novella

Missed: Rafael and Lisa

A Christmas Wedding, A Cliffside Bay Novella

Healed: Stone and Pepper

Scarred: Trey and Autumn

Jilted: Nico and Sophie

Departed: David and Sara

Blue Mountain Series

Blue Midnight

Blue Moon

Blue Ink

Blue Thread (releases September 1, 2020

River Valley Series

Riversong

Riverbend

Riverstar

Riversnow

Riverstorm

Emerson Pass

The School Mistress

The Sugar Queen

Historical Fiction

Duet for Three Hands

Miller's Secret

Legley Bay Series

Caramel and Magnolias

Tea and Primroses

Novellas

The Santa Trial

ABOUT THE AUTHOR

USA Today Bestselling author Tess Thompson writes small-town romances and historical fiction. She started her writing career in fourth grade when she wrote a story about an orphan who opened a pizza restaurant. Oddly enough, her first novel, "Riversong" is about an adult orphan who opens a restaurant. Clearly, she's been obsessed with food and words for a long time now.

With a degree from the University of Southern California in theatre, she's spent her adult life studying story, word craft, and character. Since 2011, she's published 20 novels and 3 novellas. Most days she spends at her desk chasing her daily word count or rewriting a terrible first draft.

She currently lives in a suburb of Seattle, Washington with her husband, the hero of her own love story, and their Brady Bunch clan of two sons, two daughters and five cats. Yes, that's four kids and five cats.

Tess loves to hear from you. Drop her a line at tess@tthompsonwrites.com or visit her website at https://tesswrites.com/

Made in the USA
Middletown, DE
05 August 2021